THE
TITANIC SURVIVORS
BOOK CLUB

THE
TITANIC
SURVIVORS
BOOK CLUB

A NOVEL

Timothy Schaffert

. . .

DOUBLEDAY  NEW YORK

Copyright © 2024 by Timothy Schaffert

All rights reserved. Published in the United States by Doubleday, a division of Penguin Random House LLC, New York, and distributed in Canada by Penguin Random House Canada Limited, Toronto.

www.doubleday.com

DOUBLEDAY and the portrayal of an anchor with a dolphin are registered trademarks of Penguin Random House LLC.

Interior illustrations by D'Angelo Simms
Book design by Pei Loi Koay
Jacket images: (frames) DavidGoh; (Paris) Leontura; (peacock)
visualgo; (shell pattern) debela; (clouds) edge69; all Getty Images
Jacket design by Michael J. Windsor

LIBRARY OF CONGRESS CATALOGING-IN-PUBLICATION DATA
Names: Schaffert, Timothy, author.
Title: The Titanic Survivors Book Club : a novel / Timothy Schaffert.
Description: First edition. | New York : Doubleday, 2024.
Identifiers: LCCN 2023027194 (print) | LCCN 2023027195 (ebook) |
ISBN 9780385549158 (hardcover) | ISBN 9780385549165 (ebook) |
ISBN 9780385550895 (export)
Classification: LCC PS3619.C325 T58 2024 (print) |
LCC PS3619.C325 (ebook) | DDC 813/.6—dc23/eng/20230814
LC record available at https://lccn.loc.gov/2023027194
LC ebook record available at https://lccn.loc.gov/2023027195

MANUFACTURED IN THE UNITED STATES OF AMERICA

1 3 5 7 9 10 8 6 4 2

First Edition

To Rodney

PART ONE

1

I spotted my name, again and again, on the lists of the dead. Even as the weeks went by and the reports got fixed, my name didn't budge.

Lists of those who perished, and of those who didn't, began to be published only days after the wreck. And for days after that, as facts shifted, a name might slip from one list to the other. People who lived died, people who died lived.

But my death stuck to me. I didn't write anybody about it. I didn't ask for any correction. I only waited. In dark moments I wondered: *What if they're right?*

It became a nightly habit, at a corner pub—I'd take my gin with a blast of siphon seltzer, the liveliest cocktail I could think of, then I'd eyeball the evening edition, to take my pulse.

Then one night, a few weeks in, my name was nowhere. I kept checking the reports for days after, to see if I'd someday show up on the lists of survivors. But I never did. I simply ceased to be.

Nonetheless I know, for as long as my name lingered in the newspapers around the world, people noticed me. Though I'm unknown far and wide, my name is as famous as it is uncommon. And I know exactly what they thought when they saw it. They maybe even muttered it, tried it out on their tongues. Performed it.

Alas, poor Yorick.

My dad fancied himself a Shakespearean actor, though he was merely a vaudevillian in the middle of America when he named me. My father cared only for his characters. But Yorick wasn't even that, he was only a prop, a skull for Hamlet to hold. *Alas, poor Yorick,* Hamlet says in the boneyard, gazing into the empty eye sockets of a dead clown.

You'll live forever on the stage, my father told me once when I was a little boy, when I complained about the name he gave me. *You'll donate your skeleton to the theater. Every time they do* Hamlet *forever after, they'll hold your head up high, in the limelight.*

Over a year after I was pronounced dead, I received an invitation: *To the Titanic Survivor,* it said, with only a time and a place, and nothing else.

The invitation arrived as a message in a bottle. And the message had been folded into a little paper boat, like those boats that boys and girls fold from newspaper and send drifting in a fountain. I could tell from the odd nature of the note that this was nothing at all official. I wasn't being summoned to an insurance office or called to testify.

I'd propped open the bookshop's front door with a fat medical atlas on human anatomy, and there the bottle was, sitting upright in the doorway. I heard it before I saw it, a breeze whistling across the bottle's lip.

My shop was full of novels that started this way, stories of unrequited love, lies, revenge, mistaken identity, secrets and confessions and regrets revealed in letters sent, intercepted, purloined, lost, burnt. Or maybe I was already reading into that message before I could see a word of it. I wanted to be rescued by that paper boat.

I'd bought my shop on a whim, practically, with an inheritance I would have been better off putting in a bank. And in the months I'd owned the shop, I'd managed to add far more books to its shelves than I'd sold. Whenever it was quiet, which was most of the time, I swore I could hear the weevils working their jaws, devouring the books from the inside out, eating my every word.

After retrieving the bottle, I went to the back of my shop to my workbench built from the shell of an old upright piano. Beneath the lid, where the hammers and pins had been, I kept my tools and supplies. I'd installed a narrow tabletop over the keys of chipped ivory. I sat on the piano bench, my back to the shop.

I went fishing for the message through the bottle's neck with an awl I used for repairing broken spines, but I gave that up quick, and I wrapped the bottle in a square of flocked book cloth and struck it with a mallet. When I opened the deep blue velvet, a midnight sea lay before me, the boat tossed across the glistening waves of shattered glass.

I tugged at the boat's sails to unfold the note.

Either someone had made a mistake in inviting me or they'd peeked inside my soul. Because I *had* survived the *Titanic*, despite having had both feet on dry land when the ship sank. And that survival had changed the entire direction of my life. By not boarding the ship as planned, I'd put a twist in my own plot.

You yourself are a *Titanic* survivor, you might say, because you didn't board either. You'll say that we're all survivors of tragedy, if you look at it the way that I look at it—and there is a truth to that, I suppose. When you hear of a neighbor who stumbled on the stairs to her demise, you eye your own staircase with suspicion. Every step up is a death averted. A train goes off its rails, a girl gets poisoned by a bad oyster, a thug cuts a man's throat in a dark alley. In every instance, it isn't you. You live another day. Your daily paper is full of reports of your own survival.

2

I was only twenty-six and I looked even younger, but the *Titanic* wasn't the first time I cheated death. Even my birth almost sent me to the grave, when my mother's umbilical cord tied a noose around my neck. My first cries were a desperate wheeze, my father often told me with some annoyance. As an actor, his voice thundered. He brought me onstage as soon as I could take a step, and my voice grew even weaker when people listened. *Somehow you seem even more invisible with the blaze of the stage lights shining on you,* he said.

But I'm sometimes emboldened by my invisibility. When I feel too conspicuous to leave my shop, I try to remind myself that I'm never noticed, despite the wild curls of my hair that I rarely cut or comb. And I have the saddest eyes of anyone, a handsome man once told me. He whispered it in my ear: *I could see your sadness from across the room.*

I was full of worry. I was certain I didn't belong, no matter what my invitation said. But I so much wanted to be among them. I peddled stories for a living, so maybe I would invent one of my own, I thought. I knew enough facts, certainly. I might've been on lifeboat no. 15, for all they knew; I could easily get lost in the sardine tin of it, with sixty-some passengers packed tight, weighing the thing down, the boat sunk so low in the water that the sea licked at a lady's hair when she simply tilted her head toward the side.

The meeting was in an hour, and the hotel saloon was an hour's stroll from my shop. I leaned on my walking stick, but the pins in the bones of my leg acted like lightning bolts, drawing in all the electricity of my nervous nature, putting a little sizzle of pain in my every step.

I concocted my story as I walked along the Avenue de l'Opéra. I became a character much like myself, an antiquarian book dealer, but one who'd been hired to escort a bejeweled edition of the *Rubaiyat*, the beloved book of Persian poetry, to New York City. I would tell the survivors that I was hired to guard the book with my life, and to squabble with customs agents over tariffs.

The book itself was not a lie—I read about it in a newsletter for booksellers. This special *Rubaiyat* was a gaudy thing by some accounts; it was rare, but no antique, extravagant and overwrought, bound in Moroccan leather, the peacocks on the cover strutting with embroidered wings of golden threads, the binding embedded with topazes and rubies, amethysts and emeralds. A bookbinder had been invited to indulge himself, and an American bought the madness from a London auction house. I would tell the *Titanic* survivors I cradled the book in my arms from ship to shore.

But the truth of it was, I wasn't there to rescue it. No one was. By all accounts, it was lost to the ocean.

I was fascinated by the thought of the opulent book collapsing underwater, the fish plucking it apart kettle stitch by kettle stitch. Though I might *repair* a binding in my shop every now and again, I was never really out to *fix* it. I liked to read a book's disintegration. If anything, I sought to prolong the glorious decay of a broken-down book, to keep it together long enough for it to fall apart with elegance. I liked to run my hands over the warp of the boards, to follow the unlacing of the dentelle, to touch at the frays in the calico. I loved the tarnish of gold leaf, the yellowing of ivory and bone. In my shop was a cheap old Bible bound in divinity calf, patched with different shades of leather and goat and mutton, like a coat of many colors.

As I turned the corner, my destination in sight, the pain returned to my leg, sharp. I should listen to it and not go any farther, I thought. But I kept on.

3

At the hotel, a waiter handed me a little globed glass of cognac and led me to the billiards room at the back. I'd arrived early, but everyone else had arrived even earlier. Though they all looked up when I stepped in, they just as quickly looked back down. No one met anyone's eyes, no one spoke, no one whispered, everyone seated around a long mahogany table. They fussed with the buttons on their cuffs or twisted the rings on their fingers.

There were eleven of us once I took my seat. I'd expected all women—women and children first, and all that—but there were nearly as many men among us. And I'd expected those women would be rich—the story of the *Titanic* has many morals and chief among them is "survival of the fittest." The fittest, in this instance, being the passengers of first class. We certainly didn't need the *Titanic* to teach us that.

I swore I could hear somebody's furtive glances dropping into the cognac—*plink, plunk*. But no, an old lady was plopping sugar cubes into her drink. She then stirred those cubes around and around and around with the tongs. We were all of us grateful for the god-awful racket, for the clinking of the silver against glass, because it gave us something else to worry about—*Won't her stirring ever end?* I could feel our hearts uniting over our hatred of this woman and her noise.

This billiards hall had been a chapel, and our benches were unforgiving pews whittled by monks. We shifted and sighed and plucked splinters from our silk and tweed. When church and state separated in 1905 (*Loi de séparation des Églises et de l'État*), less than a decade ago, France sold off ownership of this monastery, one of the oldest in Paris, to a hotelier snatching up sacred properties. The hotelier kept the pews, the tapestries, the stained-glass windows, and even the cold drafts that moaned along the walls like hymns of complaint, making the place a quaint relic for tourists. The hotel kept everything but the monks, who'd been swiftly evicted.

I'd wobbled an old baby pram to this very chapel to collect their hymnbooks of featherlight paper, and their prayer books with leather covers so soft you could sleep on one beneath your head, all of them bought for pocket change. I'd since been hollowing them out at my workbench, to sell as pretty little jewel boxes for your rings and cufflinks, or secret vaults to hide your valuables on a shelf. So many of the books in my shop were worth more when I cut out their insides.

When we weren't all avoiding each other's eyes, we were staring at the table's centerpiece: a toy model of a ship, most likely the *Titanic* itself. I counted the lifeboats. And then I counted them again.

Finally, the man next to the woman with the sugar cubes, a bald-headed Brit, put his hand on her wrist, stopping the stirring, but the sudden return of the silence made us miss the *clink-clank* of the tongs. The man took it upon himself to be the first to speak. "I feel we're waiting for a *detective*," he said. "We've been *gathered*, like in the last chapters of the missus's murder mysteries." He tilted his head, with a little tic, a little jerk, toward the woman, the missus herself, I presumed. Missus Sugar Cubes.

"Who said anything about murder?" came a voice, high-pitched, from a man at the end of the table.

"*I* did, of course," said Mr. Sugar Cubes. "You just heard me."

"*Nobody* said *anything* about *murder*," he said. "I won't sit here and listen to talk of *that*." But sit he did.

I wondered if I would lie after all. If we went around the table to introduce ourselves, would I admit that I'd been nowhere near that iceberg? Any group of *Titanic* survivors had every right to be disgusted by the likes of me. The ship had barely had a chance to reach the ocean floor before the frauds came rushing out like rats. Anyone could veil themselves in widow's weeds to collect charity.

I couldn't bear to deceive them, but I couldn't bear to offend them either. I could never know the fear they knew, not just as the ship went down but as they drifted in their lifeboats waiting to be lost. Nothingness was everywhere. Once you've seen a night so dark, do you ever see daylight again?

"Did everyone's invitation arrive in a bottle?" a woman asked. She wore a hat of black velvet with a brim that drooped. Her red dress shimmered and shadowed in the light of the lamp. This gave the embroidered blackbirds up and down the silk the illusion of taking flight and thrashing, as if a hunter's rifle had just popped off. She held forth, in a hand gloved in black lace, the piece of paper. "Or was *my* invitation peculiarly theatrical?" She made much of those words, *peculiarly theatrical,* the *c*'s clicking in her throat, the *l*'s and the *r*'s rolling over each other slow.

I recognized her: the great Delphine Blanchet, the *tragédienne* of the Paris stage, famous for dying a hundred deaths. Over the decades, she'd expired onstage from tuberculosis, scarlet fever, cholera, smallpox, arsenic, strychnine, antimony, despair, longing, grief.

She was known in France as *La Pleurnicharde.* The Crybaby.

Was it Delphine, though? I'd read those lists of the dead-or-alive backward and forward, studying them to see if I was still lost at sea. I would have noticed Delphine surviving. I wouldn't have had to look too hard. In Paris, she would have had day after day of front pages. *Vive La Pleurnicharde!*

Everyone brought out their invitations. One man had even brought the bottle somehow unbroken, the note somehow still inside, the boat somehow unfolded.

The squeaky-voiced man spoke up again. "Which one of you is responsible for this? And what do you want from us?"

Mr. Sugar Cubes spoke next, a jovial fellow, really, oblivious to the tensions. "The missus's murder mysteries have invitations in them sometimes, don't they, love?" he said. "And letters and such. Did you ever write a mystery with a message in a bottle?"

So he hadn't been referring to murder mysteries the missus simply read. He meant the ones she wrote. I realized that this was the woman I'd read about. She penned crime novels under the nom de plume of Penelope Quinn. She'd booked on the *Titanic* to travel to New York to meet with her publisher, but the publisher, pinching pennies, saved her life by insisting she arrange for cheaper passage.

Her anecdote had been in all the papers. A woman who peddles in stories of death skirts a death of her own. I'd wondered if it was even true, or if it was a publicity stunt. Either way, cheating fate was good for sales. I hadn't sold any of her books myself, but the shop at the end of my block had seen an uptick. And the bookshop around the corner too. (And there you see part of my poor business sense. I'd bought a bookshop in a neighborhood full of bookshops. And just a little beyond those shops was the long stretch of bookstalls along the quay of the River Seine.)

Penelope Quinn then spoke, but she seemed to not have been listening much. "You can break into a sealed envelope without anyone knowing," she said. She slurred a little, and her cheeks were so rosy they were nearly bloodred. I suspected she'd had more than just the one glass of cognac and sugar cubes. "Or you used to be able to, with some of the older waxes. Hold the seal over a flame, and then you can pry it off, intact, to glue back later, after you've read the letter and tucked it back into the envelope. Yes, it's quite simple if the wax is the right kind. After you heat up the seal over a candle, you can pry it off with a cat's whisker."

"A cat's whisker," people murmured, perhaps to be polite. I sus-

pected they were all just desperate to mutter about something inconsequential.

Then came a woman's voice, satin-smooth but tinged with a sting of sarcasm.

"Do you remove the cat from the whisker first?" she said.

Zinnia, I would find out later.

Zinnia was a tall Japanese woman with an American accent. Making her seem even taller was her hair, all gathered up and twisted around and stuck through with three long-toothed combs of ivory. I squinted at her to study the combs and realized they'd been whittled into the shape of sailboats—ivory boats in a sea of hair that was a luminous black, like it'd been washed in squid's ink.

This was before the war started nipping at the long skirts of ladies, before fabric rations and practicality and defiance led the hemlines up from the ankle and along the calf, to pause for a while below the knee. Zinnia's dress was going in the opposite direction, longer than most, covering her shoes with a train like a bride's, swirling at her feet. She wore ermine over her shoulders, and though it was a scarf of snowy fur, it somehow looked as summery as that hot August day.

Everyone at the table looked to the mystery writer for an answer. Penelope Quinn just looked back at us, quizzical, until she finally replied, in all seriousness: "Well, I suspect the task would be much easier if the cat was *off* the whisker, wouldn't you say?"

"I *would* say," Zinnia said, and then she looked right at me. She seemed to wink at me and smile. As she took a sip of her cognac, I turned my head to see if she'd meant the wink for someone behind me.

Though there wasn't anyone there, I did just then notice a twelfth person among us. A sofa faced an enormous fireplace on the other side of the room, gray stone blackened with centuries-old soot. And draped over the back of the sofa was a hand. And over the arm of the sofa, a foot. The fingers wiggled. The foot tapped at the air. The man then sat up from his lie-down to reach over to that foot, to tighten the lace of his boot. His long, dark hair reached to his collar and fell across his face. He stood from the sofa, coming into my vision piece by piece.

He was a shrug of the shoulder, a lift of the chin, the tuck of his hair behind an ear. He was a yawn, and a stretch, and a flutter of long, ladylike eyelashes. *Haze*, he would tell us later, in a voice much deeper than his pretty face would suggest.

He picked up a glass and ambled our way. He seemed somehow both fidgety and confident all at once. He saw me looking at him, but he didn't turn away when our eyes met. That lingering glance sped up my heartbeat. He looked *at* me, not through me, not past me. Usually if a man met my stare, I felt accused. Caught. But Haze seemed to accept my glance as an invitation. He looked curious about me.

I was seated at the end of a pew, so he came to my side and bumped my hip with his to scoot me over. He bumped the table leg too, which announced his presence all up the line, jostling everyone's cognac in their cups. His drink, however, was crystal clear. He sighed, and my nose bristled with the gin on his breath.

I could tell Zinnia came from money, but with Haze it was hard to say. You couldn't miss the shimmer of his cufflinks: rubies cut into heart shapes. But the cuffs themselves were a touch raggedy, with some stitches coming loose, some edges frayed. The white of his shirt had turned a shade of jaundice. He had the crisp, ocean-air scent of barbershop perfume, but his hair showed no signs of having seen a recent pair of scissors, and his chin and cheeks were stubbled.

As the others were just beginning to talk among themselves, a man came rushing in like the rabbit in *Alice's Adventures in Wonderland*, even checking his pocket watch. He was followed by two waiters, one who took his coat as he shrugged it from his shoulders, and the other who took his hat as he tilted his head to one side to knock the hat off. *"Je suis désolé,"* the man said to us. "So so very, very sorry." A third waiter rushed in, carrying a chair for him, and the man began to sit before the waiter had even set the chair down. The waiter managed to tuck it in beneath him just in time. But no sooner did the man land on the chair than he popped back up. He paced as he spoke, wringing his hands.

He apologized some more, though his late entrance seemed to me intentional.

"I have so much to tell you," he told us, but then told us nothing. He paced among us, squinting, choosing his words. He finally slapped his hands together and began. "The reason I'm late is because I'm leading a few other meetings of this kind, and I've been on the telephone and sending telegrams to assure everything's in order with my various managers. We're here in Paris, but we're also in London and in New York. I found as many of us as I could."

"Who is *us*?" asked Delphine Blanchet, drawing out the *s*, hissing it.

"I make toys," he said, earnestly, as if that was an answer to her question. "Mechanical poodles that do flips. Clockwork mice you send scurrying. Toy boats that vendors sell at the gates to a park."

Mr. Sugar Cubes piped up again. "Do you make those little tin monkeys on bicycles?"

"I do not," he said with a harrumph, as if the very notion of it was somehow insulting.

"Well, that's a shame," he said.

I exchanged a look with Zinnia, who exchanged a look with Haze, who exchanged a look with me. In just that handful of seconds that our glances fumbled around, our friendship was formed. And for the rest of the meeting, our every gesture was conspiratorial, an unspoken pact—it was now the three of us against the rest of them.

The toymaker went on: "I had a contract with the White Star Line, for the exclusive production of toys based on the *Titanic*. I have warehouses full of them. Little *Titanic*s for your bathtub.

*Titanic*s that you wind up with a key. And models you build from a kit." He gestured toward the ship at the table's center. "Even the lifeboats on the model unhook and they'll float on their own. But I can't sell any of it." In his grand-showman style, his chest puffed up and out, he added, "Except as a morbid curiosity in an underground marketplace of horror."

Delphine then spoke up again. "Were you *on* the *Titanic*?" she asked the toymaker.

"None of us were," the toymaker said. "None of us here. Like all of you, I had tickets but didn't board. My wife fell ill, as she often does. Much of my life has been strained by her fierce unhappiness. I know what you're thinking: 'Such a cheerful fellow, a maker of toys, saddled with a sourpuss.'"

I'm sure none of us were thinking that. He didn't seem so much cheerful as wound up, like one of his windup mice, which was probably why his wife was so miserable. All of it: the invitations delivered in bottles, his arriving so late and so frenzied—I was already exhausted by his joie de vivre. But at least he'd finally given some insight into our little party: I was not the only one here who'd not gone down with the ship.

He went on some more about the wife: "I nearly left without her. And when the ship sank, everything went topsy-turvy. I questioned all logic. Perhaps all those years of her sadness was . . . premonition. All those aches and pains she complained of . . . maybe they were all just . . . rehearsal. And then came that day, the day the *Titanic* left the dock, that she rescued us with her despair." He stepped up to the side of the table so that he could reach across and unhook one of the lifeboats from the model ship. He held it up before his eyes and studied it as he spoke. "Then I started noticing a few newspaper articles about other people, like me, like you, who'd intended to board the *Titanic* but didn't. I hired a secretary to study the newspapers. And then I used my contacts at the White Star Line to get access to records, so I could contact you . . . so I could form my secret societies." He squeezed the lifeboat in his fist. "I thought there might be a few things we'd all have to say to each other. I was not on the ship, so I have no business saying I survived it, but I've not recovered from my good luck. That shipwreck I avoided just keeps dragging at me nonetheless."

"How many of us are there?" someone asked.

"I believe we delivered nearly fifty bottles," he said. "I was very careful. This society includes only those who absolutely had plans to travel on the *Titanic*. Because it is a phenomenon, you know. People pretending to be like us. It's very easy to boast of such a staggering turn of luck, of such proximity to disaster. One article I read joked that if all the thousands of people who claimed to have had tickets actually boarded, the ship would have sunk in the harbor. Everyone wants a piece of that ship that's rotting at the bottom of the sea. But I know *your* stories are true. And I'd like to hear them."

"What business is it of yours?" squeaked the man at the end of the table. "I'll have none of this."

"Then *I'll* tell your story," the toymaker said. "You're Henry Dew, the American evangelist. Your tent revival show was on a European tour. You'd been scheduled to board the *Titanic* when it docked in France, but you couldn't bear to leave the spa in Cherbourg, where you whiled away hours soaking in sulfur baths while sipping pink wine. It had probably felt sinful, hadn't it? Such fleshly indulgence. But by falling under the spell of it, you canceled your return to your pulpit. And you live another day."

I looked around the table. *Everyone* was looking around the table. Were we next for such skewering? It seemed Mr. Sugar Cubes was right when he brought up the detectives in novels; it seemed we very well might have been gathered here to be accused.

Haze casually reached his arm around behind me to rest on the back of the pew. He scooted in even closer, pressing more of his weight against me. I half expected him to rest his head on my shoulder.

"Yes. Yes, I did," Henry Dew said. "Yes, I canceled my travel on a sinking ship. How could that not be interpreted as divine intervention? Hm? How is that glass of pink wine not God's greatest gift to me? In turning my back on my spiritual duties, I was rewarded with my life. I was rewarded for loitering in pleasure. What am I supposed to make of that? Hm? The angels and the devils have swapped places."

"No," said a woman in a simple blouse and skirt, a simple hat. "No," she said again, sitting up straighter, placing a fist gently atop the table. "Heaven is where it's always been. I'm no man of God like you, that's for sure, so what do I know, but let me tell you one thing that I *do* know, and that's that I'm very, very devout. I work in an orphanage, the very same orphanage I grew up in. No one ever came for me, and I never left. But the nuns gave me a job. And a cot. I cook and I clean. I read to the children. My mother never gave me anything, not even a name, but let me tell you something, Reverend Dew, I lack nothing. I have the gift of caring for children that nobody cares about . . . my place in heaven is in no doubt. My heart is so full of God's love that I sometimes feel greedy. Sometimes I feel like I've been more blessed than I deserve."

When she stopped, the toymaker stood behind her. He put his hand on her shoulder. "Tell us your story," he said.

"Some of the children leave the orphanage and go on to have lovely lives," she said, looking up at the toymaker, then around the table. "A boy of mine . . . well, a boy of ours, of the orphanage, I taught him how to cook, and now he owns several restaurants. And even a few hotels. He sent me first-class tickets for the *Titanic,* with an invitation to visit him in New York. He wanted me to meet his wife, and his babies, and to have a beautiful vacation. 'You very much deserve it,' he said. But I wrote to him asking him if I might instead take the ticket to the White Star offices and exchange it for money, for the orphanage. There were things we needed. He was very kind about it, and consented, and said it would be just fine, that he understood, and he even sent another donation. A very generous donation." She took her gaze from the rest of us and gave it to the evangelist alone. "In not boarding that ship, I saved my own life, and improved the lives of motherless children. What are we supposed to make of *that*, Reverend Dew?"

To the Reverend Dew's credit, he nodded politely and kept his mouth shut.

The toymaker nodded too, but *im*politely, with a smug grin. Perhaps this was all proving his point: our shared twist of fate kept twisting the knife.

4

Suddenly everyone wanted to tell their own stories of such grim good luck. They interrupted each other, rattled on all at once, or waited for any pause, any intake of breath that might allow them to butt in with tales of their own.

I felt this impulse myself. We all wanted to unpack our steamer trunks in those phantom suites. We longed to be both survivor and victim, despite being neither.

Delphine Blanchet, the actress: "I've always said I wouldn't be caught dead on an American stage," she told us, her breath fluttering the lace of her veil. "I shudder to think that I might've been subjected to it nonetheless. Dead on an American stage, I mean. They might have fished my corpse out of the Atlantic, tucked me into a glass coffin, then sent me on a farewell tour." Her appointment in New York City wasn't theatrical in nature: she was to make her first silent film, in which she was to play the sad clown Pierrot. "I couldn't resist," she said. "I love playing vengeful men."

The day before she was to board the *Titanic*, an actor pickled on opium warned her that silent cinema steals an actress's voice. When she returned to the stage, she'd be only whisper and rasp, he said.

"I didn't believe a word of it," Delphine said. "But as I readied for travel, I kept noticing my shadow. It kept falling in my path.

Faint. Flickering. Voiceless. And then, as slight as it was, it began to feel heavy on my ankles, as if it was dragging me backward."

Jules Beaufort, the prizewinning physician: "I should be embarrassed to tell you this," he said, and we all leaned in to hear more. "I was traveling to America to lecture medical students, as I'd done before. But before, I'd traveled on the *Olympic* and I'd made use of the ship's stenographer, to take my dictation. I was quite taken with her. Yes, she was quite pretty, but I was mostly impressed with how quite competent she was." (*Quite, quite,* he seemed to mutter, as he paused to stroke his beard.) "But for this last trip, one of the colleges booked me on the *Titanic*. I eventually got up the nerve to ask if they might book me on the *Olympic* instead, so that I might work with the stenographer again. After the *Titanic* sank, she came to seem my very salvation. I can't stop thinking about her. Since I'm a man of science, you might say that I should be above superstition. And I might have agreed with you, *before.* But the fact of the matter is, science is preoccupied with mystery. There's no scientific reason at all that my pretty stenographer— that precious, divine little soul—isn't a powerful agent of fate."

Rémy Leroy, the gambler: "I have a lover—well, she makes love for a living, so she's not *my* lover, she's the lover of many—but she tells the future with a trick knee. When it gives her fits, she sees into the days ahead. On the morning I was to leave on the *Titanic,* she wept and begged me to stay. She promised me I'd die by iceberg, believe it or not. I'm a gambler, not a man of science" (and he nodded in the physician's direction) "so I have a deep faith in chance. I gave her the benefit of the doubt, and I told her I'd let a coin toss decide whether I stay or go. *Pile ou face.* But she's American, so it's 'heads or tails' where she's from. 'I'll give you head and tail both,' she said, 'if you don't go nowhere at all.'" (Here the red-headed gambler winked at us, assuming we'd either forgive him such burlesque, or delight in it.)

The physician spoke again, and again ran his fingers through his beard. "I've been consulting with fortune tellers myself," he said. "Spirit workers. Clairvoyants. Sometimes they're the only ones who make any sense in matters such as these."

"Frauds, most of them," the gambler said.

"How can you say that?" said the physician. "Your lover's trick knee saved your life."

"I said *most*, not *all*," he said. "Surely you don't believe every fortune you're told."

"Of course not," he said.

"I've made a living beating men at cards on these ships," the gambler said. "But when I win, I win honestly. I can't say that of all the card sharps at sea. Cheaters, some of them. Charlatans. And some of these cheaters have wives who'll read your cards, or your palm, or the bumps on your head, and tell you all sorts of lies. You should be careful."

An older woman, who sat with a younger one and who had yet to say anything at all, said, "I had just such a feeling myself. A feeling that I shouldn't board. That's why we didn't." She put her hand on the young woman's wrist and told us nothing more of her story, though she did mention, as an afterthought, her name: "I'm Madame Petit."

"I had no such feeling," Haze said to that. "I was boarding in Cherbourg. With a patron. We had a spat, and we went back to Paris."

Patron. Perhaps that explained the rubies in his cufflinks. He did seem handsome enough, and beguiling enough, to attract saviors.

After Haze spoke, we learned that Zinnia was the daughter of Billy Blythe, the American confectioner.

"I was traveling first class with my father and my mother," Zinnia said, in that crisp but tender voice of hers. "But first class was only for the whites, as it turns out. My mother is Japanese. When we arrived at Cherbourg, my mother and me looking like we do, we got everyone flustered. We were detained. There were whispers, there was paper shuffling. People went behind closed doors. They took us to a room and poured us wine, and stammered apologies, and promised everything would be settled in no time at all. Finally, they told us we'd be traveling *second* class. My father protested, but got nowhere. So we didn't board. And we didn't drown." She lifted one shoulder in a half shrug, knocking her ermine off. She then raised her cognac. "Here's to a world that's rotten to its core."

I raised my glass, but I was the only one. Haze's gin was gone. I took a sip of my cognac, put the glass back down. Then Haze picked my glass up, so that he could raise it in Zinnia's direction and take a sip too. "Hallelujah to that," Haze said.

I was the last to speak. I paused as everyone watched me and waited. I'd already grown attached to the story I'd rehearsed on the way over, and to the character I'd created, the man with the book of jewels. I wasn't sure I wanted to let him go. I didn't want that beautiful book to slip through my fingers.

For a moment, I considered sticking to the story I'd already invented, but revising it, so that I was the same character, but no longer on the *Titanic,* so I'd fit in with the rest of them. I wasn't on lifeboat no. 15. I wasn't on the *Titanic* at all, I could say. I felt the character I created become criminal, creeping in under my skin. *I decided to steal the book,* I would tell them. It would be a neat little twist. I would steal the book, the *Titanic* would sink, and the book's American buyer wouldn't know it *wasn't* at the bottom of the sea. I could be racked with guilt. Imagine it: abetted in my crime by an accident that killed hundreds. How could I live with such a thing?

But I suspected, even if I did tell the story I'd come up with,

I'd end up confessing at the end of it, once I'd sputtered it all out. I only got so far as to describe the peacocks on the book's cover before I flung that spangled *Rubaiyat* back into the ocean. I ended that fiction and told them all the truth.

"I worked for the White Star Line," I said. "I started there a few years ago, wanting to see the world." *Even as I was terrified of it,* I didn't say. "But the job I got was with a ship's printing press . . . I didn't see the sea at all. I worked nights in a room without windows, slept most of the day. The news would arrive during the night via telegraph, and we'd set the type and create our own makeshift morning papers. One morning when I brought a stack of our newspapers to the ship's library, the library steward was out. So I lingered. I looked at the books in the bookcase. A woman, a passenger, came up to me and asked me to recommend something."

Rescue me, she said. *Tell me what to read. And I don't want one of your newspapers.* She sighed. *The newspapers. Once upon a time, people could escape on a ship, with a book, instead of being dragged back to shore with all the awful news of the day.*

"And I did just that. And that's *all* I did. I recommended a book. A book she then read, and then happened to fall in love with. She turned out to be the wife of a railroad tycoon, and I guess she spoke of our conversation for weeks afterward, and eventually her story made the rounds of all her various social circles, along the lines of all the world's leaders of transportation, until it landed with an executive at White Star. I got called into an office. Library steward is a plum job, but I was able to jump quite a few ranks in order to be appointed the library steward of the *Titanic*. Of the second-class library."

"I'm dying to know what the book was," Zinnia said.

"Yes," said Delphine Blanchet. "I must know of it."

"A novel, *The Awakening*, by Kate Chopin," I told them. "Very atmospheric. Even the colors of the sky reflect the character's soul. And it offers a stroll through New Orleans, in case you've never been." The novel is also set partly in an island town called Grand Isle, which certainly drew me in. I grew up in a town with a similar name, but with nothing much else in common. Though Grand Island was in the middle of Nebraska, about as far from any ocean as anywhere in America, I pictured the characters of *The Awakening* in the streets of my childhood. When Nebraska was owned by France, in those years before the Louisiana Purchase, when French fur traders settled it, they dubbed the town La Grande Île, sitting as it did on an island made by two rivers snaking around each other.

I pictured my mother as Edna Pontellier, the woman in the novel who abandons her husband and children. In Edna's face, I recognized my mother's unhappiness.

Libraries varied from ship to ship in how they built their collections. The library of the *Adriatic,* where I met the tycoon's wife, consisted only of a bookcase of castoffs, of volumes left behind on deck chairs or abandoned in staterooms or at breakfast tables.

Among the things I loved about *The Awakening* was the object itself. Such a homespun-looking thing, as harmless as a cookbook, its cloth cover featuring a pattern of green leaves on spirals of vines with dots of wine-colored grapes, all of it a little rough around the edges to resemble the prickly stitch of embroidery.

Meanwhile, *The Awakening* got pulled from library shelves in the American Midwest. It was set aflame. One preacher fire-and-brimstoned about it, calling it deadlier than sewer gas. So I was pleased to see it there in the library of the *Adriatic,* so wantonly on the shelf, especially since the book begins with the married couple taking a vacation. I liked the idea of a woman on the ship seeing herself, so alive on the page, as she read of Edna on a beach glancing out to the sea. I've often wondered if that was why the tycoon's wife so took to the novel.

"When I reported for work, on the day the *Titanic* was to set sail, I was told I was being sent home, that I would receive a reassignment. I had my theories about that . . . *have* my theories. The steward who took my place didn't survive, of course." I paused. "And it was my name, not his, that showed up on the lists of the dead for many days."

Someone among them gasped. I wondered if I seemed closer to the tragedy than any of them, closest to the bottom of the sea.

"That makes for a marvelous bit of intrigue," said the mystery writer. *Plink, plunk.* She dropped sugar cubes into another glass of cognac. "A shipwreck at the beginning of the book. A man survives it. Or so he thinks. He has a life filled with peculiar circumstance. And, in the novel's final twist, he sees his name on a list of those who perished." Penelope took a sip, then looked at us as we sat looking at her. "He was dead all along," she explained.

Haze drummed his fingers on the back of my hand. "Are you still haunting the ships of White Star?" he asked. His long, delicate, piano player's fingers were riddled with rings.

"No," I said. "I stopped working for White Star only a few weeks later." I told them about the bookshop I eventually bought, which I made sound like divine providence. The shipwreck had led me to the life I'd always wanted, I told them: a literary life in Paris.

"Can we acquire *The Awakening* from your little shop?" Delphine Blanchet asked. "There's a playwright who has been *desperate* to create just such a character for me."

I didn't dare tell her she was much too old to play Edna Pontellier. But it wouldn't have mattered; Delphine was not *too* anything for any character. While I sometimes felt incapable of convincing anyone of my existence, no one disbelieved in Delphine Blanchet. We believed her every gesture, every utterance, her every heavy sigh.

"I do keep some copies of it on hand," I said. *Keep,* I said. As if I was always running out. *Keep,* yes, because I can't sell a book to save my life. "And I can order more. I have accounts with distributors. I sell new and used."

I gave each of them my card, which had only the name of my shop and its address, all in a typeface called Clair-de-lune. I'd paid a printer a small fortune for the cards, on linen, with raised letters you could feel with your fingertips, and dabs of color: pale green, gold, rosy pink. The cards' elegance was a symptom of my predicament: I cared more about owning a bookshop than I did about running a business.

"What a dream," Zinnia said, studying the card. "*That's* my idea of a candy shop."

"Zinzins," Haze said, with a snap of his fingers, figuring Zinnia out. "The gumdrops. They're named after you, I'll bet. In your honor."

"Somewhat, I suppose," she said. "More of a punishment, really." She took from her chatelaine purse a black lacquer case with a white crane across the top of it, its wings outstretched in mother-of-pearl. As she plucked out a cigarette from the case and lit it, she said, "Daddy introduced Zinzins when I was sixteen. I'd picked up cigarettes at boarding school, and Zinzins were supposed to lure me away from them. They have a nicotine kick, or so they say." She took smoke in, then blew it out. "It's impolite for grown women to smoke, let alone schoolgirls." But she wasn't haughty about it or arrogant. There seemed even something apologetic in her voice.

I took those gumdrops sometimes to settle my nervous stomach. The Zinzins were sold in something resembling a cigarette box, a robin's-egg blue with curlicues of silver foil, and it even featured the silhouette of a woman in profile, her piles of hair not unlike Zinnia's, with a cigarette between her fingers and tantalizingly near her lips. Zinzins had always seemed more of a curative than a candy to me, and I knew they were intended to lure *every* smoker from cigarettes, to trick them into swapping one addiction for another.

"I've never liked licorice," Haze said, and something about the *l*'s rolling across his tongue sounded flirtatious. He wiggled those fingers again, this time gesturing for Zinnia's cigarette case. She held it out to him and offered a match.

Penelope, the novelist, handed me her own calling card and

asked if I might deliver the book to her. Old Madame Petit, a winegrower with vineyards in the north of France, did the same, along with Jules, the physician.

Delphine Blanchet's card was a paper doll of herself, in fancy dress, her name and an address written across her full skirts.

Zinnia asked me, "Does your bookstore have subscribers?" I shook my head no. She put out her cigarette and took on the brisk demeanor of the businesswoman she was. "Well, we could start a book society. We'll all want to meet again, but what will we talk about? How *fortunate* we are? How *guilty*? Meet again and again to talk on and on about how we don't have any words for how we feel? But if we have a *book* to discuss, we can talk about everything that's on our minds without having to talk about ourselves at all."

Here was what we learned from each other: the *Titanic* did not belong to any of us in any way, no matter what was stamped on our tickets.

She seemed to be putting into words what was in everybody's head. We felt a need to meet again, but dreaded it at the same time. And though she was being direct enough that it might have sounded rude had someone else suggested it, Zinnia's nature was gently persuasive. The toymaker seemed especially relieved.

"I'll get you the addresses of all the others in the other groups too," he told me. "Yes. I think that is exactly what the plan was lacking. An unsentimental purpose."

This unsentimental education I was to provide would bring me more customers than I'd had all month. The toymaker said he'd sent fifty invitations for these meetings of *Titanic* ticket-holders in Paris, London, and New York. With only one word—*subscribers*—Zinnia might have set me on a path toward saving my shop from ruin. I even suggested that we meet at my book-shop next time.

"We'll meet again in two weeks," the toymaker said.

Were they all as lonely as I was? As I'd imagined myself on

lifeboat no. 15, the pilfered *Rubaiyat* in my coat, I thought of the darkness, the uncertainty, how even though there were so many of us, even though we were all so close together, we were all utterly alone—that loneliness somehow became *my* loneliness, my empty shop, my listening to the bell above the shop door never ringing. I knew it was ridiculous—immoral, maybe; maybe even dangerous—to align my own doldrums with such extravagant loss.

But the fact was this: I'd survived *something*, and I think that's how they felt too. If we gathered with our collective anxiety, if we crossed all those nerves, we'd spark up a solution. But maybe that's what the people of lifeboat no. 15 thought too. Maybe they thought their shared despair had produced out of nowhere the *Carpathia*, the ship that arrived to rescue them. The sight of the ship's first tiny spot of light had been enough to pluck them from the eternal darkness.

Zinnia stood from the table and dropped her own card in my direction. Haze picked it up before I could, but leaned in toward me, holding it out before the both of us to read together. The paper was milky and almost translucent, and sparkling, like sugar syrup. "You can eat it, if you want," she confirmed. "It's made of *oblaat*, the same edible paper we use for some of our candy wrappers."

Beneath Zinnia's name was what seemed to be her title: *Candy Heiress*.

"What's it taste like?" Haze asked.

Zinnia took another card from her purse, leaned over, and held it at Haze's lips. He opened his mouth, seemingly uncertain as to whether to lick it or eat it. She placed it on his tongue. He chewed, and the sound of it was the flimsy crackle of a dry leaf underfoot. Haze raised an eyebrow, contemplating. *"Oh la vache,"* he said. "Never tasted such a flavor."

"Candied lily," she said, and with that she turned on her heel and was gone.

Haze dropped his cigarette into my almost empty cognac glass, where it sizzled and flickered when it hit the last splash of booze.

Haze followed after Zinnia, giving me a friendly slap on the shoulder on his way out. I wanted to follow too, but those who had no calling cards were leaving their addresses with me, which I was writing on the backs of the cards of others. But I was also relieved that Haze and Zinnia left before I stood. I'd been sitting so long, I feared I'd be clinging to my walking stick for dear life. While Haze too had a little swing to his hips, it was a lovely sway; it suited him. My limp didn't fit me at all.

By the time I'd collected all the streets and arrondissements and stepped out onto the sidewalk, there was no one around. I halfway hoped Haze and Zinnia had gone off together, but the thought of it gave me a little stab of jealousy at the same time.

I suddenly regretted that I'd not told anyone my name. But I hadn't wanted *that* to be the thing they all remembered about me.

5

The first library I destroyed, book by book, was in a captain's suite on a clipper ship.

My father left my mother and me in our vaudeville theater in the middle of America to become an actor in London. A year or so later, my mother punished my father for his abandonment by abandoning me, putting me on that clipper ship to toss me across the Atlantic. This was my mum's way of grabbing me by the ankle, spinning me around in the air, and flinging me, slingshot, right at my daddy to knock him down flat.

I was ten or eleven but looked seven or eight.

In New Orleans, where my mother took me to let me go, I was entrusted to a friend of my father's, a sailor named Leopold. When he wasn't working in my father's theater, he was crossing the Atlantic on one of the only clippers still sailing.

My father, the manager of the theater in London where Leopold labored over the sets, the pulleys, the scrims, and the curtains, had promised him he could finally step from the wings and into the lights of the stage—even as Hamlet if he wanted—if only he would carry me safely across the sea.

In the end, my father wasn't afraid of a Black Hamlet on his theater's stage; he just couldn't bear to surrender a lead role. Only he could be his theater's Lear, Macbeth, Falstaff. He even deprived Leopold of Othello.

But you're too dark, my father told him, coming up with an excuse. *Moors are a little more copper-colored.*

I can paint my face copper as easy as you can, Leopold said, but my father just laughed and patted him on the back. My father was not a great actor onstage, but offstage he was a master fake.

That old clipper ship that carried me was on its last legs, and its captain was antique too, often twisted up drunk in a hammock on deck. But Leopold looked after me, taking time for me even among all his management of the sails and jibs and masts, mixing for me every morning a cup of coffee sweet and muddy with molasses. He plucked the worms from my gingerbread, and gave me fresh rainwater to drink, and cooked a turtle he caught. He seemed to know the journey so well he could read even a cloudless sky for the storms to come. Before the worst of the weather arrived when there were still days of sailing ahead, he introduced me to the captain's empty suite and the library in the corner, the books lashed to the shelves with rope to keep them from tumbling.

"You'll discover your bones in this one," Leopold said. He handed me a volume of Shakespeare's collected plays. He handed me too a magnifying glass with a whale's tooth for a handle, as the print was so tiny on the onionskin. "But you should read *The Tempest* instead of *Hamlet.*" He gave me a wink, and smiled sly. "You'll see yourself in there, too, as we sail into the storm. It's got a shipwreck, and a library. And books tossed into the sea."

Magic books, no less. Prospero summons squalls and spirits with incantations. *The Tempest* would come to take *Hamlet*'s place as the Shakespearean play to haunt me ever after. It would bring Leopold and me together, and push us apart, in startling ways in the years to come. *The Tempest* even wrecked my leg, but that wouldn't be for another few years.

While on the clipper ship, though, Leopold battled storms that might have been sea monsters in my imagination, despite the ship not tossing me around much. He was already tall, but now he towered, became mythological. I hid belowdecks, away from the sleet and snow that iced the sails, to read everything in that library related to the sea, to wrecks, to whales, even nautical guides, as if to throw myself overboard, to stir up typhoons and dragons.

I found a cloisonné brazier—a tabletop furnace for burning incense or for warming opium pipes once upon a time in the ship's glory days of smuggling drugs. The fire kept me warm and lit the page, lifting the words from the dark.

I love words as much as I do the stories they tell. I can lose myself in the shape of a letter, the shade of the ink. I can get caught up in the twists of an ampersand.

But to keep the fire in the brazier burning, I had to fuel the flame. I would read a page, then tear it out, crumple it up, toss it in. The colder it got, the quicker I read. I knew, from the creaking of the ship and the roar of the ocean, that Leopold must be struggling. I imagined myself Prospero the magician, that if I just kept the fire going, I'd bring the sun back to the black sky.

As every book collapsed in my hands, I learned from its wreckage. I came to know a book's hidden architecture as its silk-floss stitching unraveled and its binding cracked. Calico, linen, calfskin. I cradled every book's shoulder and spine as I gutted it.

6

A letter arrived on stationery of Irish linen, Duchess size, in an azure tint, with the confectioner's letterhead, *Paper Crane Confectionery*, above an image of a papery crane in flight.

Dear Yorick, and no, you didn't tell me your name yesterday,

You'll see that this letter is attached to a box, and inside that box are other boxes, of Flicket-a-Flacket, the closest thing we have to pralines at my candy co. Walnuts rolled in black sugar, a Japanese sweet. You ought to put a box with every book you send out. Our Titanic survivors can gnaw on the candy and pretend they're in New Orleans.

I've been to New Orleans a time or two, and I just this moment remembered an old nurse who cured my seasickness with a cup of hot lemonade and bourbon. That was back when I sailed frequently, before the Titanic. But I haven't sailed since, have you?

I don't want to tell you how to run your own business, Yorick, but . . . You'll be tempted to be generous when you bill us for your book subscription, and you'll charge us all too little. You will, I just know it. You'll think it friendly, or you'll worry they'll think you greedy.

But let me tell you, anyone who wants something for nothing is a swindler.

You're putting together something precious. You're like the string musicians who fiddled for the victims while the Titanic sank.

And, as you well know, there's a ghoulish lust for Titanic memento mori. If you were to, say, paste a bookplate on the inside cover—"From the library of The Titanic Survivors' Book Society" or some such—then you've tripled the worth of it, at the very least. So when you think of it that way, we're getting a bargain.

(I put this letter aside after writing those lines so I could consult with the artist who designs our wrappers—within an hour she'd sketched what I've included in this envelope. You'd mentioned something about bejeweled peacocks on the book that went down with the Titanic. Just send word if you'd like me to print up a batch. And let me know also if you want that apostrophe or not. To my eye, it's a blight.)

So let your subscribers pay an arm and a leg. Or <u>pay through the nose,</u> if you prefer. (Are all the metaphors for emptying our purses about physical pain?)

Yours faithfully,
Zinnia

[Zinnia's signature was an extravagance of curlicue and spin, the Z of it especially dizzying.]

P.S. When I sat down to write you this letter, I had to stop before I could even begin. I realized I didn't know your name. I thought perhaps I'd missed it, or forgotten it, but when my secretary took down the address from your card and consulted with a librarian, she discovered you in the latest edition of the International Directory of Bibliophiles. When she told me you must be <u>Yorick,</u> I knew for certain that you'd not breathed a word of it, because if you had, I wouldn't have believed you. Such a name wasn't given to you; you surely took it. It's far too magnificent to have come by honestly.

THE TITANIC SURVIVORS'
BOOK CLUB

I wrote back to Zinnia on paper of alpine flax, octavo size, in a pale green-gray tint the stationer called "alligator"; no letterhead.

Dear Zinnia (when was the last time I wrote a capital Z in cursive? Penmanship lessons? Now it's all I want to do, just spend all the ink in my pen on a page full of z's),

You didn't send an invoice for the Flicket-a-Flacket, so I must insist you do so immediately so I can promptly lose it in my overstuffed drawer of overdue bills and deadbeat accounts. (That said, I'd give anything for a box of those Titanic bookplates, and do keep it apostrophe-less, especially if the printer charges by the punctuation.)

   (And all of this is my way of saying thank you, not only for the candy, but for the very invention of this oddball book society. I'm not at all troubled by your business advice. It must be obvious that I'm in great need of it. I've not had an easy time. When sailors give up the sea and take to land, they're said to have <u>swallowed the anchor</u>. And though the bookshop does often feel like it's dragging me into the depths, I'm also grateful it keeps me landlocked, weighing me down. I lie

awake in the night, overwhelmed by the thought of waking up in the morning one day closer to shutting my doors for good. But then morning comes, and I walk into my shop and fall under its spell, the dust of old paper floating in the rays of sun. The Flicket-a-Flacket you sent reminds me of pralines, yes, but also the brown sugar scent of pulp and leather.)

You'll see that I've sent you a box too, this one made out of a book. In London, I studied with a bookbinder, but I mostly use my tools to wreck, not repair. I make little vaults. I paste together the pages of a book—all but the first fifteen or so, so that it still looks like a book when you lift the lid—shellac the sides, install a hinge on the binding. I cut into the pages to saw away their words. When it's mostly hollow, I line the inside with some silk or flannel. I've sold some of these here in the shop. (You'll probably advise me to gut all the books on my shelves. Maybe my fortune lies in stripping away all the stories.)

People have done this for centuries, to hide their jewelry or to smuggle diamonds.

I made for you a box from a mystery by our friend Penelope Quinn: The Spinster's Smoking Gun, for you to use as a smoking kit. (One of my customers is an addict who bought my hinged copy of Freud's Interpretation of Dreams to store the needles and vials of his morphine habit.)

Yours truly,
Yorick*

*Which is indeed the name I got saddled with at birth. Inside the box I've sent you, I included a pipe with a skull-shaped bowl, so you'll feel like Hamlet when you're holding it in your fingertips.

7

Zinnia arrived early at my shop on the evening of our book club, and I was relieved to see her. Though she'd written me the one sweet letter, she hadn't responded to my reply, except for three words jotted on a little card when she sent the bookplates: *With apostrophe severed.* She'd made no mention of the pipe I'd sent, and I worried it'd been too morbid.

"I walked by the entrance twice without even seeing it!" she said, flustered, standing in the doorway. She even sighed, puffing at a curl that had fallen loose from her combs and dangled across her face. "Maybe that's your trouble . . . The shop doesn't even exist until you've passed it by."

It was true: the shop was invisible. La Librairie Sirène was on the Rue Galande, one of the oldest streets in Paris, and one of the shortest, one of the most narrow. Our avenue still showed signs of the city's old walls, all the houses and shops and gardens cinched in tight, a breeding ground for tuberculosis as we breathed each other's breath.

Every morning, the café opposite me dragged its tables and chairs out onto its stick-thin sidewalk, and the café-dwellers would nudge and scoot them out farther and farther as the day wore on, out into the middle of the street, and by evening they were on my sidewalk too, just inches from my door. The later it got, the louder it was, and their voices would fill the shop, their laughter bouncing up the walls. I didn't mind it.

"Shouldn't you have a sign?" she said. "Or something etched on the window?"

"I will," I said. Somehow I hadn't gotten to it, though it had been on my list of things to do for months. I'd managed only to scrape, with a razor blade, the previous owner's name from the glass.

Zinnia made a gesture to tuck the loose curl back, but I suspected it had been engineered to dangle. She looked somehow carefully disheveled, her hair a little undone, her long dress of silk and lace resembling a nightgown for a seaside hotel—a misty pale blue with mother-of-pearl buttons. She seemed an illustration in a women's magazine, for a story about a lady caught unawares.

And she wore perfume, its soft scent of powder and honeysuckle somewhat done in by the heavy cloud of it.

She stepped into the shop, looking up and around in slow amazement. "You would never have time to read all these books even if you lived a hundred lives," she said. She glanced back to me. "Doesn't that terrify you? All that time you don't have?" But she said it in that gentle voice, with that kind smile.

I loved seeing the shop through Zinnia's eyes. The truth was, I knew all I needed to about each and every book I owned. The upside of slow business was that I could linger with a book in my hand, and by just a glance at its first few pages, and its last few, I could learn about the publisher and its city; I could learn about the paper by its watermark. There might be a note on the printer, and the typeface, the book stitching itself together piece by piece as I held it in my hands.

But no, nothing about my shop terrified me, other than my fear of losing it. I'd even managed not to need my cane as much when moving about my books; I'd become so used to the shop's every corner and ledge, its every place to perch or pivot. And the shop itself seemed to have adapted to me, shifting and bending its architecture around my uneven steps, rendering me graceful with the warp of a floorboard or the loose spindle on the staircase banister. Stacked at the end of one row of shelves, the sixty-volume set of the romances of Alexandre Dumas steadied the sharp turn at that tight corner. I could pull myself up from my low-sitting desk chair by relying on the counterweight of a thickly illustrated edition of Italian fairy tales.

The shop owner before me had installed beautiful frosted-glass globes on the bookcases, each one glowing with electricity, with words painted to indicate the sections: *Novels, Poetry, Memoir, Geography, Science,* etc. But in the many empty hours since I bought the shop, I'd been moving things around and none of the lamps matched their sections anymore.

Nonetheless, the shop had a divine order to my mind, even the clutter—so many stacks of books that teetered, or books you had to step around on the stairsteps that didn't fit into the endless cases rising up beyond where the ceiling would be. An upper gallery lined the cases, a second floor of sorts, and yet there were still books beyond reach on the upper-uppermost shelves. Everywhere throughout the shop were ladders short and tall, and ottomans and stools, all of them rickety with shaky legs, but all there to step up on, to climb up, to get closer and closer to more and more books—a Tower of Babel that promised to stretch up through the cracks in the ceiling.

When you looked down from the gallery above, down to the tiles of the ground floor, to the midnight-black marble that had been salvaged from a ruined Spanish mission, it was like you looked up into the night sky, the marble's veins of white resembling constellations.

Zinnia noticed the table tucked in under the stairs, with my display of the books I'd hollowed out. A secret money safe made out of *The Mysteries of Paris.* A vanity kit from a biography of Marie Antoinette. "Oh, and yes yes yes," she said, "thank you so much for the book with the box in it. I tore into the package before I even opened your letter—because I'm greedy—so when I saw that it was one of Penelope's novels, I worried that you intended for me to read it." She faked a shudder up her spine. "I was so relieved to find the pipe inside instead." She then gasped. "I just thought of something. Aren't they called 'penny dreadfuls,' those thrillers that she writes? Don't we need to call Penelope that? 'Penny Dreadful'?"

"Only when she's out of earshot," I said. "I couldn't resist when I saw I actually had a few Penelope Quinns on hand. Oh, and I found *you* in one of my books too."

She tilted her head. She gently swung at her side a purse made of seashell; it hung from a chain attached to her bracelet. In her other hand was her copy of *The Awakening*. "Oh?" she said, but without any note of surprise. "What a coincidence."

"More like synchronicity, I think," I said. "People think of coincidence as an accident. But synchronicity suggests a kind of . . . harmony."

It was only in that moment, hearing my own voice aloud, did I realize how rarely I actually spoke to anyone at all. But I couldn't stop. "And that's something that can often occur in a bookshop," I said. "The books find *you,* in a sense. It can seem like a book is reading your mind, as if the question in your head shapes the words on the page."

Zinnia unhitched her bag from her bracelet and tossed it, and her copy of *The Awakening,* onto a short divan. The divan had long since worn out, its velvet rubbed away to a nubby sheen, but it was the most comfortable of those in the narrow, oblong circle I'd set up. I'd brought some rickety, wire-backed chairs down from the attic. The shop's previous owners had for a time flirted with a tearoom, and all the pieces of it—marble-top bistro tables, dessert trolleys—still weighed down the rafters overhead. But a few of the seats I'd put out were only footstools and stepladders.

"But what about me?" she said. She walked to a bookcase and ran her finger along the bindings. She seemed to be looking for something.

"Hm?"

"You said you found me in a book."

"Oh, yes, of course." I went to my desk for the cookbook and held it out to her. "A candy-making guide, with recipes. Put out by Paper Crane Confectionery. There's a little biography of the company, mostly about your father and your mother, but you get a mention. You were a little girl. One of the recipes is named for you. Zinnia's Ginger Taffy."

Zinnia came toward me and she took the book. She held it with some reverence. She ran her hand over its cover. I told her a little of what I'd learned from it: Paper Crane Confectionery emerged from her father's background in the confection industry *and* her mother's. Her father was an executive for his father's candy company in San Francisco, and he went to Japan as an *o-yatoi gaikokujin*, a hired foreigner during the modernization of the country in the 1880s. He brought milk, sugar, chocolate to where the sweets had been beans, plants, rice. Her mother's family had more humble beginnings, with a little shop on Kashiya Yoko-cho—a street they called "Candy Alley." Penny candy. Near a Buddhist temple. Now her father and mother had factories in New York, Chicago, Tokyo, Paris, London, and houses here and there too. The candy they made was spun from both cultures, marrying American gluttony with the delicate flavors of Japan.

"It goes back even further," Zinnia said, wistful. "My grandmother had a cart she peddled around; she made candy sculptures of birds and fish and rabbits by blowing through a straw, like blown glass. The prettiest, most delicate things you ever saw, handed over to children to break apart wing by wing, fin by fin." She began to turn through the pages of the candy book, but distracted, seemingly seeing nothing on the page. "If only *I* could run the company myself someday," she said.

"Why can't you?"

She handed the cookbook back to me. "Oh, my father would never allow it," she said, as if it were obvious. She returned her attention to the shelves. She picked up a book, put it back without glancing at any of it, took another one down. She held the book open and flipped through its pages, but she was actually studying the bookcase itself, and everything around and above.

"Are all your books in English?" she said. When I told her no, just some, she said, "What *if* all your books were in English? What if your shop was *the* shop in Paris for English translations? And for American novels? For all the expatriates moving here. And the tourists. And the foreign students." She held the book to her chest and put her finger to her lips, then started tapping her teeth. She looked around the shop again. "Where are all your customers?" she asked.

I shrugged. "Mondays tend to be a bit . . . slow for bookshops," I said.

"No, they're not, darling," she said. "People read about books in the weekend newspapers. They should be coming in on Mondays to buy them."

Zinnia was already so much better at my job than I was, and she'd only been in my shop a few minutes.

"And they should just want to *be* here, don't you think?" she said. "Where better to just lose yourself? Lose track of time? And they should be drawn here because of you. Look at you."

"Look at me?"

"I mean—*just look at you.* You're an eccentric. It's like my imagination invented you."

I glanced downward. I felt I had put on my best for the occasion of the book club, but now I saw myself as she likely did: my suit ill-fitting, my shoelaces frayed, the varnish of my walking stick scratched up.

"You should have seen me in my library on the *Titanic*," I said.

When I was appointed library steward, I had to purchase my own uniform, and because of the expense, I took excellent care of it. I kept it pressed stiff and the brass buttons polished. The uniform conveyed more confidence on its hanger than it did when I wore it. But whenever I put it on, I did stand up straighter, lifted my chin, and walked with a steadier gait. I didn't feel like myself in the uniform, but I did feel like *somebody*.

After the ship sank and I left White Star, I kept the uniform in my closet and even carried it over with me to Paris. While I unraveled, the suit stayed impeccable and intimidating.

"I can't see you in a uniform," Zinnia said. "I'm sure you were dashing, I just can't imagine you as anyone other than . . . who you are. A bookseller in Paris."

"I'm flattered, actually."

She should have seen me combing the city for *The Awakening* to send to our network of de facto *Titanic* survivors, pushing around my old baby pram in hopes of filling it with the fifty copies I needed. I often used the pram to stroll among the riverside bookstalls or to the homes of widows dismantling their libraries.

"I don't dare tell you that I had trouble even getting the book subscription together in time for today's meeting," I said. "I only had a few copies of *The Awakening* here, but I thought I could rely on my book distributor, a man here in Paris, or his partners in London, or at the very least I'd wire the publisher in America. But the publisher went bankrupt a few years back. Rumor has it he closed up shop to weasel out of paying his authors their royalties. So then I thought I would wire the authoress herself, but I learned she dropped dead from a sudden brain hemorrhage after a long day at the St. Louis World's Fair."

"Oh my goodness, Yorick," she said with genuine shock, her hand at her chest, as if I'd just reported the death of a dear friend. "How sad."

I began to ramble to Zinnia about the profound significance of booksellers in the history of France, "how important they were in the thirteenth century," I said as I led her up the stairs to introduce her to more of the shop, "when they were specialists, when they had to have approval from the highest ranks of society in their service to the university, and the churches, and the royals. We're literally a stone's throw from the Rue Saint-Jacques, where all the printers and booksellers set up shop at the time. Books were very expensive then. It was a very serious tradition."

I wasn't sure what my point was. I guess I wanted to suggest that a bookseller's place in Paris was of historical significance, that it was more than just peddling American romance.

Zinnia's mind stuck on my mention of the royals. "Everyone is reading books about the kings and queens of Europe," she said. "You should have a whole section devoted to royalty. Biographies. Histories. Gossip."

She ran her eyes along the rows of books on the upper gallery, and I was afraid she'd see the signs I'd had printed up for the obscure sections I'd arranged. One shelf was marked *The Playbooks of Javanese Puppet Theater*, and another *Ballet in Peru*, and another *The Decasyllabic Quatrain*. I wasn't *trying* to be peculiar. It just seemed to me that if you were looking for something so specific, then you would appreciate such direction.

I'd had the shop for less than a year, and it had already been full of books when I bought it. But I kept buying more. *Your books are going to bury you,* one of my few regulars told me as a short tower of them tumbled over. I didn't know if she meant it literally or figuratively, and I didn't ask her to clarify. Zinnia paused at the section marked *Psychography and the Metaphysical*.

Just then, the front door swung open and the gambler walked in, followed by the orphan, and the evangelist, and all the rest, one by one, as we watched from above. "Rapunzel, Rapunzel," the toymaker called up to us, seeing Zinnia at the railing. "Let down your hair."

Zinnia made a broad gesture of pulling out a comb, and it all collapsed, the tresses of her hair falling down around her shoulders. Someone down below applauded. I heard their voices echoing and a few peals of laughter, and their footsteps clicking on the tile.

I'd been looking forward to the club meeting, but I hadn't expected to be so overcome. I'd never had so many people in the shop at once. For the first time, La Librairie Sirène looked exactly like it should.

Dear Titanic Survivors Book Club:

<u>The Awakening</u>: "The voice of the sea speaks to the soul. The touch of the sea is sensuous, enfolding the body in its soft, close embrace."

Yorick
Proprietor, La Librairie Sirène

8

Not only did Haze show up, he showed up dressed for the occasion, I thought, costumed almost like a book, in a silk vest with the marbleized swirl of a book's endpapers. The vest's buttons were letters wrenched off typewriter keys: the *v*, the *w*, the *x*, the *y*.

And he was even more handsome than I remembered.

He put his hand to my left cheek, then leaned in to kiss my right one. His perfume tickled my nose with the maple syrup scent of an old library, and a touch of pipe smoke and coffee. I worried he could feel, in the palm of his hand, the heat of my blush.

"Sazerac," he said, handing me the brandy he'd brought. "Bottled in New Orleans. I have an acquaintance who deals in foreign whiskies." His voice was such a deep rumble, I could feel it tremble in my own throat when he spoke.

The toymaker intruded. "We'll drink that in these," he said. He'd brought toy tea sets with the White Star flag painted on each china cup and saucer—another forbidden object from his warehouse, though *Titanic* was only stamped in tiny print on the bottom of each cup. He ran his finger along the fine detail, along the golden hearts that lined the teacup's lip. "Such artistry," he boasted. "It's an exquisite replica. Our very best work. And no one will ever see it."

"Can't you just paint over the name of the ship?" I said.

"Then sell them to unsuspecting little girls?" he said. "Or, worse yet, to *suspecting* little girls wanting to dress up and play 'tea party on the *Titanic*'?"

"I see your predicament."

I looked past the teacups. I was distracted by Haze and Zinnia. They'd gone to sit hip to hip on the narrow divan.

When Zinnia caught my gaze, I instinctively looked away. I didn't want her to think I was watching them. But she gestured me over.

"Look," Zinnia said to Haze. "Yorick made this for me." It turned out her smoking kit was small enough to fit into her purse. She took it out and demonstrated the hinges; she held the cover open to show him the pipe inside.

Penny Dreadful took no offense at seeing her book cut up, though she did note that it was the wrong one to mutilate. "You should have used my novel that has a hollowed-out book at the heart of its plot," she said. She was already nipping at the Sazerac from her *Titanic* cup.

Her husband interjected with the title of Penelope's novel, in that manner of his that was both jolly and gruff: *"The Assassin's Guide to Perfect Gentility."*

"A bellboy gets fired," Penelope explained, "so he decides to kill the daughter of the man who owns the hotel. He takes a book of manners—*The Lady's Guide to Perfect Gentility* by Emily Thornwell—carves out a cavity, and makes a bomb. With fulminate of mercury and a spring set to trigger it when the book's cover is lifted."

"Does the poor thing go up in flames?" Zinnia asked.

Before Penelope could answer, the husband interjected again. I was now thinking of him no longer as Mr. Sugar Cubes, but as Mr. Dreadful. He said, marveling almost: "Step-by-step instructions, right there on the page in front of the reader. Anyone could turn the very book they were holding into a bomb, if they wanted."

"A perfect way to assassinate *you*," Haze told Penelope, but with a flirty wink, "when the time comes."

"Oh, I should say so," she said, and I do think her delight over the possibilities of her own assassination endeared her to us.

Haze, Zinnia, and I exchanged our conspiratorial glances, but this time with a shared approval.

Everyone found their way to a seat. We held the books atop our knees, and the cups and saucers atop the books. Everyone looked to me, waiting for me to start.

"I don't really know how these conversations begin," I said. "Should I ask a question about the book?"

The gambler piped up. "Didn't read it," he said, tossing back the brandy in one gulp. His impeccable suit, midnight blue with a silvery velvet vest, was perfectly pleated; I wondered how he'd managed to arrive without a wrinkle. Perhaps a good gambler is never caught with a hair out of place.

"I didn't either," the physician said, combing his fingers through the knots in his full beard with a very un-gambler-like look of worry and fret. "But only because I didn't have time. The book didn't arrive in the mail until a few days ago."

"Forgive me," I said. "The books were hard to come by." I swallowed. Cleared my throat. "The author is dead, by the way."

This cast a gloom. The physician even sat bolt upright, as if there was time to rush to her aid. "Since 1904," I added.

Delphine Blanchet, the tragedian, paused with the cup at her lips. "Edna Pontellier is described as having her whole being filled with a *vague anguish*," she said. "I have so many ideas for that *vague anguish*, for the stage. Critics accuse me of being much too much, but I can be much too little, if given the chance."

The orphan spoke up, but only after she'd had her hand halfway raised for a while. "I really have to tell you," she said, "I didn't much care about her anguish. I didn't have much patience with her, to be honest. I have to say: a moral book would not ask us to sympathize with an immoral character."

Zinnia's tone, though only inquisitive, did take on a razor's edge. "And she's immoral simply because she longs to chew off her paw to get out of her trap?"

"What *trap*?" the orphan said, with an edge of her own. "She's trapped by her husband's devotion? By her children who need their mother? By a house full of nameless maids and cooks serving her?"

I'd hoped for everyone to agree, on everything, and to love the book as much as I did. I'd expected we'd spend our time outlining its delights. And then, making things worse still, Henry Dew, the wayward evangelist, evangelized on his new broken-down morality. He began by reading a few lines from the book: "'She was flushed and felt intoxicated with the sound of her own voice and the unaccustomed taste of candor. It muddled her like wine, or like a first breath of freedom.' Ah, that taste of candor," he said, "is godly." He stretched out one long leg, then brought it back to cross over his knee. *"Muddled her like wine,"* he repeated, drawing it out, throwing a glance in the orphan's direction. His suit, of some slick satin, began to shimmer in the lamplight. "When you transgress, your body is set alight with electricity. It's what *The Awakening* is about. It wakes you up, transgression does. Feeds your blood. It's only then, when your eyes are open, that you can see the world for what it is. And you've all sinned, all of you. You didn't get on the *Titanic*, so you feel specially blessed. What is that, if not vanity? And vanity is one of the seven deadlies." Then another glance at the orphan.

He stopped, but it seemed only a preacher's pause, letting things settle in. So we all just kept our eyes on him, silent. And that silence seemed to feed into his showmanship.

"Only when you give in to your desires," he went on, his voice lifting, "do you feel your heart beating fast. We can only reach a higher understanding through our own tawdry flesh."

Zinnia said, "Wait, wait, wait," crouching over the book in her lap, shuffling through the pages. "There's something I marked."

We waited. *Yes, please,* I thought. *Please speak so I don't have to.*

When she found what she was looking for, she said, "Ah, here," tapping the page. She ran her finger under the lines as she read them aloud: "'She could only realize that she herself—her present self—was in some way different from the other self. That she was seeing with different eyes and making the acquaintance of new conditions in herself that colored and changed her environment, she did not yet suspect.'"

I looked over to Haze, who couldn't take his eyes off Zinnia. As I'd read *The Awakening* again, any mention of infatuation seemed to summon pictures of Haze, *of sleepless nights, of consuming flames till the very sea sizzled when he took his daily plunge.*

If anyone looked over my shoulder, they'd learn too much about me in the passages I'd underlined and in the notes I wrote in the margins. Haze's pretty lips were so full, anyone would know why I'd drawn stars around *two lips that pouted, that were so red one could only think of cherries or some other delicious crimson fruit in looking at them,* though Haze's lips weren't so much crimson as they were the shade of a faded rose.

At one point in the book, Edna Pontellier laments being overpowered *with a sense of the unattainable.* I underlined that three times.

"We look to books to articulate those feelings for which we have no words," I said to the group, a line I'd rehearsed. "We want to recognize ourselves in these other lives."

"So if you find a book to be immoral," the evangelist said, "it's perhaps more about you than it is about the book."

The orphan leaned forward to speak, and though I thought she'd object, she didn't. "Maybe you're right," she said. "Maybe *immoral* isn't the right word. Maybe I'm just worried about them all. They all let themselves get so carried away."

The evangelist nodded politely at the orphan. The orphan nodded back. That seemed like progress, and perhaps the very thing we were after. Because I wasn't yet sure what we all wanted from this club, from this connection, from this determination to be considered survivors—but I was certain we weren't looking to spar.

I said, "'The books that the world calls immoral are books that show the world its own shame.'" When they all looked at me, I said, "Oh, *I* didn't say that. That's from *The Picture of Dorian Gray.*"

"I adore that novel," Zinnia said.

"Oh, then *that's* what we should have read," I said. "Of course. I feel I should apologize to everyone. I've let you down. I should have sent a different book."

"Perhaps one that *doesn't* end with the heroine stepping into the sea to drown?" This was Old Madame Petit speaking, the last in a line of winegrowers that dated back centuries, who'd said very little at our first meeting. I was about to apologize again, but then she said, without smiling, "I'm only teasing." Her voice was hoarse, and she took a sip of the Sazerac, her pinkie lifted. But it graveled her voice more when she spoke. "She's just such a bad mother," she said. "I have to believe many women would love that about her. It must look a bit like a fairy tale. To see such dissatisfaction on the page must be absolutely thrilling."

The younger woman who sat next to her, whom I took to be her daughter, made no show of emotion at all.

Zinnia must have worried about her too. "Is *she* a good mother?" she asked the daughter, but in a friendly way, clearly wanting to draw her out, to get to know her.

"Such a question," the young woman muttered.

"I am not her mother," Old Madame Petit said, reaching over to pat the woman's knee. "I'm no one's mother."

"Oh, I'm sorry," Zinnia said. "I thought you were together."

"We are," said Madame Petit.

When the young woman sensed us making much of that *We are*, she said, "We are traveling companions."

I imagined them on the *Titanic* after all, and others like them, and myself (with someone of my own, since this was all fantasy anyway), women with women, men with men, queer and covert, everyone speculating about our arrangements: Did we share a suite? A bed? Did we share cologne? Starched collars? Did we waltz in the shadows on the farthest end of the deck?

Only a few months before, I'd treated myself to a short week in the south of France, a vacation I couldn't afford—I'd even paid too much for a summery dandelion-yellow suit. At breakfast each morning were two men at a table on the veranda, men about a decade or so older than me, and I sat so I could watch them while casting my glance idly toward the ocean. I knew in my heart they were lovers, but I longed to see some flicker of intimacy, something definitive, something beyond the laughter they shared and their ease with each other. Finally, on my last morning at the hotel, over *déjeuner à la fourchette*, I caught sight of one of the men holding a piece of toast, covered in sliced radishes, to the lips of the other, feeding him a bite.

I think they simply forgot themselves.

When another silence fell, Delphine held out her cup for someone, anyone, to pour more into it. I glanced around for where I'd put the bottle, found it atop a stack of books (multiple editions of an encyclopedia of slang and vulgarisms), and took it to her.

Zinnia turned the conversation back to me. "Why did you assign this book, Yorick?"

It was you, I wanted to say back to her. *It was your idea.* But I knew there was more to this book club, even if I didn't yet know how to articulate it all.

"The book was burnt," I said, though I was taking a roundabout way to answering the question. "It was set on fire." I didn't tell them, though, that the book's burning really just came down to one pompous minister who objected to Edna's desires, her inward life, her questions. He called it poisonous and dropped it in a furnace.

I confessed then to the damage I'd done to the book myself.

"I didn't toss it in a fire, I tossed it in the sea," I said, feeling melodramatic, I suppose. "In the days before the *Titanic* left the dock, when I was still its librarian, I snuck onto the ship books that had not been approved by White Star. I mean to say, they didn't know what I was adding to the shelves. I was curating a secret library of books that had some history of being objectionable—books that had been yanked from libraries or vilified by preachers and newspaper columnists. Or condemned by monks, long ago. *The Awakening. Manon Lescaut. Candide.*" I nodded toward Zinnia. "*The Picture of Dorian Gray.* No explanation was ever given for my reassignment, but I believe those books were the reason and, in the end, what saved my life."

The funny thing was, I didn't think the White Star executives actually cared what was under the covers, only about the covers themselves. The second-class library had been fitted with books specially bound in bloodred calfskin. It was not about taste and decency, but rather a matter of business—the company partnered with the book club of the London *Times* to stock its shelves.

Anyone happening by would recognize at a glance all the outlaw books standing apart with their bindings of cloth and tweed and flannel, of paper in shades of violet, aquamarine, canary yellow.

I did wonder, too, if my walking stick and my damaged leg set me apart, like those mismatched books. I wondered if the very sight of me threatened the executives' sense of the *Titanic* as pristine and unflawed.

Zinnia put the question to the rest of our group: "Are there books that have saved *your* lives?" But, of course, she wasn't speaking of a salvation as literal as mine.

Though not everyone had an answer for her—Haze, for example, said nothing—they all seemed to like the idea of thinking about it. A book's appeal is alchemy, witchcraft. It is nostalgia, melancholy, infatuation. For the bookish, a book can stir desire like no other set of words, not a message in a bottle, not a love letter, not an inscription carved into your heart-shaped locket. You'll never fathom the exact passion you feel for the books you adore.

The orphan spoke first. While I might have thought she'd cite a religious tract, she surprised me by naming *The Secret Garden*, a fairly new children's book. "The children are left to their own devices and they save themselves," she said. "When I first read it, I just wished I could go back in time and give this book to myself when I was a little girl. But I don't think it arrived too late. A book can reach into your past, don't you think? To heal old wounds?"

"Absolutely," I said.

The gambler told us that *Moll Flanders*, the story of a brilliant thief, had set him on the right path to wrongdoing, and though he delivered this smugly, I believed he was sincere about it. Delphine Blanchet was saved by *The Flame of Life*, an erotic novel about a young artist in Venice and his affair with an older actress.

The physician was so eager to quote from *The Life of the Bee*—which was literally about the lives of bees, but philosophical about its science—that he asked me if I had a copy. I did, of course; I had a gorgeous copy—pale moss-green cloth, gilt-tooled vellum, still in the publisher's lidded glassine box featuring the book's title surrounded by garlands of flowers, bees swarming like musical notes among two hives.

"'And there comes too,'" the physician read aloud, "'a period of life when we have more joy in saying the thing that is true than in saying the thing that merely is wonderful.'"

9

After the meeting ended and everyone else was gone, Zinnia and Haze lingered. Zinnia assembled her pipe. Once the stem was screwed into the bowl, the skull sat upside down—you were to put the tobacco in through the neck, where it would sit and burn where the brain would be. She touched a match to its jawbone.

Zinnia said, "I've been thinking of Dorian Gray ever since you brought him up. There's a place I'll bet you don't know." She reattached the chain of her purse to her bracelet and led the way from the shop. I locked up, then trailed behind her and Haze as they headed along the tiny Rue Galande toward the busy Rue Saint-Jacques.

Zinnia held her pipe before us. Haze took a deep puff. "Japanese tobacco?" he said, and Zinnia nodded. He handed me the pipe, and I put my lips where his had been.

"It was my mother who taught me to smoke," Zinnia said. "Ladies smoke pipes there as much as they sip tea. *Tabako wo nomu*. To *drink* tobacco."

"I used to be in the business," Haze said.

"A tobacconist?" she said.

"*Un ramasseur de mégots*," he said. "A cigarette collector. I was a gutter boy. I had a stick with a nail on the end of it," and he reached out for my walking stick. I handed it over. He offered me his arm, to hold me up, which I didn't really need but took anyway. He used the stick to demonstrate, to stab toward the pavement. "I'd sit on the street outside cafés, waiting for the men to toss aside their cigars and cigarettes after they were all smoked up. I could just stroll along and snatch up a stub, put it in my satchel." He pantomimed the act of it. "I could collect pounds and pounds of tobacco in a day. I'd roll it all up tight in fresh paper, and I'd return to the cafés and sell it back to the smokers cheap."

"Clever," Zinnia said, and she did indeed seem genuinely impressed.

Haze handed my cane back with a kind of gentlemanly gesture—a little nod, a turn of the wrist, a wink.

At the end of the avenue was a limousine and a driver standing next to it—a driver with the fistlike face of a thug, all scowl and disdain. This was Zinnia's car, of course. The driver opened the door, then Zinnia nudged Haze forward into the back seat, she crawled in after him, and I after her.

Haze took another puff from Zinnia's pipe. "Do you spend much time in Japan?" he asked her.

"I've only been there a time or two," she said. "I grew up in America. But there's such cruelty there, you know?"

"I've never been," Haze said. "The *Titanic* was supposed to take me there for the very first time in my life."

"I've been lucky in some ways, of course, because I have money," she said, taking her pipe back for a puff, "and I was born there, but they have laws against Japanese women. Actual laws. In some parts of the country, my parents' marriage—a white man with a Japanese woman—would be illegal."

Zinnia handed me the pipe and I breathed the smoke in. It was getting easier, with every wisp becoming more and more like a breath of icy air. I thought of that tranquil shade of pale blue in the sky above the snow-topped mountains in a book of Japanese woodcuts. "Yes, such cruelty there," I said, though I'd only been in America as a boy. "What are they afraid of?"

"They're afraid of what everybody's afraid of," she said, taking the pipe back. "Afraid there's not enough to go around. They think immigrants don't *earn* anything, they take it. Any dollar a Japanese man has is one less dollar in a white man's pocket. But let me tell you something about theft," and she used her pipe as a pointer, tapping the stem at the air. "My father's father got his start selling coffee and chocolate to the prospectors panning for gold. He started with nothing other than a grinder and a bag of beans he stole off the dock. And then he stole flavors from the miners coming up from Mexico, and in from China and Japan, and France, and Italy. Chili pepper. Plum. Saffron. His little coffee cart became a factory, and his factories helped build San Francisco. And now California has passed laws that could actually void my father's marriage to my mother. Their marriage is illegal in the town my family built."

Haze put his pinkie to a ring on Zinnia's finger, toying with her marquise diamond.

"My money allows me to keep to certain circles, so I can sometimes forget about it all for a minute. But then I get reminded— and there are *always* people happy to remind you."

I wanted her to say more about being turned away from her first-class suite. Of all the ticketholders we'd met in our little *Titanic* club, she and I were the only ones who'd been *refused* entry to the ship. Did it ever feel like a grim victory? Was the secret, unspeakable moral of *her* story that that ship went down because it left her at the dock? Was there ever a sense of vengeance achieved?

The car stopped suddenly. Did I even know this street? We stepped out toward a storefront with no awning, no window, no name. The red door streaked with rust even had a posted sign: *Entrée Interdite*. Forbidden entry.

"So that's what I call the place," Zinnia said. "Entrée Interdite."

Though this was no seedy drug den—there were no bamboo pipes and no hookahs in sight, no sailors collapsed on bug-infested mattresses—it was clearly meant to resemble one, to capture the romantic mystery without the ruin and danger.

I felt like I was inside the Chinese box where Dorian Gray kept his opium—the black and gold-dust lacquer, the patterns of curved waves, the silk, the crystal, the plaited metal threads.

There were giant peacocks, some blue, some snow white, in the wallpaper. Ceiling fans spun, kicking up a breeze, making the tasseled Venetian lampshades sway above the tables.

No sooner had we collapsed on the fat pillows of a booth than a waiter in what looked to be silk pajamas arrived, through the powdery blue smoke of incense, with a bottle of champagne.

And then I panicked. I didn't have a nickel to contribute to an evening out with someone like Zinnia. The waiter poured, then handed me a coupe of champagne I tried to refuse. "I can't— I don't— I didn't," I stuttered, but then I did, I took one sip and the bubble and sparkle of it lifted my spirits so quick I didn't care what the night might cost me. I was still feeling the few shots of brandy I'd had at the shop. I promised myself that, when I sobered up, I would regret nothing. *Don't be so hard on yourself*, I promised myself I would say.

Another waiter came along to present us each with a menu practically the size of the tabletop.

My eyes were drawn especially to the expense of the snails, frogs, turnips, dandelion salad—all pests and weeds dressed up in wines and sauces.

Our waiters seemed particularly charmed by Haze, as did any man or woman who got caught up in his attention—but maybe it only seemed so, since I myself couldn't take my eyes off him.

"*Pêches Pochées Zinnia?*" Haze said, tapping his finger at the menu. "Named for *you*, I suspect. *You're* the Zinnia of the *pêches pochées*."

"They poach the peaches, then pour kirsch over them, then drop a match," Zinnia said. "It's very dramatic. But it has nothing to do with me, really. The chef just loves to name dishes after people who eat here. See?" She pointed to my menu, and to Haze's, and indeed names were attached to practically everything. Even the stewed eels belonged to someone named Yves. "He'll name something after you too, I'm sure," she said.

Zinnia didn't even have to place an order; a waiter produced a tray of escargots.

"You can get rooked on the escargots at some places, even the finest places," Zinnia said, as she put together a plate for Haze and one for me. "The snails from the Bordeaux leaves are the best, but the Burgundy snails are cheaper, so they'll tuck a Burgundy snail into a Bordeaux shell that they've already eaten the snail out of, then charge you almost double. But never here."

Imagine being so rich that you knew the exact spiral and spin of a counterfeit snail.

As she ate a tiny forkful of escargot and swooned, tilting her head back, Haze met my eyes. He smiled sly, as if to conspire with me in our poverty. A couple of gutter boys learning their way around an elegant garden slug.

I felt him tap his foot against my ankle, though that seemed just as likely an accident, considering how his body rattled around like a marionette.

While Haze did not have Dorian Gray's gold hair and blue eyes, he was *wonderfully handsome,* as Oscar Wilde describes him in the book. And Haze definitely had Dorian's scarlet lips, as if he'd been off kissing someone for hours. As a matter of fact, when I first read *The Picture of Dorian Gray,* I'd been so curious about those scarlet lips, they stayed on my mind, and I noticed that the color showed up again and again in the novel. I even wrote down in my little notebook all the references as I caught them, the scarlet robes, scarlet flames, scarlet threads, the scarlet mat of a snake charmer. Scarlet sin. Scarlet poison on painted lips, for a deadly kiss.

No sooner were we finished with the slugs than a plate of bonbons and petits fours arrived, the sweets all in various shapes and colors, with candied violets and rose petals and frosting in fleurs-de-lis. I was still very hungry, but somewhat relieved we weren't having dinner. I knew I couldn't afford it, and I didn't want to assume Zinnia would pay.

Haze faked a swoon after biting into one of the chocolates, collapsing even farther into the pillows. I felt his shoe brush against me again.

"All the candy is spiked with liquor here," Zinnia told us. "And all the cocktails are spiked with candy." She ordered for us a round of what she called *café gloria*.

Haze had the cufflinks on again, and I couldn't resist reaching over to touch them. "They're very pretty," I said.

He touched his own fingers to the cufflinks, in that way we do when someone compliments our jewelry—our hands go to our pendants, we twist our bracelet around our wrist or ring around our finger. *"Merci,"* he said.

Zinnia noticed too. "Did someone give them to you?" she said.

"Yes," he said, and nothing more. But we waited. Finally, he said, "I was given them . . . on the train on the way to Cherbourg. To board the *Titanic*."

Zinnia gasped a little, then popped a piece of candy in her mouth. "By a lover?" she asked as she chewed.

"A benefactor," he said. "I take photographs, of all the insides and the outsides of Paris. I've been documenting the city, street by street. Its shops, its apartments. The views from the windows. To sell to artists. The artists paint pictures based on the photographs and sell them in their galleries. Many people have *my* Paris on their walls. I've sold hundreds of photographs to painters."

"I don't believe you," Zinnia said, clearly flirting. "Where's your camera?"

"I should carry it around in my pocket?" he said, teasing right back. "Like a tourist? It's not a real photograph unless it breaks your back. My cameras have stands. Glass plates. This benefactor . . . he wanted to take me to New York, to meet with galleries, to try to sell the photographs as art in and of themselves. And to publishers of postcards and such. He did very much believe in me."

He. My heart jumped at the sound of it. His heart-shaped rubies were a gift from a *he.*

Zinnia caught it too. "He?" she said.

"Yes," Haze said, and his tone shifted. He cleared his throat. He jostled the table again, rattling the plates. "A very wealthy maker of maps. Beautiful maps, with a level of detail you wouldn't think possible. Even looking right at it, every bend in every river, you wouldn't believe it could be true. It seemed if you put a magnifying glass to it, you'd see yourself right there on a street, looking back at you. And he'd been to all those places, all around the world. I'd only ever been in Paris. His art put the whole world in front of you, made miles into inches. My art does the opposite—just takes you into rooms within rooms."

Were you in love with him? I didn't dare ask.

"Were you in love with him?" Zinnia said.

"Oh no," he said. "No no no no no no no no."

Just as quickly as my heart had lifted with the sound of that *he,* it sunk.

Haze said, "I suspected that *he* was in love with *me,* but I didn't think he'd ever . . . well, that he'd ever speak a word of it."

"You must have had *some* feeling for him," I said. But I said it so softly, they both asked me what I'd said. I paused, considered just shaking my head, letting my sentence be lost. But they kept looking, so I repeated myself. And I added, ". . . since you're still wearing the cufflinks."

"When he gave them to me," Haze said, "he included a little note. A few lines from an encyclopedia page on the language of gems. A ruby is an amulet, it said. Against poison, sadness, evil thoughts. A ruby will predict danger by changing colors."

"And it *did,*" Zinnia said, "didn't it? The ruby changed colors before you got on the boat."

"Well, no," he said, "but I found myself studying the rubies after he pinned them to my cuffs. I kept watching for that shift in color. Hoping for it, almost. But then I just asked the mapmaker about his feelings for me." Haze shrugged. "It seems he'd booked only one room for both of us on the *Titanic*, with only one bed. When he told me that, I said I couldn't travel to America with him."

"Did he go without you?" I asked.

"No," Haze said. "We went back to Paris together, on the train, in silence."

"So by breaking his heart," Zinnia said, "you saved his life."

That had been a theme since meeting the other *Titanic* survivors: every decision we made, every flinch of fate—all of it led back to that ticket we didn't use.

"I'd been staying with him," Haze said. "I moved out. But then I moved back in. Then back out. But I haven't been there for a while now."

"*Could* you have loved him?" I said. "If he was someone else?" I felt emboldened by the shots of brandy back at the shop, by the tobacco on the way over, by the champagne, the incense, Haze's lips.

"Well, yes—yes, of course," Haze said, smiling, winking. "If he was a beautiful woman." He then looked over at Zinnia. Most often his charm seemed effortless, but when you could see the effort, that charm faded away. Nonetheless, Zinnia did lean toward him, and she put her hand on his.

"Oh, your hands are like ice," she said. She took his hand in both of hers and began to rub warmth into it. "Are they always?"

"I guess I've been told that a time or two." He put both his hands around Zinnia's. "Yours are so warm."

"Here," she said, giving one of Haze's hands to me. "Feel how cold they are."

I did, and when I went to let go, he held on. I squeezed his hand and he squeezed back. Zinnia then took my other hand in hers.

I'd been kissed a time or two, but had never held hands with a man or a woman. Not even my mother or my father had ever taken me by the hand as a boy. Until that very moment with Haze and Zinnia, I never knew how much I'd longed for such a simple touch. Human hands existed entirely, I decided, for this impractical act of interlocking fingers.

"Would we have found each other if we'd all boarded the *Titanic* after all?" she said. "Would this be us, holding hands, as the ship went down?"

Yes, I wanted to say, but before I could, our waiter returned. We let go of each other to watch him prepare our café glorias, which involved dropping lumps of sugar candy into our cups of coffee, then pouring cognac over the back of a spoon. As with the *pêches pochées* on the menu, the coffee was set aflame, to burn the spirit away. The waiter put the cups in front of us as their fires still raged.

"Blow it out," Zinnia instructed, so we did.

I could still taste a lick of the flame as I drank, and though the cognac had burned away to fumes, it went straight to my head. I wasn't sure I could take another sip. I put the cup down and settled farther back into the pillows. The night's mix of hunger and booze and the honeyed glow of the lamps made everything that was real turn dreamlike. This happened sometimes, a feeling of being untethered, of being my own ghost haunting my life even as I lived it.

10

Zinnia tapped her finger on my shoulder, her gentle direction that I scoot out of the booth. "We're off to the cemetery to visit Dorian Gray himself," she said. "Or his author, anyway. Oscar Wilde has a new tombstone at Père Lachaise."

I'd read about it too, twenty tons of limestone carved into a winged sphinx in flight.

I took my wallet from my coat pocket, but Zinnia waved her hand in the air. "It's fine," she said. "We don't *pay* the bill. It *gets* paid."

The limousine, of course, still idled out front. On the ride to the cemetery, we pulled up to every flower cart we happened upon. Before we were even halfway there, our arms were overloaded with roses.

"Wicked," said an old woman outside the cemetery gates when we told her the grave we sought. For a tip, she would guide you along the cobblestone paths that lined the crypts and mausoleums, offering an unofficial tour of the famous poets and soldiers. She muttered and cussed as she set off for Wilde's tomb. "Unfit," she said. "He doesn't deserve the honor of a hole in the ground. It's a disgrace to the sanctity of this city of the dead."

"Do you think a book can kill its author?" Zinnia said.

In my heart, I knew the answer was *Yes, absolutely, without question*, though I'd never thought about it before. "Why do you ask?" I said.

"In your professional opinion," she said, "did *The Picture of Dorian Gray* murder Oscar Wilde?"

A man like me best tiptoe around a question like that.

I knew about Oscar Wilde's inclinations before I even knew who Oscar Wilde was. My mother back in Nebraska, rouging the tops of her cheeks before a show, gossiped about one of the dancers in the vaudeville troupe. She said, *He's an Oscar Wilde type, if you know what I mean,* and I didn't, not at the time, I was only a little boy. But I did sense something familiar about the dancer, enough to wonder if I was an Oscar Wilde type too.

I didn't even think of it as a name so much as a condition, a diagnosis: ozkah-wild. *Wild,* I thought. Savage. Madness. When I eventually saw Wilde's name on the binding of a book, I assumed it was a nom de plume, that some daring author, some decadent, some Oscar Wilde type, had taken the name as a little wink to his readers, to sensationalize himself, to write satire or pornography.

"Absolutely," I said.

"Maybe the book club *should* read that next," she said.

"I think the poor things might see themselves in it too much," I said. Dorian, after all, lives on and on while mortal lives are lost around him. In the book's fantastical twist, a portrait behind a drape bears all his scars and damage while he keeps young and handsome.

In the courtroom where Wilde had been on trial for indecency, accused of an unmanly affection for men, an attorney read long passages of his novel aloud, passages about the infatuation one of the characters had for Dorian Gray, as if all that fable and romance was Wilde's signed confession. Wilde's own art, his own imagination, was dangled over his throat like the blade of a guillotine.

Let us go over it phrase by phrase, the attorney said.

Wilde was sentenced to hard labor, and though he was released and he retired to the fainting sofas of Paris, the damage was done, and he died only five years after his conviction. He was first dropped in a pauper's grave but eventually was exhumed and reburied in Père Lachaise. And now Wilde's devotees had installed a massive monument befitting an emperor.

So yes, indeed, the book killed its author, sentence by sentence.

"The cemetery director covered it in a tarpaulin," Zinnia said of Wilde's tomb. "To hide it away. Or so the newspaper said. I think we should tear the tarp off. Let them arrest us for vandalism." In the limousine she'd painted a heavy layer of deep red on her lips with a tiny brush, her lap full of roses. Now she kissed at the air, smacking her lips. "I'm going to leave my red kiss on the limestone," she said.

But the old woman, despite having taken Zinnia's money, had managed to escape us.

And we were thwarted further by the ringing of a bell and the bellowing of the gatekeepers. *"On ferme les portes,"* they called. *Closing the gates.*

"Oh dear," Zinnia said. "Do we even know the way out? We can't be locked in a cemetery. *Titanic* survivors, clawing at the walls of Père Lachaise." But she had no notes of concern in her voice. I think she somewhat liked the idea. Nonetheless, we turned to go. "What do you see in the moon?" she said, looking up at the sky. "Do you see a face?"

"I see a face with a rocket in its eye," Haze said. "From a motion picture I snuck into years ago. It was made by a man named Méliès. A wizard of photography. A genius."

"Who do you see?" I asked Zinnia.

"A rabbit," she said. She lifted her pinkie into the air, pointing, gesturing as if she could trace for us the shadow. "My mother always told me the rabbit in the moon is a confectioner like us. They say he's pounding rice with his fists, to make *omochi*, a Japanese sweet. And I absolutely believed her. I believed my destiny was connected to the moon." She looped her arm through mine. "What do you see?"

"It's just the moon to me," I said. Out on that clipper ship when

I was a boy, in the middle of the ocean, there was only the moon's glow in the absolute darkness of the endless night, and I could be soothed just by watching it. But when the sailors told me all the spots of gray were only more ocean—the Sea of Cold, the Sea of Clouds, the Sea of Vapors—I fell into those waters too, suddenly even more lost than I was.

"I'll read your horoscope next time," Zinnia said. "I have a book on astrology. When were you born, Yorick?" When I told her, Haze asked what year, and with that we determined we'd been born only days apart.

"In June, no less," Zinnia said. "You're both Gemini . . . the twins."

"My long-lost brother," Haze said, reaching over to squeeze my shoulder.

The bell of the cemetery rang again. *"On ferme les portes."* As we neared the exit, we dropped all our roses at the feet of a slump-shouldered widow in granite, her cheeks streaked with black tears of pollution.

11

At the cemetery gates, the driver stood outside Zinnia's limousine, leaning back against its hood, smoking a cigar, his cap at an angle. He lifted his chin just enough to sneer at us. He opened the back door for Zinnia, stepping in our way to help her with the train of her dress. He slammed the door shut, then he turned to us—*at* us, really—practically stepping on our toes. Suddenly he had in his hand my walking stick, and he jammed it up into my rib cage. "Party's over, you shitty little bastards," he said. "Tell her you're taking the Metro."

As the driver went to his seat behind the wheel, Zinnia opened her window and pushed the silk drape of it aside. "Get in, my sweet boys," she said. "Monsieur Toussaint can take you wherever you want to go."

Haze caught my eye and put his arm in mine, like a gentleman. "We'll take the Metro," he said. "The Père Lachaise station is only up the street."

"You're being silly," she said. "You don't want to go underground next to a graveyard." But Monsieur Toussaint, her protector, pulled away from the curb before she could coax us in. She stuck her hand out the window, fluttering a handkerchief in our direction, in a flirty *bon voyage*.

"I can break a man's nose with very little violence," Haze said, taking on the stance and tone of a man of fine breeding, his chin lifted, his fingers fiddling with the knot of his necktie. We both looked off and away, like spectators at a horse race, watching the motorcar move down the street. "Won't even get blood on my shirt. Or his. But I didn't want to ruin our night."

I took on his pose too, standing up straighter, chin lifted, my walking stick tucked up jauntily beneath my arm. I touched my fingers to the brim of my hat. "A very commendable chap," I said. "Doing a fine job. It's very important that he keep the likes of us away from the likes of her."

"Very, very," Haze said. "Our belittlement was a very charming thing to witness, wouldn't you say?"

"Very, very," I said.

Haze grabbed my wrist to tug me back toward the cemetery, despite more shouts of *"On ferme les portes."* He led me down a lane and then another. "There's a grave I visit when I'm feeling low," he told me. "I bring a bottle of wine and commune with the spirits."

We stopped at a stone sarcophagus, the top of it a bronze sculpture of two men lying prone side by side, their eyes shut, their nakedness mostly covered by a shroud across their waists and legs.

A naked shoulder, a naked arm, a naked foot.

Haze ran his fingers along the bronze folds of drapery. "I like to think of it as balloon silk. These two men are the patron saints of aeronauts."

The aeronauts held hands. The sight of their intertwined fingers felt profound. Other than my own hand in Haze's, back at the Wilde-like saloon, I wasn't sure I'd ever seen two men holding hands, in life or in art. And here it was, so tender and loving, memorialized, struck in bronze for all to see, forevermore. And no one was hastening to toss a tarp over it.

"Did their balloon crash?" I said.

"Yes," he said, "but that wasn't what killed them. They wanted to test how high they could go, how thin the air could get. They had bags of oxygen so they could breathe, but they didn't suck in the oxygen soon enough, and they suffocated in the sky."

"Did you know them?"

"Oh no," he said, "that was decades ago. There were three men in that balloon's basket. One survived. He said his two friends died in a state of euphoria. They were too happy to take the oxygen. They were giddy about leaving the atmosphere. Over the moon."

"That's something I want to ask our *Titanic* survivors," I said. "Did they ever think about what they would have done? How they might have been, what they might have thought, if they'd gone down with the *Titanic*?"

"Have you?" he said. "Wondered?"

I liked to think the frozen ocean numbed me, and like these balloonists who were drugged by the clouds, I would marvel at the magnificent failure of it. *Euphoric.* I would know a peace I'd never known. I believed you could even convince yourself, in such certain, final moments, that your death was a divine gift, that it was a blessing to be part of such extravagant treachery.

I would die knowing that my name would never fade from the lists of the dead.

"I think I would have been one of the ones who lived," I lied.

"What a lovely coincidence," Haze said. He took my walking stick from me and did as the driver had, pushing it into my ribs, but he did so gently. It was almost like a caress. "I would have lived too. I would have dragged a deck chair onto the iceberg. With a bottle of gin I stole from the bar."

I took the cane from him. Tapped the end of it on the tombstone. "How did you find this grave?"

"The mapmaker went up in balloons," he said. "For an aerial view of the land he was mapping." One of the arms of one of the bronze men dangled at the side of his catafalque, his hand open, his palm up. Haze ran his fingers along the man's wrist. "I learned that balloonists come to this grave for good luck. They place a flower in his hand."

Indeed, the man's hand was perfectly positioned to hold a

flower; you would just tuck the stem in next to his thumb. "Good luck?" I said. "But they perished."

"But they didn't die in a *crash*," he said. "They died in the air. Some say they got a peek at heaven first. That's why they were euphoric."

"Have you been up in a balloon?" I said.

"Once," he said. "But never again. Especially not since the *Titanic*. If you cheat death, does Death feel cheated? Does it come after you with a vengeance?"

The graveyard grew darker, the setting sun tossing the last of its long shadows.

"I'm sending you on your way before the gates close," he said. "You'll follow that path and keep leaning leftward until you stumble out on Ménilmontant Boulevard. You'll see the Père Lachaise station. Take the three to the Sébastopol station, then switch to the four. It will take you right to the Saint-Michel station. I assume you live near your bookshop?"

"Across the street," I said. "Where do you live?"

"Right here," he said. "Tonight, anyway." He crouched down onto a patch of mossy lawn next to the sarcophagus. He lay back flat and held his hands at his chest, like a corpse in his casket.

I prodded him with my walking stick. "What are you talking about?" I said.

"I have no place to go," he said, his eyes closed. "And this is as good as any. It's quiet, and the ground is soft."

"No place to go?" I said. I squatted down on my haunches.

"There's a restaurant that's open all night," Haze said. "There's a waiter who will let me sleep at my table. On the bench. So I've been doing that every now and again. I've stayed other places here and there. I make friends off and on."

"You can't stay here, Haze."

"Are you inviting me to stay with you?" he said, propping himself up on one elbow. "Do you have a sofa? An ottoman I can curl up on? A rug on the floor? A drawer in a dresser?"

"I have hardly any space at all," I said, and it was true, though I did wonder if we might both fit, tightly entangled, on my narrow bed. I pictured us as the balloonists in bronze. "I rent a *garçonnière* across the street from my shop. *Everything* I have in that room is rented. Even the cutlery. The frying pan. The dinner plate."

"I can sleep on a dinner plate," he said sweetly.

I worried I would have to explain to him something embarrassing: I was terrified of the concierge and his wife. They were ruthless. They locked the front doors and took to their beds before nightfall, and no one had a key but them. If I were to bring someone home, I'd have to twist the bell and they'd quiz me at the door, especially since I'd been drinking. They'd accuse Haze of being a thief there to take advantage of me, to not just abscond with all *my* things but *their* things too, and the things of everyone else in the building. And at that point, *I'd* be a thief right along with him.

"I do have that old barber's chair in the bookshop," I conceded. "It leans all the way back. For a shave. I got it cheap from a barber going out of business, and it's where I sit to read. Sometimes I fall asleep reading, so . . . it would probably be fine . . ."

"That's all I need," he said, with what sounded like great relief. "It's *more* than I need." He leaned over to put his hand to the back of my neck, gripped tight, and pressed a kiss hard on my cheek. His scarlet lips were as cold as his hands.

12

I bought the bookshop from an elderly man who'd owned it with his wife; when she died, he moved into the shop's basement. He'd had plumbing installed, and a cast-iron tub. He'd hung pictures, rolled out a rug, put a wing chair and a footstool and a lamp in a corner. There'd been no bed, and I imagined him simply drifting to sleep every evening in his chair as he read a chapter or two.

Though I would've saved on rent if I'd moved into the basement myself, the idea of following so closely in a widowed man's footsteps was too despairing. I'd bought his building and all his books; I didn't want to also buy his decline.

A few winters before he sold me the shop, the rivers of France filled with snow, flowed into Paris, and overflowed the Seine, sending its water down into the sewers and catacombs, then up into the cellars and streets. The bookseller's basement flooded waist-deep. He imagined the river would keep rising into his shop, and he dreamt of it every night after, of swimming underwater, the flood pulling all his books, one by one, from the shelves, turning the paper back into pulp, the ink back into liquid, all the books' stories newly untold.

I've been wanting to sell the shop ever since, he said to me the afternoon I met him. I'd newly arrived in Paris, having parted ways with the White Star Line after the *Titanic* sank. I was in search of some sign of what to do next. But I'd only gone into the bookshop to peruse the shelves. I hadn't even had any specific book in mind—it was the Café Capucine's sidewalk tables that drew me near, and I wanted to sit with a glass of wine and read.

I nearly left the shop without hearing anything at all from the old bookseller; he was taciturn and inattentive. It was only when I asked him about the picture postcards for sale, pictures of Paris flooded, that he told me of the dreams he had every night. In one of the pictures, there appeared to be books floating in the water of the street. *No,* the old man said when I asked about it. *They're wooden paving blocks, loosened by the rush of the flood.*

That night in my hotel, I dreamed the old man's dream, of swimming in his shop. But then the flood carried me out into the depths of the ocean, and I clutched at all the forbidden books I'd snuck into the *Titanic's* second-class library. The books sunk like rocks, quicker than I could catch them.

"And that was the sign I was looking for," I told Haze as we returned to the shop after the cemetery. "Of what to do with my life. I'd come into some money, and I'd brought it all with me to Paris. I made the old man a handsome offer, and he took it."

"*That* was the sign?" Haze said. "A dream that you were drowning?" Before I could say any more, Haze said, "And how'd you come into money?"

I felt a twinge of pain, but I welcomed it. My shattered leg, the money for my shop, the stories of my life were all haunted by Leopold, the sailor who cared for me when no one else did.

"A story for another time," I told Haze. It wasn't that I didn't want him to know; I just didn't want to tell him.

He asked me to show him to the basement, where he headed directly for the tub, twisted the knobs, started the water, and began to undress. "I love a long bath and I haven't had one in weeks," he said. "I've *bathed,* but mostly at the Turkish bath, because I have a friend there who lets me in, and he lets me sleep there sometimes, but there's nothing in the world like a *comfortable* bath, a long, lazy bath. At home."

I thought I should step away and leave him to his privacy, but he kept talking as he got naked before me. To be polite, I stayed. And stared. He was just as stunning naked as he was dressed, all sinew, his muscles twitching with his movement. Despite this chance sight of every inch of him, of the swing and sway of the flesh between his legs as he stepped from his trousers, I got caught up in the tattoo low on his left haunch, just above a buttock lightly furred in dark hair.

"What is that?" I said.

"What's what?" He twisted his head around to look where I was looking.

I took this as an invitation to touch lightly at his skin and to lean in a little closer. "A picture of me," I said, as I traced my finger along the black line. When Haze looked at me puzzled, I said, "I'm named after a skull. *Alas, poor Yorick.*" Haze just squinted at me, so I said, "In *Hamlet*. The Shakespeare play."

"Ah," he said, trying to twist around more to see it better, as if seeing it for the first time. "That explains the skull pipe you gave Zinnia, I guess." I'd taken my hand away, but he took my hand in his to bring it back to his skin, to touch at the tattoo again. "Feel the scar where his mouth is?" he said, pressing at my fingers. "I got knifed in the back when I was sixteen. I hadn't done anything to deserve it—at least nothing more than sleeping in an alley. A lunatic accused me of stealing his belladonna. I tried to run away from him, and that's when he jabbed me with a pig-sticker."

The tattooist had expertly worked the scar into the skull's toothy grin.

"I'm surprised you wanted to hide it," I said. "I'd think a sixteen-year-old would want a scar to show off."

"I didn't get the tattoo when I was sixteen," he said. "I got it after the *Titanic*. After I left the mapmaker the first time, I stayed with a lady friend, a tattooed lady, who walked a tightrope in a circus. She knew her way around a needle. She said a skull tattoo means you're not afraid of death." He tapped his knuckles at the side of my head. "So, Yorick the skull, this makes us brothers even more."

"Yes, I suppose it does," I said.

He winked at me again. "You're slowly starting to make sense to me," he said. Though I didn't know what he meant by that, I loved the idea of it—I loved not only that I was making sense to him, but that he'd bother to contemplate me at all. He then turned off the faucets and stepped into the tub. "Now leave me be. I'm finally taking my bath."

I actually had bathed in the shop a time or two. Despite my determination not to live as the old bookseller had, I nonetheless found myself doing so if I was at the shop late and didn't want to wake the cranky concierge at my apartment. I'd brought down from the attic one of the marble-topped bistro tables, and atop it was a cake of musk paraffin soap and some bottles of perfumed tonics and oils.

Before I reached the steps, Haze stopped me. "My things are still at the mapmaker's house. I'd like to ask him to send them all here. To the shop. My clothes. Just a few steamer trunks. And some cases of photographs. And I have my cameras and equipment in a locker I'm renting. We can keep it all down here, if that's all right."

I said yes, of course, but it did seem more of a declaration than a question. I did fear I was just another mapmaker whose infatuation he would play like a violin. But maybe I didn't mind if it meant I'd see him in his bath every now and again. And, after all, he was making sense of me, he said so himself.

Dear Titanic Survivors Book Club:

The Kreutzer Sonata by Tolstoy: "Under the influence of music it seems to me that I feel what I do not really feel, that I understand what I do not really understand, that I can do what I can't do . . ."

Yorick
Proprietor, La Librairie Sirène

P.S. I've sent along some Cinnamon Love Songs, courtesy of Zinnia, candy discs with holes in the middle you blow through to whistle. But it's been said that young lovers will pass one back and forth in a kiss, and that the kiss makes a melody of the lovers' breath.

13

"I spent all of one summer," Zinnia said, "day after day, hour after hour, reading *Anna Karenina*, consumed by it, thinking it was a love story the whole time, only to get to the end and realize it wasn't." She sucked on the cinnamon candy as she spoke, giving her a lisp and a whistle. "And now reading this, I don't think Tolstoy likes love at all."

The Kreutzer Sonata is about a man with a wife who plays piano. He becomes suspicious of the violinist who plays with her, becomes jealous, and though he does manage to keep himself from killing the violinist, he can't resist sticking a dagger in his wife's ribs in a jealous snit.

"Tolstoy *doesn't* like love," I said.

"Any romance in this book," Zinnia said, "is in a kiss that we don't even see. We don't even know if it happened. But I can certainly imagine it."

"Tolstoy was in a religious fervor," I explained to the group. "He'd renounced *Anna Karenina* and all his works that had come before. *The Kreutzer Sonata* was his condemnation of romance and poetry, of art, of love's illusions. Of lust, desire, music." Of kisses that consume. He raged against sex, I didn't say. He not only opposed sex outside of marriage but within it too. Maybe he loved someone he shouldn't, I thought.

"Did you smuggle *this* book onto the *Titanic*?" the toymaker asked me.

"Yes," I said. I'd decided I would only assign books to the Titanic

Survivors Book Club that I'd snuck onto the ship. My second-class library would live on, on dry land.

"And what made it fit in your library of the damned?" he said. Inspired by the whistle candy I'd sent with the books, he'd brought each of us a brass whistle from his warehouse, a genuine Acme Thunderer, the official whistle of the White Star Line. An officer's whistle is built to be shrill enough to rise above the fiercest gales. When the toymaker handed them around, we couldn't resist blowing through them, a flurry of noise that sent a chill up my spine. I could hear in it the frantic deck of the wounded ship, the *Titanic*'s officers blasting at their whistles to conduct the chaos.

"This book came up against more than just a country minister," I said. "It was condemned around the world, so of course everyone wanted to read it. Illegal copies were passed hand to hand. Tolstoy's disgust with love was too passionate for the Russian censors. And there's the suggestion of infidelity in it. There's murder. Madness. The U.S. Post Office banned it from the mail. An American president declared the novel to be revolting. He said it was the work of a pervert." They waited for more. "Theodore Roosevelt," I added.

"As Zinnia said, we don't even *see* the kiss that so incenses the husband," said the orphan. "We only hear it described by him, and he didn't see it either. He just describes what he *thinks* he heard coming from the music room."

Old Madame Petit of the vineyards, in that dry rasp of hers, read aloud the passage specifically about the kisses: "'I could hear the measured arpeggio and the sound of her voice, and his. I listened but couldn't distinguish any words. It was obvious the notes of the piano were sounding merely for the purpose of drowning their conversation—their kisses, perhaps.'"

Madame Petit's young companion blushed. Did she blush because of all her own stolen kisses, kisses that must by necessity be drowned out? I glanced over at Haze, who looked enraptured by Zinnia, and Zinnia did look like an arpeggio herself, her dress the tarnished cream color of music parchment, patterned with musical notes.

A poem of Oscar Wilde's, that I'd read almost daily though I knew it by heart, ended with a lament for "unkissed kisses, and songs never sung." I'd always loved the distinction, but couldn't quite articulate it. But to my mind, there was a thrilling difference between no kisses at all vs. kisses unkissed.

I imagined Haze looking at me the way he looked at Zinnia. I imagined us slipping into a candlelit room, standing next to a piano as he kissed my neck. My one hand is at the back of his head as he leans into me, my other hand tapping out something unmusical on the keys.

"How would you perform that scene?" said Penny Dreadful, and I thought at first she was talking to me, and suddenly Haze and I were caught kissing in a blast of light on a theater's stage. But she was asking the actress, of course.

Delphine Blanchet wore a fur turban, though it was only late September. When she'd arrived, and I told her it looked exotic, like something snagged on safari, she whispered in my ear, *It's rabbit skin dyed with tiger stripes.* She could certainly afford to wear skinned jungle cats, but I'd come to realize that she enjoyed illusion. Her every article of clothing was a costume.

"I would perform it just as described," she said, "offstage, just tapping at some keys on a piano in the wings." She wriggled her fingers listlessly toward some imaginary piano. "Back in my day, I would've made it so convincing, people would have left the theater debating whether they'd seen me kissing the violinist or not." After a moment, she added: "But I can't play young women anymore. When the *Titanic* went down, I aged by decades. Overnight."

Old Madame Petit spoke again. "Why do you think that is?" she asked Delphine.

Delphine cleared her throat. She fussed with a tassel on her shawl. "My ticket to the *Titanic* did not go unused," she said, looking down. She then looked up at us all. "I transferred my ticket."

The orphan let out an *"Oh,"* but everyone else remained quiet. We waited for Delphine to say more, though I think we were all uncertain she would. Finally, she said, "I did not cheat death. I assigned my death to someone else."

We all stepped in to try to assure her that that wasn't what happened, that that wasn't how she should see it, but we all had the same question we didn't dare ask: *Who?*

Now that we knew about this person who took her place on the shipwreck, it seemed to invest her every deep breath with regret.

"I think you *want* to tell us," Zinnia said, as if one of us had actually asked for a name.

Zinnia's suggestion seemed to surprise Delphine, and it was the first time I'd ever seen her caught off guard. In that moment, we saw the whites of her eyes, eyes wide with wonder and sadness. She looked, somehow, years younger.

"I haven't spoken to anyone of it," she said. But I could tell she didn't mean to discourage us; I think she wanted us to draw it out of her.

"You're among friends," said Mr. Dreadful, practically barking it in that bearish way of his.

I was pleased to hear everyone agree with him. Yes, she was among friends.

"And you should forgive yourself," said the Reverend Henry Dew. "You had no way of knowing."

"I know," she said. "But you see . . . the woman I sent to her grave was a young actress. I convinced her she should take my place in New York, on the set of the motion picture that I was to appear in."

"Then you were doing her a kindness," said the orphan.

"I wasn't being kind," she said. "I wanted her gone. The newspapers were calling her 'a young Delphine Blanchet.'"

"But you didn't want her *dead*," said the gambler, who sometimes seemed the most practical-minded of us all. He had a confidence that we couldn't help but trust. I suspected if he told any one of us that we had nothing to worry about, we wouldn't. And vice versa.

"Didn't I?" she said.

"Well, as someone in the business of murder," said Penny Dreadful, "I can tell you that you didn't go about it in a very efficient manner." She paused. "Despite the results, of course."

"Her name was Bijou," Delphine said.

"To Bijou," the toymaker said, raising his glass. "*To Bijou*," we all said. We were drinking Russian vodka since Tolstoy had written essays about the evils of it.

"Bijou was a lovely young woman. Very kind. She probably gave up her own seat on the lifeboats."

"You're just haunted, is all," said Reverend Dew. "We're all haunted."

"Now it's my turn," Penny said, almost giddy, unable to wait another minute. "My turn to tell you all something I've not told anyone." She cleared her throat. "I can't kill my characters," she said, enunciating each word. "Not since the *Titanic*. I used to write one or two murder mysteries every year. But now, when it comes time for the victim to die, I just can't pull the trigger. I've written some short stories, and I've made sure the victims are dead before the story even starts, but then they just show up alive before the story ends. I somehow bring them back."

"It'll be the end of her," her husband said.

A few others of us tried to comfort her too, with stories of our own hauntings. The physician said every heartbeat he listens for through a stethoscope is uneven, arrhythmic, beating with a diseased *tick-tock*ing, as if his ears knocked every healthy heart out of whack. The gambler said he sometimes secretly slipped money into the pockets of people he beat at the casinos—he'd become a reverse pickpocket. Even Haze, who tended not to say anything, spoke up:

"I can't take pictures of people anymore," he said. "Only empty streets. Empty rooms. I don't even really like to *look* at pictures of people. Their stillness sends a chill through me."

Until he mentioned it, I hadn't realized how much I wanted Haze to take a picture of me. I began to imagine it, him posing me, studying me, adjusting my light, the set of my hands, the tilt of my chin.

We eventually found our way back to the book, and we spent some time discussing whether or not we believed the wife to be innocent of kissing the violinist, and then we spent some time discussing why it did or didn't matter. We reached no conclusions but ended the evening anyway, though I don't think anyone really wanted to go.

The shop had come to be inhabited by the spirit of the book society. I could swear their shadows lingered behind them, falling this way and that as the sunlight shifted. In the evenings, the shop was lit only by lamps in glass shades, giving the room a glow the color of the pages of a book left open too long in the sun. And in the days after a meeting, I would continue to hear the echo of their voices and the sound of paper against paper as they turned pages. Certainly all that night's whistling would hang in the air for a while.

14

After I locked up the shop following our talk of Tolstoy, Haze went to his steamer trunks to fetch a bottle of brandy for Zinnia and me. "An 1878 Cognac Camus," he said, cutting into its sealing wax with a penknife and a gentlemanly bow. "I snagged it cheap when the Maison Lemardelay closed, when they auctioned off all the guts of its cellar."

Since Haze had moved in, I saw little of him. He spent his days photographing the collapse of old Paris, and we'd have about an hour together in the evening, at Café Capucine, where he'd show me some of the pictures in his portfolio. He'd documented the last gasps of many fine restaurants and cafés. For years, the city had been falling, the rotting buildings a century old knocked over with a feather, new businesses springing up in their spots. And the Paris flood had played its part in tugging at the bricks.

His photographs made it seem like a city we'd already lost. An elegy. He was drawn to torn awnings and alleyway walls blackened by licks of flame. He had pictures of old posters peeling from brick. His favorite subject seemed to be dismal little shops: there was an optician's, the spectacles on display behind a filthy window, and a shop with corsets strapped to sickly mannequins, and an *antiquaire* with all his shoddy goods displayed on the sidewalk—a taxidermied lynx, a crystal chandelier, frames without paintings.

No people.

So when Haze said he wanted to photograph my bookshop soon, I was a little troubled. Was he drawn to the dying, like a circling crow? Could he hear something ominous in the creak of the stairs and the wind through the walls? Or was it the picture itself that cursed you—you were doomed once you got caught in his camera's sights.

He turned the shop's water closet into a darkroom, the sink full of bottles with smudged skulls and crossbones on their labels, the air of the entire shop sometimes humid with poison. Haze's trunks—one of them full of his liquor collection—had been delivered that morning, along with some suitcases and a few hatboxes.

"Tastes like bad apples and cologne," he said after a sip of the cognac, but he wasn't being critical. He moved his jaw around, looking up, contemplating. "Molasses cake. The skin of a fig."

I was relieved he was in a better mood. He'd been cranky when all his belongings arrived—I suspected they'd not been easily gotten back from the mapmaker. I already knew Haze well enough to know those low, sleepy eyelids of his could both draw you in and cast you out. So I didn't ask questions, and I didn't object when he dragged all of it over to his barber chair in the corner. He did at least drape a few silk handkerchiefs over the trunks in his feeble effort to hide them away.

"Mushrooms. Apricots," Zinnia said, after taking a sip.

I went to the phonograph to play a recording of Beethoven's Violin Sonata No. 9. "Also known as *The Kreutzer Sonata*," I said.

"After the novel?" Haze said.

"Didn't you read it?" Zinnia said. "It says in the book that it's Beethoven."

Haze seemed to blush from his error, so I spoke up. "Beethoven named it for a famous violinist of the day. But Kreutzer never performed it, because he didn't like it."

"I hope someone names something after me someday," Haze said, leaning back against a bookcase.

"Nothing will be named after me, that's for certain," I said.

"Someday," Zinnia said. "Someday you'll marry, and you'll have a child."

"How could I ever afford a family?" I said.

"Oh, stop with your sad story," Zinnia said. She kissed my cheek. "You're breaking my heart."

"You could name your shop after me," Haze said. "You haven't even painted a name on the window yet."

Zinnia walked away from us, over to the window, studying it as if she could already see the words painted there.

"Or Zinnia could name a candy after me," he said.

"*Haze?*" she said. "What would it taste like? Fog? Mist?"

At the mention, I thought of *Wuthering Heights,* a book I'd read again and again in the windowless rooms of the ships I'd served, breathing in air dank and moldy, like the brandy we were drinking. And suddenly Haze took the role of Heathcliff, stepping into my imagination, sweeping across the moors to replace whatever face I'd cast in the role before. *I have not broken your heart—* you *have broken it—and in breaking it, you have broken mine.*

"My name is actually Hansel," Haze said, and Zinnia and I exchanged a look. "I had a mother for a while, until I was ten. She told me I was named after my father, a German soldier. But I don't know if I believe any of it. I don't even have an *acte de naissance.*"

"Well, candy was your destiny, then," I said. "With a name like Hansel."

"How so?" Haze asked. Zinnia and I exchanged the same look again.

"You don't know the fairy tale?" I said. "About Hansel and Gretel? Lost in the woods? They find a candy house. Eat some of it. Turns out a witch lives there. She decides to eat *them.*"

"Well, I didn't really need fairy tales, I guess," he said. "When you grow up on your own, there's no one sweetening up the terror. Every door has a witch behind it."

"You're breaking my heart," Zinnia said again, but this time she said it sincerely.

Haze turned to me. "What about Yorick?" he said, his smile half-cocked. "What's his candy taste like?"

"Ah, I love that idea," Zinnia said. "'Alas Poor Yoricks.' Candy shaped like a skull. Tastes like vanilla, like the smell of old books."

"Does Zinnia know about the skull on your back?" I asked Haze.

Zinnia said, "Zinnia does not."

I shot back the rest of my cognac, which put some swagger in my step. I put down my glass and leaned my cane against the phonograph. I then pulled Haze close, like in an embrace, and put my chin on his shoulder to look over at Zinnia. I tugged up at his shirt, untucking it from his trousers. I felt his heart beating against my chest, his breath on my neck. I was afraid he could feel my own heart speeding up.

Zinnia stepped forward and put her fingers to Haze's scar, the grin of his skull tattoo. She seemed transfixed by it, but said nothing for a while. Finally, she said, "I wish I could go back in time and rescue all three of us."

Haze disentangled himself and went to the bookshelf where he'd left the bottle. He poured us all more. "I'll bet your dance card was always full," he told Zinnia. "Pretty girl like you."

"No, not at all," she said. "The boys didn't ask me to dance. They flocked to the lily-white girls."

"One thing that I remember about my mother," he said, "is she tried to teach me good manners. She said that if I ever went to a dance, I should dance with all the undanced-with girls."

"Oh no, that's all wrong," Zinnia said. She unwrapped a cinnamon whistle candy and held it to his lips. He opened his mouth and took it from her. "Someone who looks like you shouldn't dance with the undanced-with girls. They'll all fall tragically in love with you."

Haze started to whistle through the cinnamon candy. He said to Zinnia, "So the boys and girls of America kiss with this candy?"

"Preachers in little towns have tried to outlaw it," she said.

He then leaned in toward Zinnia, and he put his lips to hers. The kiss went on long enough that I didn't know where to look or if I should step away. Or could I step forward? I was jealous, but I knew I shouldn't be. I knew I shouldn't want anything from Haze.

Before I could decide what to do, they stopped kissing, and Zinnia whistled a few shrill notes with the candy he'd passed her. She turned to me.

She put her lips to mine. I'd never kissed a woman before, only a few men, and only a few times, in a few rushed moments down an alley of the Champs-Élysées, where I'd heard men like me leaned back against the wall, waiting. But the police knew about those alleys too, so the more desire I felt, the more illegal I was, the more ashamed and afraid.

When I stepped away from her, the candy in my mouth now, I was too shy to look at Haze. I just sucked on the candy, blew a few weak, feeble whistles. I was about to just break the candy with my teeth when Haze stepped toward me. He put his lips to mine, and I stumbled back against the phonograph, knocking the needle from the groove, putting a skip in the sonata. He clinked his glass of cognac against mine.

Even as the kiss was still happening, I was thinking of the memory of it. I would be unable to think of anything else for days. As we kissed, I imagined writing about the moment, writing as quickly as I could, as if everything might fade away, like a breath on glass: the way he put his hand to the back of my head, the way he parted my lips with his tongue. The cinnamon, and the scratch of the scruff of his chin and the *sound* of it. Not the whistle of the candy, but the sound of his lips on mine, like the sound in the novel, the illicit kiss the husband listened for.

"The cognac is making the room spin," Zinnia said, feigning a faint, stumbling into us, ending our kiss. "I need to go right now."

"Don't go," Haze said, putting his arms around her.

Her back against Haze's chest, Zinnia looked up and around at the shop. She said, "What's your favorite book, Yorick?"

I nearly said *Wuthering Heights,* as it had been on my mind. *I just kissed Heathcliff,* I thought.

"I don't really know," I said. "I've fallen in love with so many of them." She shrugged Haze off her, then took my hand and began a clumsy waltz with me.

"Yes, of course, but it's still fun to pick a favorite," she said, "so when someone asks what your favorite is, you have something to say."

"Maybe *Nicholas Nickleby,* I guess," I said. "When my mother put me on a ship to Liverpool, to live with my father, she gave me a toy theater in a little suitcase. And the paper dolls, and all the sets, were all based on the novel. And there was a little script. The story's full of actors and unwanted children who get flogged. I suppose it was a terrifying story to send along with a little boy you were abandoning."

"And that's your favorite?" Zinnia said. I only nodded. I didn't tell her that I came to love it later, when Leopold read it to me as I lay in a bed backstage for weeks with my leg in a vise, the bones broken to pieces.

I still had the book, but I'd cut out its insides, making it into a box to store what remained of that toy theater I'd been carrying around for years, though the pieces had dissolved even as I played with them, the characters curling in on themselves, from the damp ocean air that hovered like a cloud within the ship's walls.

"And what's your favorite, Haze?" she said.

"Ah," he said, nodding, nodding, nodding. He poured himself more cognac, took another drink. "Yes. Yes." Another sip. And then it occurred to him. *"Notre-Dame de Paris."* He crouched forward, lowered his head, lifted his shoulders, shut one eye tight. He was performing, taking on the hunch of Quasimodo.

"The outcast," I said.

"Yes," he said again.

The night ended soon after, and no one said anything more about the kiss that I couldn't stop thinking about. Zinnia kissed us both again, but only our cheeks, and Haze and I walked her to the end of the block where Monsieur Toussaint waited for her. When we returned to the shop, Haze then collapsed in his barber chair—"Sanctuary!" he called out, quoting Quasimodo when he rescued Esmeralda from the gallows and carried her to Notre-Dame Cathedral. Haze drifted off to sleep, right in front of me, still fully dressed in all his clothes.

15

When I returned to the shop late in the morning, nearly noon, Haze wasn't there. He often left early to take pictures, his camera strapped to his back, to capture Paris in the ashen light of dawn.

I remembered I had a first edition of *Notre-Dame de Paris*, bound in emerald green. I could understand why Hugo's book was Haze's favorite; Haze and Hugo shared a passion for old Paris. The book describes Notre-Dame Cathedral in great detail, in an effort to preserve it, and to pay tribute to the city's Gothic architecture, so much of it at risk for destruction or hideous repair. Before there was the printed page, poets built buildings, Hugo argued, writing across the skyline, composing their poetry in steepled belfries and stained glass, sending stone griffins and gargoyles into the clouds.

After I put on the coffee, Haze returned with a paper bag in each hand. "A fried potato," he said, dropping one of them on my desktop, "from the woman with the furnace in the alleyway. You're so thin you're making me worry." But he didn't sound worried. He sounded vexed, exhausted.

Zinnia might have enjoyed fine restaurants, but my gut had become accustomed to the goods bought cheap off carts. The crude smell of the potato—dirt, salt, heat—was heaven. I made a tiny tablecloth with a linen napkin from my top drawer, where I also kept a few knives and forks. He'd bought himself a potato too, and he pulled up a little bench to sit opposite me.

"In a minute there'll be coffee," I said, nodding toward the stove near the window. I always used the grounds from the day before that had festered all night in the pot and added some fresh. "It'll either stop your heart or make you feel more alive than you ever have."

"Yes," he said, distracted. "Stop my heart."

We finished our potatoes without another word, and after I poured him his coffee and he took a gulp, he straightened up, his eyes wide, as if he'd been jostled from a nightmare. "This is a nasty brew," he said, and he took another deep swig of it, then fell back into his blue funk with a shiver.

I put the first-edition *Notre-Dame de Paris* in front of him.

"What's this?" he said.

"Your favorite book," I said. "This copy was bound by Francisque Cuzin, one of the most famous bookbinders in the history of Paris." Most French books had only paper covers, so wealthy Parisians sought out the finest bookbinders to bind their novels in leather, with lettering in gold leaf. "Some bookbinders bind their books so tight, you can't get at the book itself, like it's their job to lock everything up, to keep you out, make the book itself untouchable. They make you afraid you'll crack the spine and all the pages will fall apart. But not Cuzin. He was a genius at binding a book so that it's . . . graceful . . . in a way that invites you in."

"I've heard of a bookbinder who binds lewd diaries in the skin of dead prostitutes," Haze said. He then pushed *Notre-Dame de Paris* across the desktop, back toward me. "I don't know the book. I saw *Notre-Dame de Paris* at the cinema, at the theater that used to be a skating rink, by the Arc de Triomphe. A lady I liked wanted me to take her to it." He took a deep breath. He sighed.

I got up from behind the desk and walked around it, to stand next to where he sat. He reached over to put his hand over my kneecap, as if feeling for the damage done.

"Something's on your mind," I said.

"It's nothing I should tell you about," he said.

"Why not?" I said. I sat down next to him on the bench.

"I know what you'll say," he said.

"What will I say?"

"That I shouldn't."

"Shouldn't what?"

"Shouldn't be in love with Zinnia."

"Why would I say that?" I said, though, of course, it was exactly what I would say. Zinnia had everything; he had nothing.

But maybe he thought I would protest because he sensed *my* feelings for *him*. He had to have known what his kiss had done to me.

"How could somebody like Zinnia know that somebody like me was . . . honest? Wouldn't she be suspicious of me, a man worth so little?"

"How do you even know that you're in love?" I said.

"What do you mean, *how*? How does anyone *know* anything like that? It's beyond knowing."

"But how can you fall in love so . . . quickly?" I said.

"You've never fallen in love quickly?"

Quickly was the only way I'd ever fallen for anyone, but I didn't tell him that.

"I'm just asking the questions that Zinnia might ask," I said. But they were actually questions I'd asked myself. As I sat up in bed every night after an evening with Haze, I tried to convince myself that love was something different from what was keeping me awake. Love was entirely denied me, so my feelings for Haze could be nothing more than affection. But his kiss had tossed a spark in.

Haze put his hand to the base of my spine, to press at the small of my back, and then put his other hand to my shoulder, pushing me to straighten up. "You're going to break your back with your awful slouch," he said.

Things like *that*. He paid attention. He recognized things about me that I didn't even know were worth noticing.

He then rested his head on my shoulder. "I don't have words," he said. "But Zinnia has words for everything. I just want her to talk to me. I could listen to her for hours."

I patted his knee mostly as an excuse to *stop* patting it, to let my hand rest there. When he took my hand, I was afraid he was pushing me away. Instead, he brought my fingers to his lips to kiss them. "You could rescue me," he said, giving me those eyes again.

"What do you mean?"

He reached over to drum his fingers atop the book I'd given him. "We could do something like this," he said. "Zinnia loves talking about books with you. Maybe we could send her a book along with a letter? Just something that makes me sound like I know what I'm talking about."

"Well, I can . . . *help*, yes, I suppose."

"You can help me pick the book, and help me write the letter," he said. "You know me well enough."

"Oh, Haze," I said. "I don't . . . I don't know about that. If you're worried about honesty, then I don't know if I should be the one to . . ."

"I didn't write the *book* I'm sending," he said. "Men send ladies perfume that they didn't bottle. They send bouquets of flowers put together by a florist."

"So send her perfume," I said. "Or flowers." I already felt like I was deceiving Zinnia just by having this conversation. Yet, at the same time, I was already puzzling out which books to send. "Won't she know?" I said. "Won't she see through it?"

"That's part of the charm of it all. It's flirtation. It's playful. You're my cupid. You're just flinging darts."

"I wouldn't know what to write," I said.

"Of course you would," he said. "You would know exactly what to write."

"But I wouldn't know what to write *as* you."

He put his hand to the back of my neck. "But you're my brother," he said. "You would know better what I want to say than I do myself."

Muddled as that was, I was convinced, or I *decided* to be convinced. When he straightened me up from my slouch again, I would have trusted him with my soul. He did make it all sound like a romantic folly, as harmless as a masquerade ball. And I was already complicit in such things, I reasoned: I had a whole shelf in the shop devoted to books on composing love notes. *The Complete Art of Writing Love-Letters. How to Write Love Letters. North's Book of Love Letters. The Lady's Love-Letter-Writer.*

And Haze was right, really, about the perfume and the flowers; so much of romance did rely on art and artifice. In those first days of falling in love, we don't want to be only ourselves. We want to be exactly the person they want us to be. And that might mean being someone else entirely.

Dear Zinnia,

At Wuthering Heights *everyone reads their books by candlelight, which I hope you won't do, because I'd hate for you to trouble your beautiful eyes, eyes I would describe if I was a poet, eyes that flicker and spark, like dapples of sunlight caught in drops of honey. That's what I saw as you sipped your cognac last night, and though I might not be a poet, I know pictures, I know light and shadow.*

And light and shadow plays all throughout this book. After the cognac, I began to fall asleep in my barber chair in the bookshop and I thought of the book's beginning, when the narrator sees Cathy's name carved over and over into the paint of the windowsill. He wakes later to the smell of a candlewick leaning against an antique book "perfuming the place with an odor of roasted calf-skin." He sees Cathy's name, her signature, scribbled in white light across the dark of the room.

Nothing good comes of anything in the story, but its romantic hero is a dark-souled devil you love nonetheless.

À tout à l'heure,
Haze

16

"I like how you make me sound," Haze told me, when I read the letter aloud to him.

If there *was* any damage to be done, I'd be the one at risk, I figured. If helping Haze find his way into Zinnia's heart helped me find my way into his, then there was nothing lost.

I wanted to be used. Over the next few days, I got caught up in our intrigue. And I couldn't wait to hear all his words for love.

Haze would stand behind me, leaning against me to read the letter as I typed it, sometimes reaching around my shoulders, his lips at my ears, putting his hands over mine, as if poised to type something himself.

He shaped my words to his voice.

At the flea market, a secondhand jeweler peddled the old intaglio rings people used for sealing a letter, for pressing an imprint into the hot wax—an initial, or a crest, the profile of a lady, the head of a god. I chose a heart cut into rust-colored carnelian stone, to match his heart-shaped cufflinks.

The day after *Wuthering Heights,* Haze wanted to send Zinnia another book, and another the next, and the day after that. We had an accomplice. To deliver the books, we hired a girl of about seventeen who ran errands for the seamstress on my street. I'd seen her strolling past my shop many times, a repaired dress over one arm, a half-eaten green apple always in her hand both coming and going.

I stopped her, *Wuthering Heights* wrapped up and be-ribboned. She told me her name was Alice. "What's yours?" she asked. When I told her, she cocked her hip and became Hamlet. She gazed at the apple she held aloft. "Alas," she said with a wink.

Dear Zinnia,

My favorite letters, by my favorite author, in <u>The Love Letters of Victor Hugo</u> *are the letters where he begs his ladylove to burn them.*

But I don't think he truly wanted her to. By telling your love to burn your letters, you've set fire yourself, haven't you? You've given your words a lick of heat. And if she doesn't burn them, which she didn't, they seem illicit. If anybody ever sent me a letter begging to be burnt, I'd lock it up forever in a fireproof box.

In his letter of Tuesday, April 18, 1820, he writes to his Adèle:

"Burn all my other letters, but keep this one. They may part us, but I am yours—yours for eternity. I am yours—your property, your slave. Do not forget that. You may always make use of me as if I were a thing and not a person. Wherever I may be, near or far, write to me and tell me what I am to do for you. I will obey you or die."

À tout à l'heure,
Haze

Dear Zinnia,

I did try at first to write this letter with a matchstick dipped in red ink like the opera ghost did in <u>The Phantom of the Opera,</u> but I didn't get far with that. Think of me though not as the phantom but as Raoul, who so loved Christine, the opera diva. They sent letters to each other daily though they met every day in her dressing room too. He'd bring her violets.

(In the tin I sent with the book are crystalized violets to dissolve in your champagne.)

À tout à l'heure,
Haze

Dear Zinnia,

Books about Paris written by writers who aren't French should never be read unless they're as ridiculous as this one is. Marie Corelli writes as if she gets paid by the exclamation point. Wormwood is a love letter to absinthe, but it pretends to be anti-absinthe, a sermon against its dangers, but the dangers are the book's best part.

The book is even dressed up like an absinthe bottle, with the cover a sickly green. The red ribbon on the binding means to suggest the red wax that seals the bottle. The serpent that coils on the cover is the same serpent that coils on the labels of the liquor.

À tout à l'heure,
Haze

17

We hadn't seen Zinnia since the night we'd gotten dizzy on the antique cognac and kissed. And she hadn't responded to the books we'd sent. Haze blamed me.

"It's not even been a week," I said.

I'd closed the shop for the night, and we'd taken our favorite table at the Café Capucine, the one next to the cat the café was named for. A small table, with a full glass of red wine, was always reserved for Capucine, who would curl up in the chair and effortlessly hold court as she napped.

"Maybe we've sent too many books," he said. "Or there's been too much talk of love in the letters."

"Or maybe we haven't sent enough books," I said. "Or we've talked about love too little." I'd already had a few glasses of Holland gin, and Haze had too, but booze always went faster to my head than it did to his.

Now that we'd begun this courtship, it was all I could think about. As much as I adored La Librairie Sirène, I'd worried every day, from the way the shelves bent and warped from the weight of too many books, that the walls of that house of paper were only inches from falling apart, everything tumbling in on me. But now I just wanted to spend all day strolling through the shop, reading the bindings, contemplating each book's romantic prospects, considering which book to send next.

Of course every letter I wrote to Zinnia was my letter to Haze. Or maybe I wrote the letters I wished Haze wrote to me.

"I bet Zinnia doesn't believe I could have sent those books," Haze said. "So we have to get better at it."

"I thought you wanted her to know it was both of us," I said.

"I do," he said, reaching over to tug at the knot of my necktie, to loosen it. "But we don't want her *certain* of it, do we? We want her to wonder. That makes it all the sweeter."

Haze requested from the waiter a fountain pen and a sheet of paper. All the cafés of Paris provided their patrons pen and paper, a great service to the distracted poets of the city who were always without a notebook but nonetheless forever struck with inspiration a few drinks in.

"I wonder how much French poetry has been written by absinthe," Haze said. "How many poems are just hallucinations."

"Write that down," I said.

"You write it," he said, handing me the pen.

"Words," I muttered. "I don't have a single word left tonight." I pushed my glass of gin away. "I can't drink any more of this," I said, but then I picked up Haze's glass of gin and took a sip. "The Dutch have practically a whole dictionary of words related to gin," I said. "There's a word for someone who drinks gin, and a whole other word for someone who gets drunk on gin." I started counting off the various words, but on Haze's fingers, not my own, taking his hand in mine. "There's a word for the apoplexy caused by gin. A shop where they sell gin is a called a gin 'palace.' There's one word for a *barrel* of gin, and a whole other one for a *cask* of gin."

"I bet if I walked around inside your head," Haze said, "it would look just like your shop. Every odd thing about the world is written down somewhere in there." He tapped his finger on my temple.

"You know everything about Paris," I said. I put the pen in his hand.

"I know everything about a Paris that's fading away," he said, putting the pen down.

"Tell her about one of the old cafés. Where did the poets hallucinate?"

"Café Vachette," he said. "It just closed last summer. I bought a bottle of its 1863 Château Mouton Rothschild for a song when they auctioned off its cellar."

"Write it down."

But he just kept mumbling about the cafés dreamily, his glass at his lips. "Newspapermen would meet at the Café de Madrid. I got its 1888 Château de Laubade Armagnac. The Café de Suède was where the actors would go. Bouchard Père & Fils Montrachet, 1890."

"Poetry by Rimbaud," I said. "That's what we'll send next." I said it with some conviction, which seemed to lift Haze's spirits.

I'd recently stumbled across an article about the literary partnership of Arthur Rimbaud and Paul Verlaine in a newsletter for booksellers. Verlaine was married, a father, older than Rimbaud, who was dangerous and troubled. "Rumor has busied itself with this friendship," the article said. Rumor? Could they mean *those* rumors? Usually, the idea of a friendship between men being more than it might appear was something so unspeakable that there weren't any words for it. I read the line over and over—*Rumor has busied itself with this friendship*—gorgeous with suggestion.

Busying the friendship further was opium and absinthe. In the end, Verlaine shot at Rimbaud, hitting his poetry-writing hand. Verlaine then chased him down the street, hoping to shoot more holes into him.

I certainly didn't want anyone gunning me down, but I wouldn't mind a man loving me just short of that. I envied the kind of passion that led to such desperate acts.

I looked at Haze and thought of how Verlaine once wrote that Rimbaud had the face of "an angel in exile."

I didn't really select the book for the poetry itself. I selected it because Haze would have to translate for me. We returned to the shop, and he and I sat on the divan. He slung his left leg over my right one, my broken one, and I read Rimbaud's poetry aloud, holding the book open, pressed against his knee. French poetry felt lush on the tongue, even more so when someone else was listening alongside you.

Together we translated a poem called "Dawn," but had some debate about what the poet wanted with the word *éclat*—was it a splinter? A gleam? It was important to our purposes, because it was in a sentence with a flower in it. We settled on: *I follow a path strewn with fresh shimmerings of light, to a flower who tells me her name.*

"I dedicate this translation to my own lady named for a flower, my shimmering Zinnia," I wrote, as Haze.

I wrapped *Illuminations* in pale blue tissue and bound it with a white ribbon, to have Alice deliver the book to Zinnia's door. But it was not the copy I'd read aloud to Haze. *That* copy I intended to keep to myself forever. I wrote on the title page the date of this evening of ours together on the sofa. I described how he'd sat with his leg slung over mine. I noted that he'd translated the French for me, his deep voice somehow soothing and dangerous both, and his smell of musk and sweat both sharp and intoxicating.

18

This time, Zinnia responded.

"My house needs music" was the only thing she said when she arrived at my bookshop wearing a broad hat busy with feathers: swansdown, glycerined ostrich, white egret, a few dramatic plumes of peacock. She took us to the *marché aux oiseaux*, a bird market only open on Sundays.

In the limousine, she had to sit with the hat in her lap.

"Your driver doesn't like us," Haze said.

"Is that true?" Zinnia called up to him. "That you don't like these boys?"

"I have no particular feelings one way or the other," he said.

Zinnia gasped comically, and she tugged on my sleeve. "Oh, did you hear that? He *does* like you!"

"That's a relief," I said, sarcastic.

"He's been with the family since I was a little girl," she said. "He gets a little overzealous." She raised her voice again. "But your heart is in the right place, isn't it, Monsieur Toussaint?"

"If you say so, mademoiselle," he said.

Zinnia patted Haze on the knee. "Monsieur Toussaint wants me to be happy, is all," she said. "We can't fault him for that."

We judged the birds by their songs. Haze, Zinnia, and I carried off a nightingale, a bishop finch, and a linnet, all in cumbersome cages, one of nickel, one of zinc, one of bamboo, "their pretty little prisons," as the bird seller said. Haze bought a windup organ full of simple songs of easy notes we were told the birds would learn.

Zinnia had two cars waiting: one for us and one for the birds.

It was only that afternoon, at the Café Capucine, that she referenced our letters at all, and only briefly.

"Haze said I had eyes like honey," she told me, referencing the letter we'd sent with *Wuthering Heights*. "Do you agree with him, Yorick? How would *you* describe my eyes?"

Haze tapped my ankle with his foot, and I didn't know what he meant by it. Did he want me to be lyrical, or did he want me to fumble around, to be the one of us who was the most inarticulate about love?

"Oh . . . oh, I . . . I . . . I don't know," I said, though I did know. How could you not? She had gentle eyes, and when she looked your way, you felt like she was the only one who'd ever seen you for who you were. No wonder Haze was in love.

Yellow-brown eyes like ginger tea, like the petal of a sunflower late in summer, like the feather of a goldfinch.

The waiter then appeared with the beer I'd ordered. "Eyes like a *bière blonde*," I said, hoping to sound unpoetic before taking a swig. This seemed to be the right thing to say, as Haze gave me another toe tap on the ankle.

After saying good night to Zinnia, Haze and I spent the rest of the evening writing a letter. We sent Alice off to Zinnia's with a copy of *Dickens's Dictionary of Paris,* with a feather marking the page about the bird market. I also hid a message of my own, in a way: I very slightly bent the corner of a page in the *B* section of the dictionary, the page that describes the cravings of the book collector.

We saw Zinnia every evening after that, always the three of us. We felt tranquil in each other's company, a moonlit calm during those autumn nights that arrived earlier and earlier, the daylight hours fading away. We hadn't kissed since the whistle candy, which seemed to make that one and only kiss almost mythological. It floated in the air every evening like a promise.

With Haze so enraptured by Zinnia, I could watch him watching her without him seeing me. I now knew the look in his eyes when he was in love, I knew his gestures of affection, the way he leaned toward her as she spoke, watching her lips.

As Haze, I sent Zinnia *The Kiss and Its History,* a book by a Romance philologist.

Zinnia,
~~*The candied perfume of plum blossoms in spring.*~~
~~*The light, clumsy flutter of the midnight-blue wings of a*~~
~~*drunk butterfly.*~~
~~*Soft birdsong at sunup.*~~
~~*A strawberry steeped in jasmine tea and honey.*~~
~~*Those first two sips of gin of an evening.*~~
~~*A poem written in lilac ink on a white rose petal.*~~

I keep trying to describe your kiss very particularly, but nothing comes close. I'm sending you all my failed attempts with the hope you'll help me get it right. Maybe the only way to describe a kiss is with the kiss itself.

À tout à l'heure,
Haze

Our nights out were always followed by Haze and me alone in the shop, composing our letters as I gazed upon Haze's beauty, as he lay back on the divan in stocking feet, as he took tiny sips of his nineteenth-century liquor.

Without any doubt, I'd never been happier.

Dear Titanic Survivors Book Club:

Here is Monsieur Vénus, *by the lady-scoundrel Rachilde,
a novel confiscated by Paris police after it was outlawed as
obscene back in the '80s.*

*Go looking for the obscenity, though, and you won't find
much. A rich woman in a gentleman's suit takes as her lover a
poor, pretty man. She calls herself "he" and calls him "her." And
there's a brothel and hashish. But you really do have to read
between the lines to see up anybody's skirt.*

*The author herself wore a man's suit, and you probably
already know that ladies can't wear pants in Paris. She told
the police, when they ticketed her, that she was just doing
business, just promoting* Monsieur Vénus. *She wasn't a serious*

wearer of pants, she insisted; she was only playing a part. She was just kicking up some publicity.

Yorick
Proprietor, La Librairie Sirène

P.S. Because the poor, pretty man in the novel makes paper flowers, I've sent along a paper flower of your own, a camellia made of rice paper, a very delicate candy that will dissolve on your tongue (again, a gift from Zinnia).

19

Zinnia arrived for the next book club meeting distracted. She'd dressed for the occasion, as she always did, inspired by the book. Her pants were only an optical illusion, her dress pleated in such a way as to give the impression of billowing trousers. Her bodice had lapels and a vest like a man's suit, and she wore a scarf knotted into a cravat. "Kimono silk," she told Haze and me, holding out her sleeve for us to pet. It was iridescent, blue-black, like the back of a scarab. But her heart wasn't in it.

"*Belle comme un coeur*," Haze told Zinnia.

"If women want to wear *actual* pants, they can apply for a permit," I told her, nodding toward her pretend-trousers. "It's generally only legal, though, if you're disguising an infirmity." I smiled, but she didn't smile back.

"Is being a woman not enough of an infirmity?" she said, then stepped away.

Before I could ask her what was wrong, the toymaker arrived carrying that bag he always brought with him, always full of toys. He took from it a gray paper box. "Thought you'd appreciate it especially," he said, "as a White Star steward yourself." The doll, about the size of my hand, wore a greatcoat of navy blue with two rows of gold buttons and *Titanic* in an infinitesimal stitch across his tiny pocket. The sight of it was startling, though it didn't look much like me beyond the uniform: it was nestled inside the box in tissue paper, like it had been tucked into the silk of its coffin. "Such life in those glass eyes, don't you think?" he said.

When I first met the toymaker, he'd seemed to me something like a circus barker, all hubris and pomp, but I now sensed he'd been much saddened by these toys locked in his factory cabinets. Once again I tried to offer a solution: "Just remove *Titanic* from the pockets. Unstitch it."

"You can't pluck away its soul with a pair of tweezers," he said.

Several of us took our dolls from their boxes and we looked a little perverse with our stewards in our laps, or on our knees, or in our arms, as we sat in our haphazard circle. I did sometimes wonder if we all envied those who'd sailed the *Titanic, all* the passengers, dead or alive. *Our* survival of the *Titanic* could only ever be theoretical.

Haze sat on the divan with Zinnia, whispering in her ear. I could tell he was trying to comfort her, and to coax her into confiding in him. As with everything else, he wore sympathy with such allure.

Zinnia didn't respond to him, though. All her attention was on the *Titanic* doll. She smoothed her finger over his swoop of genuine human hair. Was she angry at Haze? At me? Had we given ourselves away? Had I put too much of myself in my letters?

In the margins of my *Monsieur Vénus* were notes I'd taken, to lead our discussion of it. *Almost supernatural beauty,* I'd underlined—a description of the pretty boy who sewed together the paper flowers.

But the gambler, as always, began.

"I couldn't get at it," he said. He held his copy of the book up and open, to show that the publisher had not trimmed the fore edges of the pages.

"My pages weren't opened either," the physician said. "I just took a scalpel to it."

"Used to be," Haze piped up, "that when you bought a book, it wasn't finished. You took it to the bookbinder, and he'd do the business of putting a cover on it and opening it up." This insight, which he'd picked up from me when we'd discussed the binding of the book I'd given him, was clearly for Zinnia's benefit. I wondered if he was feeling nervous too, feeling he should demonstrate that he was bookish by nature. He glanced over to her to gauge her response. She had none at all. She kept her eyes down, on the pages of the book open in her lap.

"A guillotine," I said. "That's what they call the blade they use. To cut through the folds."

That brought Zinnia's eyes up. At my mention of a guillotine, she looked my way and tapped a few fingers at her throat, as if to suggest her beheading.

I ran my own finger along my own throat, slashing my jugular. This got a smile, at least, and I was very relieved to see it, even as melancholy as it was. Zinnia's wistfulness drew all my attention away from Haze.

"I wish I hadn't gone to the trouble of cutting the book open," said the orphan.

"Too shocking, was it?" said the fallen evangelist. He wasn't sarcastic about it; I think he genuinely wanted her to detail her objections.

"No," she said, shaking her head slowly. "No, it's not that . . ."

"Then what is it?" He said it so softly, it seemed he meant to speak only to her.

She looked at him, then turned to me. "In all the books you've had us read," she said, "people are so cruel to each other."

"Oh . . . I wouldn't say so," I said. But no sooner had I denied it than I realized she was absolutely right. "Well, it's not intentional, anyway."

"The *unconscious* is the culprit," the physician said, tapping a finger at his temple. "Have you read *The Interpretation of Dreams*?"

"I haven't," I said, though I had a "Dreams and Dreaming" shelf up on the second gallery, with copies of Freud's book in German and English, alongside a dream dictionary, sonnets about dreams, an encyclopedia of dreams by notable people, and an illustrated edition of *A Midsummer Night's Dream* with gilt-edged pages and fairies in sepia.

"We're reluctant to talk about our most private thoughts," he said. "We're afraid of being misunderstood. So all the wishes we make when we're awake come true when we sleep." His fingers returned to the rat's nest of his unruly beard. "But for me, there are only nightmares every night anymore. I dream about my patients. I'm always killing them. Smothering them. Giving them a fatal dose. Sometimes I bleed them. And drown them, of course." After a moment, when he saw us all looking at him with concern, he said, "Oh, no, no, I don't *wish* to kill my patients. I'm *afraid* I'll kill them."

One book on my "Dreams and Dreaming" shelf, *A Treatise on the Incubus*, diagnosed nightmares as disease.

"Why is your unconscious sending us books of cruelty?" asked Old Madame Petit of the vineyards. Her tone wasn't accusatory, and it didn't even sound like the question was meant for me. She was analyzing out loud.

Delphine Blanchet said, "A French critic called this book an entreaty against love." She too gave me an analyst's sidelong eye.

"Against love?" Zinnia said. "Shouldn't a novel be a plea *for* love?"

Was *this* what Zinnia was upset about? That I would choose such a book?

"Well," I said, "I guess I was ... at least ... *entertained* ... by how the book casts women as men and men as women. The book flirts with the possibilities for romance." I stopped there. Though all the characters came to a bad end, I was grateful for the tender deviance that led up to it—that deviance seemed a strength, not a weakness. "Isn't a book like a dream? A mystery to be unlocked?"

Perhaps in all those books that surrounded me every day, my story was told somewhere in the margins. I *did* live outside of my unconscious; I wasn't a figment of my own imagination. I was the unkissed and the unwritten; but I was not nonexistent.

I added: "At least it's an interesting artifact, perhaps? It's something derelict for your secret library?" There was a reference to just such a library in the book itself: a chest with velvet-lined shelves and doors of inlaid ivory hiding away "unacknowledgeable" authors: Évariste de Parny, Brantôme, Voltaire.

"Too many villains," Delphine Blanchet declared, her long string of smoky pearls twisted around and around her finger. "Theater, literature, cinema. Too many heartless monsters, all conspiring against love. It's a lack of imagination. Playwrights throw in villain after villain to give the illusion of suspense."

"Yes, and the newspapers are all trying to stir up war," said Penny Dreadful. "I've come to find the whole enterprise of death to be dispiriting."

"I nearly died minutes ago, on my way here," said the fallen evangelist. "Because of this hat." With each meeting, the fallen evangelist seemed to be emulating more and more the style of our gentleman gambler, yet he couldn't quite carry it off. His clothes seemed ill-fitting, untailored, his pleats in need of pressing. Even his boots were trying too hard to please, polished to a shine that seemed intended to be conspicuous.

"Your hat?" the gambler said.

Henry Dew fussed with it, bending its spine, picking at the pinch of the crown. "The wind caught it. I ran into the street to fetch it and nearly got clipped by a taxicab."

"Perhaps our sunken ship will drag us all under at some point," said the orphan. "Maybe when your time's up, your time's up. Maybe we avoid ten deaths a day."

"So many of the cafés now pull their tables closer to their walls," Haze said, "away from the streets, because too many people stumble into the paths of automobiles. The Paris morgue has tripled its business since people started driving motorcars."

"This again?" Zinnia said, practically hissing the *this*. "Is this why we get together? To turn our good fortune into a curse? Ten deaths a day . . . more like a hundred. A thousand. Yes, we're lucky, we survived our own births. Everyone who lives another day survives until they're dead. What I want to know is what will you all do with these endless, countless second chances? You should all go home and frame your unused ticket and hang it above your doorway. That way, your ticket will go unused every time you go outside, and maybe it will change the very world you walk out into."

Some of them looked to Zinnia as if about to speak; others looked down, and inward. I could see them all taking it under consideration, but it was a battle of instincts. We're often inclined to defend our misery and fear. Do you celebrate all that you have or do you lament all that you don't?

Before anyone could say anything, Zinnia stood, flustered. "Forgive me," she said. "I've forgotten . . . I'm needed . . ." She looked around for her things, but all she'd brought was her book. She tucked it beneath her arm and stammered some more: "I was supposed to . . . to meet my father. I just . . . just remembered . . ."

I followed her to the door, and Haze followed me.

"Zinnia," I said.

"It's nothing," she said.

"Is something wrong?" I said.

"Oh no, not at all," she said. She stopped to think a moment. "Cherries," she blurted. "Chocolate-covered cherries. My father has to . . . he has to pay penalties in America because of the . . . the paraffin that gives them their glow. It's dangerous, they've decided." She looked into my eyes, and over to Haze, and she seemed on the verge of tears. "The chocolates are pretty, though. You can practically see your reflection in the glaze."

After she walked out, I followed her into the street, but her long stride was taking her away quickly, her legs kicking apart the illusion of trousers, sending her dress billowing out behind her. "Zinnia," I called out, and she waved a hand in the air.

"I'm fine," she called back.

"We don't believe you!" Haze yelled down the street. But she only just waved us away once again.

Back inside, Haze slapped me on the back. He squeezed my shoulder. "She's in love with me, old fellow," he said.

I wasn't sure that was what he should be taking from it all, but I didn't discourage him. I did so adore his confidence. I even half-way believed in it.

20

Haze was perhaps right to be optimistic. The morning after the book club, Haze came up from the cellar, his hair still irresistibly damp from the bath. He'd doused himself in a cologne that smelled of lawn clippings and menthol. He wore no suit coat, just the canvas jacket of a fencing uniform with a flannel heart sewn over where his own heart was, like an open invitation to wound him fatally with the point of your sword.

That day Zinnia had arranged for Haze to be let into the hidden staircases and studios of the Louvre, where artists used to live before Napoleon chased them out. She told him there were still easels, stretched canvases, empty frames, as if the artists had fled a fire. It was preserved like Pompeii.

"Did you know that?" Haze asked me. "Artists crawled around in the walls like rats." He pulled onto his back a contraption he'd strapped together, a knapsack with his cameras, his tripod, his flashlamp. "I suspect Zinnia will meet me there." After Zinnia had left the book club in a rush, he'd gotten her note about the Louvre by morning, which had been blown our way through the gusts of the postal service's pneumatic tubes. "I'll take her for a stroll through the galleries. I've always wanted to kiss someone in front of that marble sculpture, the one with the curly-haired angel about to kiss the woman in his arms."

"Cupid and Psyche," I said. "He's not *about* to kiss her. He kissed her already."

"Should I tell her that, that I've always wanted to kiss a girl in front of Cupid and Psyche? Should I tell her that, then kiss her? Or should I kiss her, then tell her?"

I looked at his lips. "Kiss her," I said. "Then tell her."

I went to the rare-book vault beneath my stairs and took from it a volume of librettos. Among them was a French *tragédie lyrique* about Cupid and Psyche. When you bent the binding back, you could see that the fore edges of the pages had been hand-painted with a portrait of Psyche in Cupid's arms. When you bent the binding forward again, the lovers disappeared.

"Take it to her," I said, handing him the book. "Tell her you found it on my shelves. Tell her you discovered the hidden painting yourself, that I didn't even know about it."

Haze put his hand on my wrist as he took the book, pulling me close to put his cheek to mine. I thought he might be about to whisper something in my ear. He didn't, so I whispered something in his, the exact name of the sculpture: *Psyche Revived by Cupid's Kiss.*

But he didn't hear me. Or he wasn't listening. He stepped away, said goodbye, then left the shop, the book beneath his arm.

All of this did make me wonder if *I* was the one being deceived. Why would someone like Haze look to someone like me in matters of love?

Zinnia walked in so soon after, I wondered if she'd been watching nearby, waiting for him to leave. She was followed by a woman all in black. We all exchanged hellos.

"Noémi's my secretary," Zinnia said.

"Your secretary?"

"Yes," she said. "I have a secretary and I have an office. I just don't have much to do." She said this with more than a little disdain. "Noémi will keep an eye on the shop," she said. "You're coming with me."

"Where are we going?" I said.

"All I can think about is the Mermaid Bookshop, Yorick," she said. "I want to help you. And I genuinely believe I can. Today you're getting your mermaids on your windows."

"What do you mean?"

"I mean a window painter is coming."

"Oh, that's too much for me to ask," I said.

"You *didn't* ask," she said.

"Shouldn't I approve of the design?" I said, too meekly, I knew.

"Oh, you *have* to approve of it," she said, and she took my arm and led me to the door. "Oh yes, absolutely, you must approve. If you don't, you'll break my heart. Oh, I would be destroyed, Yorick. There's no question of your approval."

Though her spirits had lifted considerably since the night before, she leaned into me when she took my arm. She walked as close to me as she could. "Is this about yesterday's book club?" I asked. "Are you going to take everyone out and fix their lives, one by one?"

"No," she said. "Just you."

Her limousine idled at the end of the block, and Monsieur Toussaint held open the door. Once inside, Zinnia took from her pocket a piece of Paper Crane candy, Happyaku, with a drawing of a mermaid with a flower in her hair. "I enlisted my candy wrapper artist to design *your* mermaid too, for your windows, but it's quite different than this one," she said, carefully unwrapping the candy, giving it all her attention, tearing delicately at the seams of wax paper. "There's a folktale in Japan, 'Happyaku Bikuni,' about a little girl who eats some mermaid that a fisherman cooked. Then she never ages."

She held the open wrapper out to me and I peeled off the sticky candy. It was chewy, a fruit flavor I couldn't place.

I raised one eyebrow.

"It has the flavor of pickled plum," she said. "But it's actually a piece of squid stretched thin."

"You feed children squid and tell them it's mermaid?" I said.

"*And* eternal life," she said.

After a moment, I said, "I don't think it was the chocolate-covered cherries that had you upset yesterday."

"You're right," she said. "The cherries are nothing to be upset about. Barely a dewdrop of poison. You'd get sick from all the candy before you could get sick from the paraffin." She reached over to put her hand on mine. "You do know me, don't you?"

"I like to think so," I said.

21

Zinnia took me to a shop for a new suit and bought three. Rows and rows of impeccable suits just dangled on hangers, up in a fourth-floor loft, bespoke suits ordered from the finest tailors around town, then refused for some reason or another, simply abandoned, orphaned, and they all ended up at Madame Latreille's, still with their labels sewn in, miles and miles of empty costumes promising the appearance of prosperity. "Expensive suits for next to nothing," Zinnia said.

I was too embarrassed to tell her that I couldn't even afford next-to-nothing, but I did want to get lost in Zinnia's logic. She had a way of convincing me that my empty wallet was just a state of mind, just a failure of imagination.

I left the shop wearing my ratty old tweed, leaving the new suits behind to have some hems and cuffs lifted and lowered by the in-house seamstress. We then went down the street to a boutique to buy *American* shirts—"better made than the French ones," she insisted. Zinnia then took me to a barber who operated outside, under the bridge, with just a bistro chair and scissors, a blade, some tonic in his back pocket. "A genius, an artist," she said.

She instructed Monsieur Toussaint to unscrew the ornamental radiator cap from the front of her car and bring it along, so that she could advise the barber to cut my curls to match those of the little silver statue of Hermes, or Mercury, or whoever it was leaning forward into the wind, his hair blown back.

My thicket of curls that wouldn't be combed, curls that always toppled my hat off my head, were clipped and pomaded into an elegant swoop. For next to nothing.

I barely knew myself. Looking in the barber's hand mirror, I tried to imagine Haze looking back at me.

My transformation wasn't complete, it seemed. She took me to a shop that sold walking sticks and umbrellas, and she gave the shopkeeper a nod. He went behind a curtain and returned with an ivory-colored cane made of shark's backbone, with a silver handle in the shape of an octopus. Zinnia took it from him, then handed it to me.

"Did you commission this too?" I said, trying it out, gripping the octopus, tapping the whalebone on the floor tile.

"Do you like it?"

"It's beautiful . . . and strange," I said. "But I worry that it's just too . . . it's a little ostentatious . . . for me." I handed it back to her, and she handed it back to me, taking my hand and pressing it around the octopus handle.

"But you want people to remember you," she said. "The owner of the Mermaid Bookshop, a survivor of the *Titanic*, should have a whalebone walking stick. You need to be a character in your own story, Yorick."

"I'm not a survivor of the *Titanic*," I said. "It's all just a little brazen. Isn't it?"

"So what if it is? The first rule of business *and* of art, Yorick: you'll get the loudest applause from the cheapest seats."

Before I could object further, she paid for the walking stick and bought herself a parasol. Outside, she dismissed Monsieur Toussaint and the limousine. We would be walking back to the shop.

"It's called jamwood," she said of the handle of her parasol as we walked arm in arm in its shade. "If you cut a knife into it, we'd smell raspberries."

At the mere suggestion, I thought I caught the scent of raspberry jam. As we strolled along, I couldn't quite get accustomed to the walking stick. It seemed the wrong length, or it made the wrong *tap-tap* on the pavement, or it crooked my elbow at a somewhat awkward angle. I wished I hadn't left the other stick behind, and I was about to suggest we go back for it, when Zinnia said, "What do you think about the books Haze sends me?"

"Books?" I said.

"Books," she said.

"Books, yes, well, yes . . . Yes, the books he sends . . ."

"I didn't mean to confuse you," she said, amused, squeezing my arm.

"I don't know if I'm supposed to know about them," I said. "Am I?"

"Are you?" she said.

"Now you're making fun of me," I said, leaning into her, smiling.

"Never," she said. "Whether or not you're *supposed* to know about them, you *do* know about them, don't you?" Before I could answer, she said, "It's your typewriter. His letters have the same quirks as the letters you send the book club. The lowercase *h* tilts to the left. The *m*'s float a little, lifting above the line."

"Yes," I said. "He uses my typewriter."

"But you're worried that he wouldn't want me knowing that you know." She then said, "He must get the books at your shop, too. Do you recommend them?"

I considered inventing a story. Would Haze be decisive, knowing at once what book to send her? Or would he roam the shop slowly, looking up and down the shelves, tapping his fingers on the bindings, waiting for inspiration? But I realized I'd told enough lies with the letters themselves; it was best not to embroider. "No," I said. "I mean, yes, they come from my shop, but he doesn't ask me for advice."

"But you've read the letters," she said, keeping at it. She said this with such certainty, I wondered if she already knew. Had I already spoken of them?

"Yes. I mean, he's *read* to me, is all . . . just a few lines here and there, or not even, a few *words* here and there, for my advice, but . . . not really for my *advice*, just my thoughts. And only a time or two. Not even a time or two, really. Almost never."

Though I'd been clumsy about it, falling over my own words, Zinnia seemed convinced. "How charming," she said, dropping her glance to the sidewalk. "And I think it's sweet, the two of you talking about me."

"You know, I think he's falling in love with you."

"He probably falls in love ten times a day," she said.

"He thought he'd see you at the Louvre," I said. When the day began, I thought she might still be planning to meet him. Now I felt pangs of guilt imagining him waiting for his kiss next to Cupid and Psyche.

She didn't seem at all surprised to hear this. "I do love his attention," she said. "When he's looking at you, into your eyes, saying nothing at all, it's like the rest of the world falls away. Do you know what I mean?"

"I do."

"But what about you?" she said.

"What about me?"

"Who are you in love with?"

"Oh, I can't be in love. I can barely look after myself."

"Love isn't a *practical* consideration, Yorick," she said. We walked a bit farther, saying nothing. She said, "I'm *not* falling in love with Haze, Yorick," as if only just deciding that very moment. "But who knows, I might later." She leaned into me again, against me. She lowered her voice. "Can I tell you my theory?"

I leaned toward her too. Lowered my own voice. "Absolutely."

"Desire can sometimes lead to love. But love never leads to desire. Does that make sense?"

"Not quite," I said.

"I mean, if you desire someone you don't love, you might come to love them eventually. But if you love someone without desiring them, then there's no hope. You'll *never* desire them."

"And when we say *desire,* we mean . . . ?" I shrugged one shoulder.

"Sex, of course," she said. "Am I right or wrong? And *don't* quote from a book."

"Well, I guess I don't know that I agree with you. As you get to know someone better, as you get to know them intimately, as you grow closer to them, it seems quite possible that would lead to . . . a flicker of something." As I attempted to explain myself, I realized I was expressing my own hope, or fantasy, or whatever it was, that Haze's affection for me could lead to desire. I knew it wasn't likely, but I liked to imagine it at least possible.

I added: "But I couldn't say one way or the other. Like I told you, I don't fall in love."

"You didn't say you *don't.* You said you shouldn't."

"I said I can't."

"But you do *desire,*" she said.

"I do desire," I said.

"I've seen the way you look at him," she said.

Though she'd spoken just barely above her breath, she might as well have shouted it. I felt my cheeks burn, my skin tingle. My heart sped up. "And how's that?" I asked. "How it is that I look at him?" I pretended to be perplexed.

She began to rub at my arm, which had stiffened up. "You've been a good friend to him," she said.

"I hope so," I said.

I could tell Zinnia wanted me to say more. And I *wanted* to say more, to say more and more, to tell Zinnia everything about desires of my own, for us to rhapsodize on Haze's handsomeness. At the same time, I wanted to say even less than I already had. That very familiar inclination to confide, to confess, was always followed by anxiety and fear that I'd said too much, even when I'd said hardly anything at all.

22

After we turned the corner, my shop getting closer, Zinnia stopped me. I could see the windows, but the mermaids were still faint, the glass catching the reflection of the early evening sunlight. She unknotted my necktie. Removed it. "You're undressing me right here?" I said.

She covered my eyes with the necktie, wrapped the ends of it around the back of my head, and tied a knot into the silk. She then led me, blindfolded, down the middle of the street.

"Why are we doing this?" I asked. When we reached the tables of Café Capucine, she pulled out a chair for me. I reached down to feel the seat beneath me before sitting.

"I want you to see the windows all at once," she said. "And you're going to have a few sips of something so that you're in good spirits."

"You're starting to worry me," I said.

"Don't be worried."

Zinnia hadn't disentangled from me when we sat down; she kept her arm in mine. She rested her cheek on my shoulder.

"Zinnia," I said, "what had you so upset yesterday? Will you tell me?"

"I already told you," she said.

"No," I said. "You didn't." I began to lift my blindfold so I could see her, but she reached up to tug the blindfold back into place. I put my hand to her hand, held it at my cheek, kissed her palm.

"Oh, Yorick," she said. Once again, I pushed up at my blindfold, and again she tugged it back down. She kissed my cheek. I heard the waiter come up to the table and the sound of the glasses on the tabletop, though we hadn't ordered anything. "Drink," Zinnia said, and I felt the glass at my lips. "I know you've come to have a taste for Haze's gin."

Haze's gin. Now *that* was poison. It raised the hairs on the back of your neck, sent a chill up your spine. It worked like a love potion, making you susceptible after only a few sips.

"To be honest," Zinnia said, "I blindfolded you so I could just sit here and stare at you, and admire your haircut, without you noticing." She fed me more gin.

"I'm taking my blindfold off," I said.

"No one's stopping you," she said.

So I did, and I blinked the sun from my eyes and looked toward the shop. One window was in French, the other in English, and both had the same mermaid at their center, the *sirène* of my shop's name. A mermaid of my very own. She brought to my mind all the mermaids of my seafaring days, the ones etched into the wood signs of seaside taverns and painted on the sides of ships and tattooed on the arms of sailors.

The tips of her tail fin were pointing upward, giving her the shape of a hook at the end of a fishing line. In one hand she held an open book at her chest, hiding her naked breasts. She looked straight ahead with wide cartoon eyes, casting her spell.

"Say something, Yorick," Zinnia said.

"It's like that mermaid was always there," I said. "I already can't remember what it looked like before."

"Does that mean you like it?"

"I . . . I don't know what to say."

"Oh, Yorick, please don't be at a loss for words. Not now."

It was like a mirage lost sailors would see on the horizon, the Fata Morgana, a sign of life where it was unlikely—a vast island or the full sails of a rescue ship. Mermaids frolicking.

"Imagine," I said, then stopped. I was on the verge of tears myself. "Imagine your own bookshop in a city like Paris. Imagine it just . . . appearing before you one day."

Suddenly the windows seemed more fragile than they ever had. Not once had I worried about them breaking, but now all of Paris seemed full of flung bricks and clumsy birds.

The artist used pearl leaf for the letters, which he outlined in thin lines of silver foil. At the top of the window was written *La Librairie Sirène,* and at the bottom was my name, comma, *Propriétaire,* and beneath that: *Intendant de la Bibliothèque du Titanic.*

I looked over to the English translation of my window to make sure I was seeing straight. And there it was: *Library Steward of the Titanic.*

23

I walked into the bookshop so I could see how the mermaids looked backward, and to see what kind of shadows they cast; once inside, I saw there'd been more than just a window engraver at work. There were a few new wing chairs of burgundy leather, and new lamps with stained-glass shades of dragonflies and irises. But most astounding was the space overhead: hanging from the ceiling were what must have been twenty-five toy ships, maybe fifty, of various makes and shapes; they appeared to be hovering, floating far overhead, the strings too fine to see.

Only minutes later, men walked through my open door with cases of champagne already chilled, and waitresses with trays of glasses, and yet other men with cakes and pastries all in the same pastel colors of the candied almonds served at baptisms and first communions—those shades of pale rose, of blue clouds, of the silvery green of lamb's-ear leaves.

"We're christening the shop," Zinnia said, suddenly at my side. "With a little party."

It had all come together behind my back. I couldn't take my eyes off my windows, and looking out of them seemed to transform the city itself. The city outside my windows was suddenly a place I was welcome. I felt like a true denizen of Paris for the very first time.

People stopped to look, but they weren't seeing me. They were running their eyes along the lines of my mermaids. And then the faces became familiar. The orphan, the evangelist, the toymaker, and the rest: one by one they came.

Strangers came too. Noémi beckoned them all in, offering champagne. The regulars of Café Capucine left their tables and wandered in, carrying their own cocktails. All the ballerinas from the little opera down the street joined the crowd after their show, their hair still riddled with pins, their faces glistening with cold cream.

Of course, it was Haze I was waiting for. When he finally showed up, my first instinct was to apologize for keeping Zinnia all day, but as he walked up to me he smiled wide, took my hand, kissed my cheek. *"Belle comme un coeur,"* he said—*she's pretty as a picture*—and he meant the mermaids in the windows.

He advanced into the crowd that had gathered, to find Zinnia. People moved about the bookcases, up and down the stairs, walked along the gallery overhead. They took books from the shelves, paged through them, and either put them back or held them in their arms. The sight of customers browsing made the shop seem even more fragile than before.

I sat behind my desk to do business. I sold so many books, I worried I charged too little. When one person left, two would arrive, and the party went on.

Zinnia insisted I give a speech. She sent me up the staircase to snake in and around the people who'd gathered on the steps. I stopped midway. Haze whistled sharp. Everyone quieted.

"I don't know what to say," I said into the silence, to laughter, to applause.

"Tell us your name," Zinnia called up to me.

"Oh yes, yes," I said. It was then I realized, despite having had dreams of being an actor when I was a child, that I'd never in my life announced myself to such a large gathering of people. *Lend me your ears.*

"Tell us your story," Zinnia prompted.

"My story," I said. My story was that I didn't dare tell them what my story was. I didn't dare tell them because it was too fanciful and grim: I had become a bookseller only to discover that I was a book *collector*. A hoarder of books. No matter what book they wanted to buy, and no matter what price they wanted to pay, I didn't want them to have it.

I was every eccentric shopkeep in every children's book ever written. I was the doctor of a doll hospital, with drawers full of glass eyes and horsehair wigs.

La Librairie Sirène, I wanted to say, *is only sea mist and delirium.*

But I didn't say any of that. Instead, I said:

"I was the steward of the second-class library of the *Titanic.*"

I looked to Zinnia because I longed to see her face glow with approval. Before I could continue, there was a smattering of applause. A glass of champagne was passed up to me, person by person. "But just so you know, I only selected the books. I wasn't on board the ship when it set sail. But it was a dream come true. I spent weeks developing my library. The passengers of the *Titanic,* second class, would be my captive audience. I included books that had been boycotted, banned by libraries around the world. *The Picture of Dorian Gray. Madame Bovary.* A book by Karl May that was removed from libraries in Dresden after someone calculated all the death in it. There were more than two thousand characters dead by the end. Someone made a list. A certain number were scalped. A certain number poisoned. Three were eaten by crocodiles. One was buried alive."

I wanted to take a sip of my champagne, but my hand was shaking, so I was afraid I'd spill it all down the front of myself. All these people were listening to me and I wanted to tell them everything. But I didn't want to watch them watching me, so I spoke into my glass.

"I snuck in books about shipwrecks, and mutiny, and nautical disaster: *Lord Jim, Robinson Crusoe,*" I said. "I had every intention of being on board. And I *was* on the ship, in the days when it sat docked. I placed every book in the cabinets myself. And then I strolled the ship one day, along the long promenade, which seemed to go on for days and days, and I could feel the pain in my leg. I was no longer a young gentleman with a walking stick, but an old man with a cane. Even with the cane in hand, I was limping. I could hear it . . . my uneven footfalls, the *tap* of the cane, echoing as if the ship was under glass. A few White Star executives happened along, leading a tour of five or six men, and they all looked at me as they passed, none of them saying hello. One executive stayed behind while the others moved along, and he demanded to know, rather impolitely, who I was and what I was doing. And why I dragged my leg so. So when I was denied entry to the ship a few days later and told that someone else had been assigned to my library, I thought it might have been my limp and my cane that did me in. That's not what they said. What they said was that bringing in my own books was a kind of insubordination. But what I believed, and what I still believe, is that it was decided that I was not up to the exacting standards of such a grand ship. Not even in second class. Whatever the reason, I did not board the *Titanic*." The room seemed impossibly quiet. "And I did not die."

24

The party was over, everyone gone, and the sudden absence of noise made a noise of its own, a silent ringing in the ears. I poured more champagne for Haze and Zinnia, but when I brought it to them, Haze kissed my cheek, Zinnia kissed the other, and they left me behind holding a glass in each hand.

"I'm just walking Zin to the end of the block, to her limousine," Haze said on his way out. "I'll be right back."

They left the door open, letting in the warble of a woman singing at Café Capucine, where she weaved among the tables fluttering a sky-blue scarf. I leaned in my doorway and listened. I took a sip from one glass, then a sip from the other. She had no musical accompaniment, and I couldn't tell if she'd been paid to sing or if she only sang in order to be paid to stop. As with all the songs likely sung in Paris at that very minute, the sadness she sang of, the anxiety, was from a love that was lost.

It got later and later, the wine grew warm, the bubbles lost their pop, and the singer stopped singing. But I kept drinking, and the more I drank, the more jilted I felt. I looked at the clock and saw that more than an hour had passed since Haze had said he'd be right back.

I knew, of course, that this had been inevitable. This was *their* love story, and I was little more than a matchmaker. It had been only a matter of time before they went off without me.

This was what we wanted.

Under the spell of the wine, and of the woman's song still in my head, I wallowed in my abandonment. It felt luxurious, even sensuous, almost like love itself. I longed to be inconsolable, so that Haze might beg for my forgiveness.

I walked to my workbench—the empty piano where I kept all my book-wrecking tools—my walking stick in one hand, the last bottle of champagne in the other. Beneath my arm was a recent edition of *Les Liaisons dangereuses*, first published in 1782 and never out of print since, a story of jealousy and revenge, of sex and lies, told in letters sent back and forth.

Les Liaisons dangereuses had been among those novels I'd smuggled onto the *Titanic* in my carpetbag. For a hundred-some years, it had been outlawed by more than one French court; it lingered for decades on the Vatican's Index of prohibited books.

What I wouldn't give for Marie Antoinette's own volume. In his memoirs, her favorite hairdresser insisted he was the one to slip the licentious book onto her dressing table.

Some historians boasted that the book was so illicit, the title did not appear on the cover of her copy of *Les Liaisons dangereuses*. But the fact of the matter was, none of her books in her library in Versailles—all of them specially bound in a Moroccan leather the color of pomegranate skin—bore titles. Each book's cover had only the golden stamp of her coat of arms.

I took a pot of glue from the back of the piano, and I sat on the bench to begin pasting the pages together. I would cut out all its depravity, line the inside with red silk, and give the box to Zinnia. I would tell her it was for keeping the love letters Haze sent her.

"Hello?" Haze called out.

I considered ignoring him, but I said hello back, with the same question mark on the end of it.

Haze tapped my shoulder for me to make room for him on the bench. He sat next to me and picked up the champagne bottle to take a swig.

"It's gone warm," I said.

"I like it warm sometimes," he said. Then, "How could you abandon me tonight?"

"I didn't abandon you," I said. "I wasn't invited."

"You don't have to be invited."

"You didn't seem to want me along."

"Well, you should've come along anyway," he said. "I was tongue-tied the whole time I was with her. She probably thinks I'm an idiot." He took another swig.

"You've been gone a while," I said, running my camel's-hair brush over another page of the book, then dipping the brush back in the glue. "Did you sit in silence all this time?"

"Almost."

"Where did you go?"

"Nowhere," he said. "We just sat in the back of her limousine."

"With her driver up front?"

"He wandered off. Left us alone."

"Ah," I said. "Finally alone." Haze said nothing to that, so I asked, "Did you kiss her?" I wanted to know everything and nothing, all at the same time.

"We kissed some, yes," he said. "And we did talk some. But mostly we just sat there holding hands. I spent most of the time looking into her eyes and trying to think of something to say."

"She must not have minded much," I said. "The quiet." *And holding your hand. And looking into your eyes.*

He leaned against me and spoke softly. I felt his breath on my cheek. "I couldn't stop wishing you were there, whispering in my ear, telling me what to tell her. It was like your words were on the tip of my tongue." Then he said, "Oh," and he leaned back to reach into his pocket.

He set before me a cameo bottle with a purple flower painted across it. "When I told her I loved the smell of her perfume, she told me to tell her what I loved about it, and I couldn't describe it at all. Not at all. All that came to mind was *perfume*. 'It smells like perfume.' It's beautiful, a beautiful scent, hypnotic . . . *hypnotic!*

That's what I should have said. But I didn't say anything. *Pine*, I thought. I smelled a little pine in it, but I didn't want to say that. What's poetic about pine?"

"Evergreen," I said.

"Yes. Yes!" He put both his hands to my shoulders, to give me a gentle shake. "Yes. See?" He then picked up the bottle and removed its glass stopper. "So she gave me the bottle from her purse, and she told me to take it with me and to think about it. To *muse upon it*, is what she said." He held the bottle to my nose.

I put my hand over Haze's, to hold the bottle in place. There *was* a hint of pine needle, but only enough to counter the tuberose, which might be oversweet otherwise. I began writing Haze's letter to Zinnia in my head. "Camphor is cut from trees in India," I told him. "Buddhists wrote that snakes coiled around the trees in summer because the bark was cool, so they called camphor 'dragon-brain perfume.' The camphor is like a vein of silver ice through the wood when they cut it open."

"How do you know these things?"

"I just do. I've been off on my own, reading books, since I was a boy."

"You're *still* a boy," he said. He turned my hand up so that he could dab a fingertip of perfume on my wrist. "What book will we send her? We can send it tonight, can't we?"

When Zinnia gave the perfume bottle to Haze, was she sending me a secret message? Was she telling me she knew for certain his words were mine, despite my denials? I realized, of course, that *Les Liaisons dangereuses* was my own secret message to *her*. I would be inviting her to tuck Haze's love notes into a book about letters of seduction and deceit.

When I didn't answer Haze, and continued to glue pages together, he began pinching at my elbow. I jerked my arm away, but he just started in again. "Don't," I finally said, not looking up.

"Don't be that way," Haze said. I kept working. He said, "You're upset with me."

"No," I said.

"You had all day alone with Zinnia," he said. "I had a few minutes. Maybe *you're* in love with her too."

I met his eyes. "Maybe," I said. I waited for him to be the first to look away, but he didn't.

He said, "Something's different. Did you used to have a beard?"

"I got a haircut," I said, exasperated.

"Le bel homme," he said.

And just like that, my exasperation went away. *"Le bel homme,"* I said back to him.

"Means 'handsome,'" he said. He thought I was asking what he meant.

Le bel homme. I imagined him saying it with his lips at my ear. I held my wrist to my nose so I could marry the scent to the sound of him saying *le bel homme* to me.

I stood from the workbench to go find a copy of *The Art of Perfumery* by the chemist Septimus Piesse.

Piesse aligned perfume with music, writing of its octaves and harmony, I wrote as I sat at the typewriter, the sound of the keys a music of its own. *And whenever I breathe in your perfume, I'll think always of the music of the night just past, of the clamor of Paris just outside the window, a city that might as well have been miles away while we hid from it, in the middle of it all, under glass.*

When I read it to Haze, he said, "I should apologize." I thought he meant to me, and I was touched, and ready to forgive him, but then he said, "Tell her I'm sorry that I didn't have much to say."

I'm embarrassed by how tongue-tied I was with you tonight, but I have to confess that I love being quiet with you. Please don't think I have nothing to say. I'm only silent because I'm listening so closely.

25

As I lay in my bed and stared at the ceiling, I resolved to forgive Haze. But I fell asleep and woke up upset with him all over again. I fell back to sleep, and when I woke, I realized that his friendship and affection were better than anything I'd ever known. And Zinnia's too. How childish to be angry simply because they found happiness. I fell asleep once more, and when I woke in the morning, I couldn't remember whether Haze was forgiven or not.

The day after Haze disappeared with Zinnia alone, he slipped off to be with her again, and again the night after that. I had a feeling things would never go back to the way they were.

We did still spend time together, the three of us. But before we'd always orbited around each other, sipping from each other's drinks, taking food from each other's forks; now every night together it felt like the two of them and the one of me. I often wondered if I was only along so their secrets felt more secret, so they'd have someone to not see them holding hands under the table, to not hear what they whispered in each other's ears.

I did manage to keep myself distracted; the mermaids lured people to my shop. *How have I not known about this?* they asked me, sometimes with a tone of annoyance, as if they'd been uninvited all this time. Others were critical in other ways: *You can't just up and buy a bookshop in Paris. It requires an apprenticeship.* You have to know all the old laws, they told me, even those that no longer apply. Booksellers were legally obligated to be knowledgeable, to sell books with dignity, in proper shops, to keep these vital objects out of the hands of those who'd mishandle them, lose them, sell them for cheap.

Zinnia had already encouraged me to raise my prices. People expected to pay more in a Paris shop, she reasoned, that it was a kind of luxury tax. *You're an agent of culture*, she told me.

Though I couldn't say I'd become *friendly* with the other book-sellers in the fifth arrondissement, they did at least stroll into my shop to growl with disapproval. Even when they admired a rare and unusual book on my shelf, they might be dismissive of its condition, or the price I was asking, or a repair I'd made.

I didn't mind their grumpy appraisals, though, because it felt like a kind of acceptance. They even introduced me to a tradition of closing up shop for a few hours in the afternoon to sit in a café with a bottle of wine. They often joined me at Café Capucine, and I felt they were performing for me, teaching me the vernacular of the used and the rare, a glorious poetry of collapse: *sunned and fox spot, split bite, rubbed feet, cracked spine with frayed nerves.*

They called me Hopalong, after Hopalong Cassidy of the cow-boy novels, to mock not only my limp but also my voice—they swore they could hear in my shy mumble the dusty drawl of Nebraska, one they'd come to know from Buffalo Bill's Wild West show that had enraptured Paris. *Guillaume le Buffalo.* And they knew all about the frontier; French translations of dime novels sold swiftly in their shops.

"Booksellers are constantly at war with book buyers," said Monsieur Escoffier of Escoffier & Cie. "People of Paris expect to return books after they've read them. But I'm in the business of selling books, not hiring them out."

Madame Mondragon of Chez Mondragon, in a fur coat ratty with mange, wished she owned all the old books lost to history, imagining an abattoir of volumes wrapped in the cracked skins of all sorts of creatures: lamb, goat, walrus puppy. "Ah, the *libri elephantini* of ancient Greece," she sighed, swooning, touching her glass of wine to her heart. "It had a cover of carved ivory; its pages were of elephant intestines."

While I did sense that some of them disapproved of my using my *Titanic* stewardship as a lure to my shop, others admired the tactic—or, at least, respected it as a tool of business. We carried our shops on our backs, as a part of us, like a snail's shell. And their own eccentricities had certainly served them. Zinnia had been right—book lovers loved bookshops that took on the character of their owners. *I know so much more about you than you could ever tell me,* Zinnia said, *just from the books on your shelves. And the order they're in.*

My book subscription service had expanded too, beyond just the *Titanic* ticketholders; now that my shopwindow announced my connection to the tragedy, people wandered in curious. What books might the passengers have taken to their beds that night? What did they read on the deck that day? My customers wanted to slip into the imaginations of the victims in their last hours. The *Titanic*—all its elegance and horror—had always seemed a nightmare we all dreamed up together. So I gave them a peek, for double the price of each book's worth plus a steep monthly fee.

I think many of them thought I'd been on the ship when it sank but were too polite to ask me about it. They eyed my limp with sympathy.

I watched the people in my shop and memorized their habits. I loved how a lady might clutch a book to her chest, or how she might carry one around with her, then put it back after finding something else. I loved watching people read: one man kept flicking at the corner of the page he was on, as if anxious to move on to the next; one woman seemed to need to know the ending before she'd begin. And there were two handsome gents who came in from time to time together—one would hold the book open in front of himself and the other would read over his shoulder. I could've watched them standing there for hours.

I could even afford to hire Alice, our delivery girl with the green apples, to work in the shop part-time. She looked seventeen but claimed to be twenty. She took to the job right away, and proved quite sharp—so sharp that she quickly caught on to our letter-writing scheme. I tried to tell her I was only transcribing letters for Haze, but she could see that Haze was never anywhere around. And he wasn't asking for letters anymore—he'd already captured Zinnia's heart, he reasoned. *It was fun while it lasted,* he said to me, with a kiss on the cheek. He saw it all as a game of flirtation, as innocent and playful as the whistle candy that young lovers passed in a kiss.

But I was addicted. It was a kind of consolation, the letter writing was. With the letters, and the books, I could still be a part of it all. I could linger in their romantic imagination. In this disguise, I was entirely myself.

Alice saw over my shoulder as I sat at the typewriter one day, the page blank except for Zinnia's name.

Feeling caught, I improvised. I typed Hamlet's *Alas, poor Yorick* monologue, which I'd memorized as a boy, and it came back in a rush, though I couldn't remember the last time I recited it.

I stopped after I typed, *Here hung those lips that I have kissed I know not how oft.* I took the paper from the typewriter and sat back to run my eyes along the line, over and over. How was I just noticing it now, Hamlet remembering Yorick's many kisses? *I know not how oft.* I thought of Haze's lips, lips like a cupid's bow. No, that wasn't right at all. Was that a cliché? The sentiment of a valentine? Were his lips like the petals of lilies, like the slices of peaches? Had there ever been more kissable lips in the history of Paris?

Alice stepped away, so I rolled in another sheet of stationery and typed exactly that: *Have there ever been more kissable lips in the history of Paris?*

Along came Alice, with *A Room with a View,* about love that blooms on a trip to Italy. "There's even a vendor of souvenir photographs in it," she said. "And a romance novelist." Myself, I remembered the book for its scene of young men swimming naked in a pond, *only a pond, but large enough to contain the human body, and pure enough to reflect the sky.* One of the men was described as *Michelangelesque.*

"Kissable," Alice said, looking again over my shoulder. "This book is full of kisses. There's a stolen kiss in a field of violets. And in the garden. But the best one's at the end." We marked that page with a snippet of typewriter ribbon, the scene in which the *Michelangelesque* George puts his face to Lucy Honeychurch: "Kiss me here," George says. *He indicated a spot where a kiss would be welcome.*

As luck would have it, Alice was a bit wicked in a good way. She took a dislike to Haze, a dislike that pleased me. *He's picking your brain,* she said, *like he picks people's pockets.*

He doesn't pick pockets, I told her, though I suspected he had in the past. But this portrait of him—derelict, vagrant—only made me desire him more. I wanted him wanting whatever was in my head.

I got so caught up in my own sentiments, I became better at reading the sentiments of others—and better at selling books, especially the rare ones I kept in the vault. I'd come to know how a man's emotions could betray him. I never penciled a price on the rarest of the volumes. I would negotiate with an otherwise buttoned-up gentleman, say, and I'd set my price based on the uptick of his heartbeat that shivered the linen of his shirt or his nervous swallowing that knocked at his collar. He might even start blinking from the sweat beginning to bead at his temples. For every fraction of an inch that his forelock drooped, my price would lift.

While I saw little of Haze in my shop in the daytime, his corner seemed to expand. He'd closed it off with an old folding screen. Where there should've been silk in the panels were pages of newspaper as patchwork. Behind the screen was his barber chair, now covered in tasseled pillows, like the chaise in an opium den. And across the bookshelves next to the chair were little things he'd salvaged from the streets of Paris—a finial shaped like an artichoke, the ball-and-claw foot of a bathtub, a demon's-head door knocker, old glass, dice of carved bone, cigar bands. He'd even propped up the doll we'd gotten, the *Titanic* steward, which struck me as so sweet, I forgave him once again.

Soon enough, Haze was back. He needed me. "I have to send a letter to Z tonight," Haze said.

It was already late, but in the underground of Paris, among the catacombs and phantoms, were networks of pneumatic tubes like organ pipes, sending letters through the city with gusts of air.

Among the things I now sold were the stamped cards marked *Carte Pneumatique*, on paper the pale blue green of pond water. It was just as fast as a telegram, maybe faster, and far more intimate— you didn't have to confess your sentiments to an operator.

While I loved the idea of Haze asking again for a letter, I wanted to seem aloof. "Zinnia could have your letter within an hour," I told Haze. "But you should write it yourself." I sat him down at the desk, handed him a pen, and put the *carte pneumatique* before him.

"I don't know what to say," Haze said.

"Write whatever is on your mind."

Haze sat stone-still, the pen hovering above the paper, all the words stuck in the nib. Finally, he said, "I could just send it blank. A . . . a . . . um . . . a *symbol* of how overwhelmed I am, how there are no words enough to express . . . et cetera, *et ainsi de suite.*"

"Start with that. What you just said. 'I should leave this page blank . . .'"

"No, it's a terrible idea," he said, throwing the pen down on the desk and leaning back in the chair.

"What is this all about, Haze? What happened?"

Haze rocked the chair back and forth on its squeaking springs. "She took me to her house," Haze said. "She keeps all the books we sent her in a red cabinet. She brought out the poetry book. The one in French. She wanted me to translate one particular poem for her."

"Like we did that night . . ."

"Except you read it to me," he said. He kept rocking, but watched me, waiting.

"You couldn't . . ." I paused. "But I've *seen* you read . . ."

"I can read a café menu," he said. "I can read the writing on a shopwindow. But something as . . . *motley* as a poem . . . I can't untangle a word of it. The sight of it . . . how locked up it was . . ."

I felt Haze's anxiety fluttering in my own gut. "What did you do?"

"I tried to kiss her," he said. "I said I'd rather be kissing her. But she insisted. So I told her I wore spectacles, but not around her, because I didn't want her to see me in them. I was too vain, I told her. So she brought me a magnifying glass. I ended up getting frustrated. Told her she wasn't listening. And I left."

I felt a touch of pity. I realized there was no way he could unravel this complication without me.

"I'm not an idiot," he said.

"I know you're not."

"I ran away from school so much, they finally didn't let me back in. I've never owned a book of my own, not in my life. But until now, I've never had a reason to much regret it, you know? Now every book in this shop haunts me. All those words I've never read just keep echoing."

I jerked my head to the side, gesturing for him to stand from the chair so I could type his letter for him. He stood and stepped over to me. He put both his hands to my head. I thought he might let me kiss him. But I also thought *he* might kiss *me*. So I did nothing.

"*Tu es un homme bon, mon doux garçon,*" he said, in a hush. "I do love Zinnia, Yorick. I hope you believe me. Because some days it feels like it's the *only* thing that's true anymore, my love for her. But I'm nobody. I'm nothing."

Haze leaned forward to press his forehead against mine, and I could feel his breath on my lips. "*J'ai besoin de toi,*" he told me. *I need you.*

Z—

I have to be honest with you.

I was embarrassed.

I didn't want to translate the poem tonight because I didn't want you to see how slow I was about it.

The letters I write you are more lucid than I am myself.

I make a ritual of it. I sit at the café and they bring me a pen and paper and an inkpot. The pen's broken nib and the watered-down ink do less for me than the gin, which tilts my brain at a proper slope to tumble words around.

I scratch out so many missteps the paper's full of holes before the café closes. I take my notes to Yorick's typewriter and I try to make it all sound like it all came easy.

Growing up, I had to teach myself everything. I learned how to read by standing outside cafés, studying their chalkboards, memorizing their menus, all the eloquent dinners I'd never know the taste of.

Please forgive me for being rude.

À tout à l'heure,
Haze

26

Zinnia came to the shop a little before lunchtime. "The restaurants in Robinson will be closing for the season soon," she said. She'd even brought woolen sweaters and scarves for Haze and me.

Monsieur Toussaint drove us to the village south of Paris for lunch in the branches of a chestnut tree—it was a literary destination, Zinnia explained, inspired by *Swiss Family Robinson,* a novel about castaways who live in a tree house after getting shipwrecked.

The village had four or five restaurants in trees, platforms nestled in the trees' branches, staircases winding up and around the trunks. "Do you think you can make it to the table at the very top?" Zinnia asked me after we'd chosen the tallest tree.

"Yes, of course," I said, but I took Haze's hand anyway, when he offered to help me climb the steps.

Waiters sent dishes and casseroles up in a basket on a rope and pulley—a bottle of wine, a pot of *lapin de garenne,* some young turnips.

Everything about our lunch lifted my mood. Maybe I hadn't lost them both after all. "There's no one I'd rather be shipwrecked with," I said. "Zinnia, especially. I suspect she'd have a knack for keeping us alive."

"I'd trap a better rabbit than this sad, scrawny thing, at least," she said, poking her fork in the pot. "He must have died of starvation."

Haze studied the wild rabbit. "I'd say syphilis."

"Oh no," I said. "He was a terrible morphine addict. Look at the euphoria on his face."

We ate what little there was, then tugged on the rope for the waiter to send up more wine. Haze had finally relented and bought himself a tourist camera, and we posed for snapshots. He took several of Zinnia and several of me, and I loved how particular he was. Instead of straightening my hair up, he tousled it, running his fingers through my curls. He then took my wounded leg in his hand and lifted it to cross it over my other leg. He unknotted the lace of my boot. He situated my wineglass in my hand just so. I could picture myself in his viewfinder, and I liked the look of it. But when I straightened up in my chair, he instructed me to slouch back down.

I could've spent hours letting him pose me. I wanted to ask him endless questions. I would happily spend every minute of my future hearing about every minute of his past. I could see us in a rowboat on a summer lake, with a bottle of champagne, a basket of grapes, our legs intertwined, Haze confessing. I had a sense that getting into his head would be as easy as picking the tin lock of a girl's diary.

Haze told me to move my chair next to Zinnia's so he could photograph us together. *"Mon bouquiniste et ma confiseuse,"* he said. *My bookseller and my confectioner.* She kissed my cheek, her breath warm with red wine. "Haze is in love with me," she said in my ear.

I spoke in her ear. "Are you in love with him?"

"I haven't decided," she said, and she said it with some melancholy.

Haze overheard none of it. "Have I told you what I want Z to do with her life?" he said. He put his camera away, but Zinnia stayed put as if still posing, her arm in mine, leaning against me, her head on my shoulder.

"He wants me to be more like you," Zinnia told me.

"She should take her own advice, make good use of her second chance at life," he said, sitting across from us, pouring us all more wine.

"What's wrong with the life you have?" I said.

She shrugged. "In France the wives and daughters work in the family business," she said. "But my father is American through and through. So I have an office and a title at the Paris factory, but I have little influence. Very little. My father was cursed with no sons, but he has a nephew. The nephew will someday run it all."

"So she should give it all up, start her *own* business," Haze said. "She makes the most beautiful Japanese sweets. You should see them. The colors. The shapes. It's an art. They belong in a shopwindow."

"You cook?" I said.

"Oh, heavens, no," she said. "I can't *cook*. But I can make confections. I learned from my mother, who learned from her mother."

"What a wonderful secret you've kept from me," I said, though I felt a little sad I was only just learning of this talent now. I didn't think it was the wine—though I drank much of it—tipping me toward sentiment. "I don't want to lose either one of you," I said.

"How could you ever lose us?" Zinnia said.

"We're from such different worlds," I said. I took another sip. "We wouldn't even know each other if it wasn't for the toymaker bringing us all together."

"We would have found each other some other way," Zinnia said.

Without me, it all falls apart, I wanted to tell them.

27

Zinnia invited Haze to the opera, but he had nothing to wear. So we set off to see the gambler, who'd boasted a time or two of his wardrobe closet. At our book club, he always seemed aloof, unconcerned, even a little callous, but his apartment showed another side of him.

"An impeccable suit does useful damage," he said of his success at casinos. He walked us down his rows of coats and trousers that seemed to go on for a city block. He was still dressed for bed, in pink pajamas and a red robe patterned with golden cheetahs, but his hair looked freshly washed and set. "It unsteadies the nerves of your opponent. No matter how honest you are, you want them to think you're crooked. If you look good, they think you've been bad, and they'll make mistakes they wouldn't otherwise."

The swallowtail coat the gambler plucked from its hanger fit Haze perfectly, and he offered up a *chapeau claque*, an opera hat that collapsed with a tap. The gambler snapped it back into shape with a flick of the wrist. "You knock it flat then tuck it under your chair," he explained.

On our walk back to my shop, Haze practiced popping the hat up and down.

"You're going to wreck the springs," I said.

Haze reached over to hold my chin. "Alas, poor Yorick," he said. "You live in a world where everything's about to break, don't you? Your ships are sinking, your shop is flooding. Your top hat's gone flat."

"Haze, my ship did sink," I said. "My shop did flood."

"Well, yes," he said. "In *actuality*. But I'm talking about your state of mind. You're in your own head too much."

"Whose head should I be in?" I asked.

He said nothing, but I knew the answer. I should be more like him. Whenever I walked with Haze, I became preoccupied by the glances of every woman and man we passed. I saw myself through the eyes of those who looked at him with awe and longing, and I stood up straighter in their sight, my walking stick mere decoration, not a crutch.

I asked him what opera was playing, mostly to put some creak in his armor. I knew he wouldn't know. We stopped at a news kiosk to investigate.

"It's a good thing I asked," I said. "It's *La Traviata*. What do you know about it?"

"I know slightly less than nothing," he said, without a care in the world, fascinated with his hat again.

"The man that Zinnia is falling in love with would know it's based on a novel," I said.

Back at the shop, I showed him the gorgeous copy from my vault—a limited edition printed by Maison Quantin, a publishing house with a workshop of some of the city's finest binder-gilders. The book's title, *La Dame aux camélias*, was low on the spine, beneath three long-stemmed camellias in bloom, four in bud, mosaicked with spots of pink and green. There was no title on the cover, only a raspberry-colored swirl.

As the hour of the opera neared, Haze came upstairs fresh from a bath, his hair still damp and smelling of sandalwood oil, the same scent as the actors backstage after they'd wiped away their makeup for the night. As a boy, I would sit in the corner swooning as they ran the oil through their hair to revive curls tamped down by their wig caps so that they could go out to charm barmaids at taverns.

"Zin wants me to take her dancing after," Haze told me. He

then handed me a rolled-up magazine. "She wants me to learn the dance that's in there."

It was *Femina,* a fashion magazine. "Did you?"

"Of course not," he said. "Teach me."

He opened the magazine to a page featuring the *maxixe brésilienne,* a Brazilian tango, the pattern of the steps mapped out. I opened it and placed it on the floor for us to glance at, my hand in his, my arm around his shoulder, our fingers intertwined.

His grip was strong, but his hand at the small of my back rested featherlight. The tango was awkward at first, a lot of stop and start, but soon enough we knew our way around. We kept dancing, practicing. I wanted it to never end.

"You're dancing with everyone else on the floor," I instructed. "You'll catch their eye, to keep from bumping into them."

"I want her to marry me, Yorick," he said, out of nowhere. We kept dancing.

"Do you think she would?"

"Her father would never allow it," he said. "But I want her to know I don't want her money. What I *want* is for her to give it all up. It would prove how much I love her. We could move into a cabin in the vineyards of Old Madame Petit. We could pluck aphids off grapes."

How could you ever lose us? Zinnia had promised me, only moments ago.

28

You must arrive for the opera as gentlemen have arrived for the opera for two centuries, the gambler had told Haze. So we arranged for a horse and carriage.

Meanwhile, I secretly arranged for a carriage of my own, an extravagance I couldn't really afford, even with the success of the shop. But I could not stop thinking about Haze and Zinnia leaving Paris. I instructed my carriage to follow Haze's from a distance. When we got to the theater, I had the driver stay back so I could watch Haze and Zinnia through my opera glasses. Zinnia looked like a countess stepping from a Russian train on the whitest day of winter, in a beet-red gown and a sable coat of steel gray.

I'd heard tell of a ticket broker who worked near the box office of the Paris Opera whose prices got cheaper the closer it got to curtains-up. So I was able to watch them from inside too, from my place in the dark of the farthest seats, my binoculars aimed at the *fauteuils d'orchestre,* the balcony box that seemed just inches from the stage; it seemed if they leaned too far forward they'd fall into the diva's deathbed as she wailed about her consumption.

They were as distracted by each other as I was by them. They whispered to each other, or looked into each other's eyes, or kissed each other's necks. At the same time, they seemed enraptured by the opera. Zinnia was in tears by the end as the lady of the camellias coughed up her last tragic note.

After, in my carriage, I asked the driver to take me back in a roundabout way—up the Rue Auber, then along the Rue des

Mathurins, then down the Rue de l'Arcade—without giving him any specific address.

I guzzled champagne right from the bottle and sank low into the silk pillows. I thought not only of Zinnia and Haze in their balcony, but of the opera itself, its story of death by heartbreak. Their love—Haze and Zinnia's, and even the fictional characters' on the stage—was genuine; mine wasn't. My shop was full of the love stories of men and women, but most of the stories of men loving men and women loving women were in medical textbooks and criminal records.

I'd now read many times the gentle story of a man describing his passion, his longing for another man, all written down as part of his treatment and published in a psychology journal. The doctor's conclusion: such men were prone to melodrama. Their love was not real; it was an overwrought performance, a replica of the love shared by men and women. The love felt by someone like me could only ever be a pale imitation.

But as we turned the corner onto the Rue de l'Arcade, my heart pounded, my hand shook. I checked the address again in the booklet I'd brought along in my coat pocket, an illicit guide with lists of brothels, parlors, agencies, all cataloged according to sexual fetish and phantasm. The pages were pale pink, in imitation of the classic guidebook *Le Guide rose des étrangers à Paris,* sold to foreigners to help them navigate train schedules and tipping the staff at hotels. There was no date stamped on my pink booklet and it evaded any appraisal—it might have been from years in the past or years in the future. On page sixteen were a few addresses I didn't expect I'd discover in any book of any time.

Just up ahead was a salon where men could meet other men. There were rooms to rent by the hour should you meet someone you liked. I listened to the *clip-clop* of the horse's hooves, and their rhythm on the pavement seemed to grow slower and slower. I didn't yet know whether I'd let the building pass or if I'd call up to the driver to stop.

The idea of stopping the driver and going inside felt like both salvation *and* self-destruction. An evening in this space—which I knew nothing about, nothing more than an address and a brief, sexless, banal description in this underground booklet—might bring me serenity or despair.

All the possible consequences ran through my head when I spotted the salon through my opera glasses—*The place is raided, I'm arrested, my name's in the newspaper, my shop is shunned, I'm broken, destitute, alone, dead in the streets before I'm thirty.*

After I'd carried all my anxieties well past the salon, I only then told the driver to stop. I ducked into a tobacconist's to buy a pack of Gauloises, a short, stout cigarette, then returned to the carriage and back to my bookstore. I felt a rush of relief. I convinced myself that it wasn't fear that had brought me home, but love. I didn't want anything to overshadow Haze, so handsome in his top hat and suit, so beautiful in the balcony, captivated by the opera.

I sat down at my workbench with the booklet and began to cut out its insides before I'd even glued the pages together. I decided it would make a quaint cigarette case for Haze, with its rose-colored cover and an illustration of a pretty lady in a negligee—a scribble of ruffle and lace.

I rummaged through Haze's trunk of liquor for a bottle of absinthe. I wanted something lethal. With every sip, the room tipped a little more, and I fell back in Haze's barber chair.

The more absinthe I drank, the more aroused I was by my friends' indifference. I shut my eyes and pictured them all the times I'd seen them without me. To feel betrayed is a kind of lust. You make yourself sick with jealousy hoping to sicken the one who made you jealous. You watch your lover love someone else, and the rush of poison in your veins reminds you you're alive.

Zinnia,

Yorick writes this letter to you. Same as always. Yorick wrote <u>all</u> our letters to you. I'm not even here.

These letters and these books are just Yorick's idea of who I should be. I don't exist at all.

You're in love with nobody.

The miserable monster I created . . . His jaws opened, and he muttered some inarticulate sounds . . .

That line above is a lie too. I didn't write it. I stole it from Frankenstein.

I'm sending the book along to you, my favorite edition, with black hearts all up its spine, and hearts on the cover too, heart-shaped blooms at the ends of long stems with heart-shaped leaves.

It's a love story. The monster longs for love. To be loved. But everyone turns him away.

Everywhere I see bliss, from which I alone am irrevocably excluded.

That's from Frankenstein again, right from the monster's mouth.

I leave no signature.

29

Alice's voice wove into my dream, a dream I often had, of water rolling down the walls of the shop, knocking the books off the shelves to fall into the flood. *"Debout là-dedans,"* she said, "wake up, wake up," standing on the stairs, reaching down for my hand as I tried not to drown.

I woke, feeling like the sunlight was holding me to the barber chair. "I've been trying to wake you," Alice said, leaning over me. "It's almost noon."

"Yes," I said, blinking spots from my eyes. "I'm up."

"You're not up," she said. "You're down. It's time I should open the shop."

I'd tried to stay awake, waiting for Haze, drinking more and more, almost hoping to make a fool of myself when I saw him. I would be too drunk to make sense or to care about consequences. For all I knew, I might tell him I was in love with him. I might beg him to never leave me.

When I realized Haze hadn't even come home, the whole night went dark. And the darkness gave way to dim images of Haze and Zinnia alone together. I not only felt left out, but completely lost.

A few people were already strolling through the shop by the time I stood up. I nodded at them as I passed on stocking feet, leaning on my cane, my shirt untucked, unbuttoned—*Pardon me, hello, let me know if I can help with anything.* It wasn't until I got to the front desk, where Alice was tidying up, that I remembered the letter I'd typed. The night came back in tiny fragments, glistening like broken glass. I had tucked the letter into an envelope, and the envelope into the pages of *Frankenstein,* intending to taunt Haze with it when he arrived. My plans, in my drunkenness, had been to embrace him *and* to push him away. I had intended to tell him I was only teasing, I would never send such a thing, but it was more than that. It was a threat. I'd show him how, with just a few lines on paper, I could change everything.

In the light of day, I was realizing I was the villain in their story of romance, which troubled me as much as anything else.

When I saw there was no book where I'd left it, I felt a flicker of relief. Maybe I'd only dreamed it. But the relief quickly gave way to panic; perhaps Haze had been by after all and he'd read the letter. I tapped my finger on the corner of the desk. "The book that was here . . . ," I said.

"Yes," Alice said.

"Did you put it away somewhere?"

"I delivered it."

"No."

"Well, yes. I couldn't wake you this morning, and I saw Zinnia's name on the envelope, so I took it to her. Like I always do."

It was as if the monster himself had just walked in and socked me in the jaw. "You have to go," I said. "You have to go retrieve it. Did you leave it on the front step? Or with the maid?"

"I left it with *her,*" Alice said. "She came to the door herself. She did seem . . . perplexed to see me. Oh no . . . Was Haze there with her, do you think?"

I held one hand to the throbbing in my head. "It's not your fault," I mumbled, mostly to remind myself that it really wasn't her fault at all. I knew she didn't like Haze much, but she couldn't be blamed for all these weeks and weeks of our deceiving Zinnia.

I dropped into one of the leather chairs and clutched the octopus handle of my walking stick to my chest. "Is it really so bad?" I said. "If you found out that a man you loved didn't write the love letters he sent, would it matter that much?"

"We tell all kinds of lies to get people to love us," Alice said. "There's an art to it. I would find it flattering, to be honest."

And that was exactly why I loved Alice's advice: she could make any mistake seem the right thing to do.

"I wish I could remember what I wrote," I said. "I think I meant for it to be a little abstract . . . and I was drunk, after all . . . Maybe it won't make any sense to her?" I looked to Alice as if she might have an answer.

She opened her mouth to speak, then closed it back up. Opened it again, closed it again. Finally, she said, "If I tell you something, you can't be mad at me."

"How can I promise that if I don't know what you're talking about?"

"You just have to. Or I won't tell you at all."

I sighed. "I won't be mad at you."

She looked down to her hands folded atop the desk, and she kept her eyes there. "So . . . I *did* read it, actually. But you can't be mad at me, because I'm putting your mind at ease." She looked up. "I read the letter, and so I can tell you: it *was* vague. You can fill in the blanks however you want." She shrugged. "You can make something up. Tell her you just wanted to send her a book, like Haze has been doing. You can say you were trying to be mysterious."

But even if Zinnia couldn't find the confession in it, Haze would. If Zinnia read the letter to him, he would know my intentions.

"There's something else," Alice said.

"Nothing else, please," I said.

"I just want you to know . . . I opened them all. *All* the letters that you and Haze wrote to Zinnia, not just the few I helped you write. When you first hired me to deliver them, I always read them along the way. Actually, I read the letters over and over. I couldn't take my eyes off them." She shrugged again. "What can I say, I'm a romantic at heart."

"I would never have known," I said. "You didn't have to confess to all that."

"Sometimes when you don't tell the whole truth it feels like a lie. And I don't want to lie to *you*. Not you. Yorick . . . it may not be much, this little job of mine, but . . . it's everything to me. You took me in off the street. The fact that you trusted me . . . you can't imagine what that means. A very small thing, maybe, but a very small, kind, generous thing." She looked back down to her folded hands. "You rescued me."

I had no idea. I thought all I'd done was assign her tasks. "Well, you've been a godsend yourself," I said, but she just shook her head. I was curious; knowing that her eyes had been on the pages seemed to change all the letters somehow. "So you just . . . opened them?" I said. "They were all sealed shut." Sometimes I would take Haze's hand in mine and turn it, so that his intaglio ring would leave the imprint of the stone heart on the wax.

"Your wax is old," she said. "You can pop the seal off, take the letter out, read it, put it back, then lick the seal and stick it back to the envelope. I read how in a novel. You can jimmy it loose easy, with a cat's whisker."

30

When Haze failed to return to the shop that day, and that night, and the next morning, the letter I'd written rewrote itself in my imagination, revealing more and more, until I was certain it had not been vague at all.

Alice helped me compose a letter of explanation to Zinnia—but I couldn't explain too much, or I'd implicate Haze. I needed yet *more* vagueness, a note in which I neither confessed nor denied. At the typewriter, Alice and I wrote of absinthe, of dreams. I thought back to the book club's discussion of Freud. I could blame my unconscious.

I hope I caused no confusion by sending you Frankenstein. *It would be peculiar to receive it, I now realize, and I don't think I even know why I sent it. I hope you did not make too much of the monster's monstrousness. I suppose the monster is a creature cobbled together, like the three of us in our friendship. I really only meant for the letter to be sweet . . . like the letters Haze sends you.*

I typed it on the blue sheet for the pneumatic tubes of the underground, in hopes that she'd respond the moment she received it. But the rest of the day passed and I heard from neither of them. I went to Zinnia's house, where I'd never once been invited. I felt certain she'd not been embarrassed by *me* by any means, but I did wonder if she was embarrassed for herself, for the excess of such a grand mansion taking up so much of the city.

When I arrived, I wondered over the candy-box frill of it. The wriggle of shingles suggested ribbon candy, and the brickwork was pink, with balustrades of tarnished copper the color of mint nougat. I knocked at the door, and knocked again, and waited. Only when I began to walk away did the maid answer. She ignored my request to see Zinnia, but did so politely, without a word, only a nod, her eyes lowered, and she held out a silver plate with an envelope on it. My name was written with such flourish I was heartened by the sight of it, by the loopy, almost meandering curves of the *Y*, and how the leg of the *k* had some kick to it, running right off the edge of the paper.

Entrée Interdite. In our booth. At 7.

Entrée Interdite, the little Oscar Wilde–like den where she first took Haze and me. So she wasn't angry. That letter I'd sent accidentally retreated back into vagueness, taking all its threat and accusation with it.

I got a fresh haircut under the bridge, and as the evening neared I put on one of the suits Zinnia had bought me. I tapped some perfume on my cheeks and neck—something decidedly candy-like, with notes of burnt sugar and almond.

Maybe Haze and Zinnia hadn't been avoiding me at all—maybe they'd just been caught up in their love affair, like always. Suddenly their romance didn't trouble me. It meant I'd done no damage. Once again, with all those hours by myself, I'd invented turmoil from nothing. To console myself, I'd imagined myself not ignored but at the very heart of their silence.

I decided, with this second chance, I would never do that to them again.

But when I walked into the saloon and was led to the banquette where we'd sat, I saw Haze morose, slouched, still in the suit the gambler had loaned him for the opera. Haze sat in the curve of the booth, and I took a seat on the other side of the table, in a wing chair of silk chinoiserie patterned with monkeys in trees.

When he looked at me, then looked away, his jaw stiff, I felt my heart speed up and I fell right back into my panic. "Please tell me what happened," I said. He just shook his head. I brought out the cigarette case I'd made for him from the rose-tinted guidebook. He did take it from me, and he held it in his hands, but with disinterest, as if he was looking past it.

"She has a garden behind the house," he finally said. "Can you imagine? Being so rich that you have a whole house, and a garden too, in the middle of Paris?"

"I can tell Zinnia whatever we—"

"It's over, Yorick," he said with a look of pity. He picked up the snub candle from the center of the table to light a cigarette—not one of the cigarettes in the case, but one from a box in his pocket. When he put the candle back, the flame lifted and sputtered, shifting the light around in his eyes.

"What's over?" I said.

"All of it."

"Please tell me what happened."

He breathed the smoke in and blew it out toward the cloud that hovered near the ceiling, all the fog stirred slightly by the fans. He paused longer, picking a fleck of tobacco from the tip of his tongue. Finally, he said, without looking my way, "We were sitting in the garden the morning after the opera—we'd not even been to bed, we'd been out all night—and Emi, her maid, came out to tell Zinnia that Alice was at the door asking for her."

"Alice *asked* for her?" I said. I didn't recall Alice mentioning that part of the delivery. "Haze, you have to believe I didn't send her out with the book." Another lie came easily to mind: *Alice* wrote the letter, I could say. She's a troublemaker, I'd say. *I plucked her off the street.* I even convinced myself in the moment that Alice wouldn't object to my lie, considering what she had only just told me about her gratitude for the job. The lie could fix everything, for all of us. And, when it came down to it, maybe it wasn't such a lie. Maybe Alice wasn't so innocent after all; she read the letter, and she knew I was passed out drunk, but she delivered it anyway, insisting on placing it right in Zinnia's hands.

I stopped myself before I uttered a word of this plot. *I'm pathetic,* I thought. The poor girl thanks me for trusting her, and the very next day I sit poised to accuse her of a crime she didn't commit. How desperate.

"It doesn't matter whether you sent the letter or not," he said. "It's all over. When Zinnia came back out, she handed the letter to me and she asked me if I wrote it. I did recognize something about it—your name, and hers—so I said yes. 'Why would you ask?' I said. She told me to read it to her." He shrugged, as if there was no reason to say anything more.

"And she was angry?" I said.

He shrugged again. Shook his head. "No," he said, almost with a smile. "Not angry, really. I could tell she was hurt, and confused. And so I told her the truth. I told her everything. I guess I had myself convinced that she already knew, or suspected, that we'd written the letters together. I wanted to believe that she had already overlooked it all . . . that she was just playing along. But when I couldn't even read the letter back to her, not a word of it, then she knew—without a doubt—that I knew nothing, *nothing,* of the books we sent. Nothing."

"But she loves you," I said. "She just needs time, Haze. Don't you think? The two of you just need to talk."

"We've *had* time," he said. "We've talked. She confessed a few things herself."

"What does she have to confess?"

He just shook his head. "I spent all day begging for her forgiveness. And most of the next night. I only ever had the best intentions, I said. And it seemed she would start to understand, but then she'd fall apart. I've hardly slept at all. She asked me to leave this morning, but told me to meet her here tonight. But she told me, very tenderly, very gently, that after tonight she never wanted to see me again. Or you."

We continued to wait for Zinnia, but in near silence, long enough for him to finish his cigarette and to get halfway through another. I asked again what she had confessed, but he wouldn't say. He wouldn't even acknowledge he'd heard my question. But I sensed that, despite his frustration, he did truly need me there. He needed to tell me everything, even if he couldn't bring himself to do it.

When Zinnia arrived, I couldn't help but see her long red coat as the costume of friend *and* enemy. She wore red because she knew I'd appreciate the symbolism of it—but she knew also I'd understand she meant fire, blood, war.

Charlatan came from the Italian *scarlattino*, for scarlet, the color of the cloak worn by a man from Milan who sold quackery in the Place Dauphine, powders and elixirs he promised would cure all. Scarlet robes, scarlet lips, scarlet flames, scarlet poison. I considered mentioning *Dorian Gray* again, to remind her of our first night here together.

When I stood to greet her, she slipped past me and dropped into my wing chair. She nodded for me to sit across the table from her, alongside Haze. Before she could begin, the waiter arrived with the café glorias we'd drunk on our first evening out together, the coffee cocktail with the lumps of sugar candy and cognac poured over the back of a spoon. After he set our drinks aflame, we blew the fire out, each of us with a lazy puff. I even had to blow at the flame three times before it went up in smoke. Zinnia then took from her pocket a velvet pouch where she kept her skull-shaped pipe. Like Haze had, she picked up the candle. She touched the flame to the bowl of her pipe.

"Did you get the letter I sent?" I asked, meaning the letter I'd sent most recently, but she said, "Oh yes, I've received all the letters you've sent."

"Zinnia . . ."

"Just let me say something, Yorick," she said. She put the stem of her pipe to her lips, but then set the pipe in an ashtray. "I just want you both to tell me the truth, and I promise I won't punish

you. I won't scold you. I just want you to admit: you don't love me."
She looked from Haze to me, then back to Haze. "You never did.
You're in love with each other. I was just a pawn in some game."

"In love with *him*?" Haze said, with more disgust than I thought
was necessary. "Zinnia, it's you I love. With all my heart. I've never
known such love. I've told you over and over."

"Yes, yes, over and over," she said. "You're very, very good at
these things. You're good at getting people to love you. So yes, you
say you love me, but what else *would* you say? You've intended
to deceive me. Maybe you want my money. It's all part of some
scheme. Maybe even this is the scheme, somehow, this confession Yorick sent. How does it all come together, boys?" She took
a breath, calmed, took a sip of her café gloria. "At least show me
some respect," she said softly. "Tell me what you had up your
sleeve."

"You know better than that, Zinnia," I said. "You know, in your
heart, we've not been scheming."

"You followed us to the opera," she said, leaning back into her
chair. "I heard you, before I saw you, in the lobby. And it wasn't
just the tapping of your walking stick on the marble; I know you,
I know the exact rhythm of your steps."

"You *followed* us?" Haze said, with even more disgust, more
seething. "To the opera." He turned his attention back to Zinnia.
"You didn't tell me that."

"I keep things to myself too," she said.

"Stop this, please," I said. "This isn't *us*, the way we're talking
to each other. Blame *me*. Just punish me, can't you? Cast me out.
And then the two of you can . . . you can go on. You can work
this out between the two of you. Yes, I went to the opera, and
I *watched* you through opera glasses, and you should have seen
what I saw . . . two people so in love. I started all this, all this trouble, out of jealousy."

"Which of us were you most jealous of?" Zinnia said, taunt-
ing. But she must have regretted the question. She didn't want an

answer and I didn't want to offer one. She gathered up her coat and pushed her chair away from the table. "I only came here to tell you that I'm not speaking to you," she said, standing. "Either of you. I need some time alone." I began to stand too, but Haze put his hand on my arm to keep me from following her.

After she left the saloon, I took my first sip of the café gloria and I was carried back to that night when we held hands in this booth. The powdery perfume of the incense, rising in curlicues of indigo smoke. Haze's ice-cold skin. A lock of Zinnia's hair falling loose from her ivory comb as she leaned forward to look into my eyes.

"I need a bath," Haze said, dropping his cigarette into his coffee, extinguishing it with a hiss. "And I need to change out of these clothes."

"Go to the shop," I said. "I'll leave you to it. I'll stay here."

"No, just come along," he said. "But I don't want to talk anymore."

The shop wasn't far, so we walked, and we walked in silence. He kept several steps behind. I sensed him picking up his pace to get closer. I just wanted to keep walking for days and days, a pair of *flâneurs* in Paris, strolling the city until we grow old, Haze my quiet, brooding shadow.

31

Haze went to his corner to gather some things before going downstairs. I went to Café Capucine for two tulip-shaped glasses of Haze's Holland gin. I locked up the shop and turned out all of the lamps but one. I sat on the divan and set the gin atop the chessboard before it, and I lit a candle for its glow. I took one sip of the gin, which sent a tingle down my spine. I waited. I'd often listened for the splash of the water as he bathed, the sound of his movement. Among my many romantic imaginings, I'm on the lip of the tub, running a cloth along his shoulders and the back of his neck. I pour a pitcher of water over his head and wash his hair.

As always, Haze carried the cloud of his bath up with him, that masculine scent of the thick of the woods, both humid and sharp, of cedar and fallen leaves, the bristling of ice as you breathed in the thin air.

He sat next to me on the divan, his hip against mine.

His pajamas were beautifully ridiculous; the silk, top to bottom, was printed with color-tinted photographs of women wearing next to nothing, smiling not so demurely.

"Now you can talk," he said.

I pinched at the silk at his knee. "Where'd the pajamas come from?" He crossed his leg, moving his knee away from my pinch.

"I don't want to talk about my pajamas," he said, but I knew that wasn't true. He loved that I loved what he wore. So I kept quiet until he spoke up. "A pornographer I know makes naughty handkerchiefs. He can print photographs on silk. These are the ladies of a bordello."

"Were you the photographer?"

"These are my pictures, yes."

I could almost tell from the women's eyes that Haze was the one they posed for.

Haze swiftly returned to his task at hand: punishing me with his silence. He lit a cigarette and held the match before himself to watch it burn.

"I honestly thought about setting the place on fire yesterday," I said, exaggerating some. I *had* looked at all the crumpled paper across my desk—all my failed attempts at writing an apology—and it had crossed my mind how easy it would be to set this house of dry paper and kindling ablaze, just by dropping one match. With my shop in ashes, they'd have to take pity on me. "I felt terrible about what I'd done."

"All the brittle old buildings on this street would go up at once," he said, dropping the match in his gin, that *hiss* I knew so well. But usually he only dropped his *cigarette* in the glass, and only after he'd drunk the gin. "You might burn down half of Paris. It would be madness."

"I sometimes think I've *gone* mad."

"You *did* follow us to the opera," Haze said.

I said, "You abandoned me."

"We would never abandon you," he said, with such sincerity that I felt even more foolish for being jealous.

He must have regretted his spiteful gesture of ruining the gin I'd brought him, because he picked up my glass and took a drink. He looked up and around. He said, "I came to think of this as my shop too. You know? And I know Zinnia did."

"It *is* yours," I said.

"Before I met you and Zin, everything in my life seemed like it *started* with an ending. Nothing was meant to last—whatever bed I slept in, when I even had a bed, was only for the night. Even when somebody said 'I love you,' it sounded like goodbye. I would hear the words, and I'd think, 'Ah, you won't love me for long.' I have an affliction that I afflict on everything and everyone around me. People are drawn to me somehow, but when they get close enough, they can see the same ending I do."

"*I'm* not ending anything," I said.

He looked at me with such kindness in his eyes. He put his hand to the back of my neck and squeezed. "I loved being alone in the shop in the middle of the night, listening to its creaks and moans, all the old bones of the place settling in around me. The middle of the night here? That *definitely* belonged to me." He took his hand back. "But we all love the shop, of course. All of us in our little club of survivors. We don't belong together, we don't belong anywhere, but something makes sense when we're all here, puzzling over everything."

I now wished I'd not let the club fall behind; I hadn't assigned a book in a while. Perhaps that omission was just enough to send us spinning out. Though our club might never have any answers, it was sometimes just nice to be around people with the same questions.

"You know what makes it all so much worse?" he said. "Through all this, the person I've most wanted to confide in is you."

"She'll forgive you, Haze. I promise you."

"I don't believe anything you say anymore." He put his glass down. Dropped his cigarette in the other glass with the spent match. He brought both his hands to his face. He spoke into his palms. "That's not what I mean. It's not your fault. You were telling the truth. I just don't know why you did it the way you did it."

"You don't believe me," I said. "You still think I sent the letter off with Alice myself."

"It doesn't matter."

"It does, Haze."

"I'll have the mapmaker send someone for my things."

"The mapmaker?"

"He likes to look out for me."

I said, "You *are* angry with me."

"I'm really not, Yorick." He reached up to give my chin a little pat, and he kept his hand there. "When we leave people, it's not always out of anger."

I put my hand to his, to hold it, to press it to my cheek, to kiss his wrist. I began to cry, which I tried to hide, but I couldn't keep my hand and my head from trembling. When he kissed my cheek just then, I assumed he was kissing me goodbye, that he would stand to leave. But when I turned my head to him, he leaned in, not away. He put his lips to mine. He returned his hand to the back of my neck, and with his other, he pushed my necktie aside and undid the buttons of my shirt.

He kissed my neck as he put his hand beneath my undershirt, to touch my naked chest. I knew this wasn't the start of anything; it was another of his endings. He returned his lips to mine, his tongue to mine, and he leaned into me, pressing his weight against me.

32

We lay naked on the rug on the floor. I put my head on his chest and listened to his heart, still beating fast. He sat up and pressed his hand against my wounded leg. "Your scar is beautiful," he said.

"It's grisly," I said.

"Grisly and beautiful," he said. "I've heard of surgeons who are so arrogant they stitch their names into the gashes they sew shut. At least you don't have that."

"I don't know," I said. "I wouldn't mind it. I don't remember his name, if I ever did know it. I'm probably able to walk because of the work he did."

I couldn't stop looking at Haze. I wanted him on me again, in me, his lips on mine, on my neck, my chest, my stomach. I'd committed it all to memory as it was happening, letting myself slip away, hovering above, watching, even as I wanted to get as close as I could, to be part of him.

"Before I go," he said, "I want you to tell me what happened to your leg."

Before you go, I thought, *stitch your name into my flesh.*

"So if I don't tell you, then you won't go," I said.

He said nothing to that. He ran his fingers along the line of the scar.

But maybe if I *did* tell him, he wouldn't go. Maybe he truly didn't want to leave me at all. "I hadn't been in London long," I said, touching his hand, the hand touching my scar. "I was just a boy. Leopold—the sailor who'd looked after me on the ship over—he helped my father build the sets in his theater. A production of *The Tempest* was to begin with a shipwreck. Leopold built the most beautiful thing I'd ever seen—a gorgeous ship. I don't even know how he did it. It was to sail in from offstage, but it didn't seem it could possibly fit in the wings."

I want the audience afraid of it, my father had told Leopold. *I want them to feel the storm thundering in their blood. I want the ship to crash in their laps.* Leopold had sailed through a hundred storms, so he knew all the moving pieces of such destruction. And he'd fashioned so many vital repairs from flimsy supplies that he could build for my father not only a shipwreck but a ship that would wreck night after night without a scratch. The very act of dragging it back into the wings put it back together, uncollapsing it piece by piece, its every broken board clicking back into place.

Even the figurehead, a wooden mermaid bare-breasted at the prow, would perish again and again, her fin clipped off, her arched back cracking, her arms that reached upward sent diving down. But when the curtain dropped, she rose from the depths like a contortionist unraveling.

I'd already torn apart all my books by then, and I knew how to build one from scrap and string, so I wanted to learn all the hinges and springs that made the ship wreck and unwreck with such grace.

"I was told to stay back," I said. "But I didn't. I stumbled into some rigging and got pulled onto the track that the ship moved along."

I wasn't sure I'd ever seen Haze so interested in me. He sat for a while with his jaw dropped, his eyes open wide. He then looked back down to my leg. He said, "Did you scream?"

"I did. And my screaming was just in chorus with all the noise of the storm and the shipwreck. It was the best acting of my career."

"And ships have been trying to take you under ever since," he said.

Leopold had always told me the sea keeps singing to you once you get the taste of its salt. And though he gave me books about the sea, he hoped to discourage me from becoming a sailor like him. He gave me books because he wanted me to be a professor, or a librarian, or an author, and he knew the sailors' tales would draw me in and make me read more and more.

But in all those stories of peril, of killer whales and giant squid, of pirates with peg legs and eye patches and hooks for hands, I saw something of my own endurance.

"Though he'd told me to stay out of the way that night backstage, he blamed himself for my leg. In all the weeks after, when I was confined to my bed, he would come to my side and read to me, in his actor's voice, so deep it felt like it was rattling my busted-up bones."

"What did he read to you?"

I stood right up, without my cane, and walked to the vault where I kept not only the rare books for which I charged a fortune, but the books I would never sell, my own sentimental artifacts. It was in this vault where I also kept my copy of Rimbaud's poetry, the one that I read aloud to Haze, and Haze translated. "This was his favorite," I told him as I returned to his side, to lean against him, holding the book before us. "A memoir of Ira Aldridge, a Black actor who'd played Shakespeare. And not just Othello. He played King Lear. Macbeth. Hamlet." And this was the *actual* book Leopold read from; he'd even written his name on the inside cover.

"Who published it?" Haze asked, to my complete delight.

"Well, you see, I think that's why I never have any copies for sale," I rattled off. "It's decades old, and it's never been reprinted, and the publisher, Joseph Onwhyn, was first and foremost a bookseller, and a newsagent, and he made maps and things, and tour guides, and though this illustration of Aldridge as Othello has no signature that I can find anywhere"—I opened it to the engraving and tapped my finger at the page—"I do know that Onwhyn's wife, Fanny, did illustrations of all the famous actors of London at the time. So maybe the book was a very personal project."

Whatever drugs they gave me to keep me from fainting from pain colored my memories of my days in bed. When not gripping at my pillow and begging for death if death was the only end to the agony, I hovered above my own broken body. I could remember Leopold holding a mask to my face, from which I breathed in clouds that turned my bones and flesh to mist, a feeling not so far from this night of nakedness with Haze.

Imagine an Ethiopian Romeo, I could hear Leopold reading from the actor's memoir, *and an Ethiopian Juliet.* In my intoxication, Leopold became my Romeo (*But soft, what light through yonder window breaks?*) and I was his Juliet (*I will kiss thy lips; haply some poison yet doth hang on them*).

As if he'd read my mind, of those poisoned lips, Haze put his cigarette to my mouth. He perched it there, and he started to stand. I put my arm around his waist and kept him to me.

"I have to go," he said softly, "or I never will."

"You never have to," I said.

"Maybe I'll be back someday." He linked his fingers with mine and held my hand. "You never know with me."

"Just stay a little longer," I said. He took the cigarette from me and reached over to drop it in the gin glass. He then picked up the candlestick and brought it to the side of the rug.

"I'll stay until the candle ends," he said.

I ran my hand along the inside of his thigh and kissed his neck. I was determined to seem aloof to his leaving me, but the sputtering flicker of the flame kept drawing my eye.

33

A few men came along to take away Haze's trunks and suitcases. I tried to reason with myself: he loved me more than he did the mapmaker—his heart just needed to heal before he could see me again.

I sent Zinnia more letters of apology. I went every now and again to her house and knocked on the door.

I also sent notes of apology to the Titanic Survivors Book Club. I'd fallen behind, I explained, but I would be assigning a book soon.

But I sent no books.

I would some evenings have a glass of wine with Alice, my spirits always lifted by her twisted theories on love, little greeting card sentiments of dysfunction. *Zinnia secretly loves it all, I'm sure,* she said. *People can only toy with your affection if you play along.*

Finally Delphine Blanchet came to the shop in the thick of winter. "Iceland fox," she said of her coat. "Trimmed in chinchilla squirrel."

"As stunning as always," I said.

"But surely I look days and days older," she said. "You've been avoiding us all for weeks."

"It hasn't been so long," I said. And it hadn't. It had been only a little over a month.

"They're all coming to my farewell performance," she said. She handed me an envelope. "You'll hate yourself if you miss it."

"Surely it's not your *farewell* farewell performance," I said.

"I'm afraid that it is, Yorick," she said. "Might I have a little nip of something before I go into it all?"

"Of course, of course," I said, taking the bottle of cognac from my desk drawer. "Take off your coat and have a seat."

"*Mais non*, I only have a minute." She shot back the cognac with one snap of the wrist. "Nothing's the same, Yorick. It used to be I'd look out into the theater and see nothing. I was only my character, not myself. I wasn't an actress. I was a vessel. It was like a possession. But now when I look out at them, I can see the whites of their eyes. It's like gazing into the night sky, at the constellations. So distracting to see everyone seeing you. And it's not, I've realized, that I've failed to fall under a spell; I've failed to cast one."

She nodded toward my bottle and held out her glass for another shot. "All my other farewell performances were only mild threats. I only wanted them all to beg me to stay. They'd imagine Paris without me, then let me play any role I wanted."

"So who are you playing?" I asked. I began to open the envelope. She only smiled, waiting for me to look at the ticket. *Delphine Blanchet et Hamlet*. "Hamlet? Is this coincidence?"

"I won't be holding your skull," she said. "French audiences are too delicate to stomach Hamlet raw—the translation leaves out the gravediggers."

"A Hamlet without Yorick," I said. "That's worth the price of the ticket alone."

But then she arrived at the real reason she'd come. "I've spoken to Zinnia," she said. "You need to go talk to her."

"She won't."

"She will. I've arranged it. We meet often these days. We like to go to the tavern with the dead rat painted on the ceiling, where we can get lunch for two francs fifty. She likes to sit among all the actors and artists who wear those terrible velvet trousers."

She took the envelope back from me, and took another slip of paper from it. "You'll go to her tomorrow, at the skating pond of the Bois de Boulogne. Get on the *ligne une du Métro* at the Châtelet station and take it to the end of the line." She tipped her empty glass toward me. I gave her another splash, she drank it back, and she was on her way.

34

Zinnia sent a note of her own, on the morning of: *I'll be waiting in a sleigh at the edge of the pond. I'll be wearing black velvet like Anna Karenina.* It seemed a gesture of forgiveness, this mention of a character in a novel. I thought of the scene where Anna sits reading in the light of a travel lamp as the train drives into the heart of a blizzard.

It was early evening, but already dark, and the temperature had dropped enough for the night air to have a bite to it. Zinnia had rented a sleigh with a wicker bench and a little roof like a rickshaw. A paper lantern on either side of us knocked the shadows around as a driver on skates pushed us across the ice.

Before I said a word to her, I handed her a blue velvet box. "Anna Karenina reads with a paper cutter in hand," I told her when she opened it. Inside was an ivory knife you'd use to cut the uncut pages of a book. The handle was a jade dragonfly.

"I happen to remember that scene very well, as a matter of fact," Zinnia said, "because I always love it when we see characters in books reading books."

"That must be why I remembered it too," I said. "Anna didn't like reading novels about people doing interesting things because it made her want to do interesting things instead of reading novels."

On the coldest days, which were very few, the ornamental ponds of the park froze over. Compared to my boyhood on the prairie, winter in Paris seemed an opera house stage with paper snow, all the actors sweating in winter coats under the blast of lights.

Zinnia returned the knife to the silk lining of the box. "Aren't you tempting fate," she said, "giving a knife to someone who's angry with you?"

"*Are* you angry with me, Zinnia?"

"Not like I was," she said. Our sleigh nearly nicked a skater who'd dipped into our path as he rounded the curve of a figure eight. Zinnia grabbed hold of my hand. "Pardon!" she shouted back to the skater as we slid past. To me, she said, "The ice broke a few years back. Broke right out from under everyone's skates. They all fell in, all tumbling over each other. The water is shallow, but a few people died."

I gripped her hand tighter. "Zinnia," I said, my voice weak, my mouth muffled by my woolen scarf, "I'm so sorry that—"

"My mother always told me that *her* mother always told *her* that accidents and unhappiness in this life are because you're being punished for something you did in a previous one."

"Zinnia . . ."

"I know," she said, taking her hand back. "I know that you're sorry. I've read the letters you've been sending." She fiddled with her glove, with the buttons at her wrist. "I suppose Haze told you everything," she said.

"He didn't tell me anything," I said. "And I haven't seen him."

"He's not staying in your shop anymore?"

"No," I said. "I don't know where he is."

In the faint light of the lantern, I saw her words turn to frost. "I didn't mean for everything to fall apart, Yorick," she said.

"Wouldn't everything be better if you just forgave him?"

"It's not really a matter of forgiveness, Yorick. Not *my* forgiving *him*, anyway."

I waited for her to say more. When she didn't, I said, "What do you mean?"

"When he confessed after *you* confessed—when he told me

that you'd written all the letters—I confessed a few things myself." She kept her eyes on mine, waiting for me to guess at her confession. She tilted her head. "You're growing a beard."

"Do you like it?"

She tilted her head in the other direction. She contemplated my chin, then seemed to fall into reverie. Finally, she said, "I told him that I've been in love with you all along."

"Why would you say such a thing? To punish him?" I said.

She seemed surprised by this. She even seemed a little amused. "Not to punish him, no," she said. "I wanted to be honest with him."

Even once I pieced it together, I wasn't sure I had it right. How could *I* be the one she loved?

"You love *me*?" I said, but hesitantly. I'd feel like a fool if I'd heard her wrong.

"I never told him that I never wanted to see him again. I said I just needed some time. I needed to"—and here she turned her wrist around in front of herself—"to unravel, or untangle, all my feelings for him from my feelings for you. All the books you sent me, and the letters, they were all so much a part of who I thought *he* was."

"You *do* love me?"

"How could you not know that?"

I didn't know how to answer. I couldn't quite believe what she was telling me was true, so I decided not to believe it at all.

"So *that's* why you invited me out tonight," I said. "To mock me. This is your revenge."

"You really think that of me?"

"The two of you cast me aside," I said. "I thought you didn't care about me at all."

"Oh, Yorick," she said. "I wish you'd stop pretending. I *know* you know something about love. All those letters you wrote for Haze. You swept me off my feet."

"But you can't love me for the letters," I said.

"But I can. Maybe you were pretending to be Haze, but that was no disguise. I shouldn't have been fooled. I've read them again, and I can hear you reading them to me. Your voice is everywhere in them."

"You can't deny that you were in love with Haze," I said. "I won't believe it."

"Of course I love Haze," she said. "You're the one with all the words, and he's the one who doesn't have to say a thing." She added, with a snip of sarcasm, "Together, you're a wonderful man." She pulled up on the black fur of her coat's lapel, nuzzling her chin in for warmth. She said, "But if some of what I loved about him is actually what I love about you, then . . . how do I make sense of that?"

"But maybe what you *think* you love about me is actually what you love about him."

She lifted her chin from her coat to smile at me. "You see, *that's* why I adore you. That's exactly something you'd say."

"Zinnia—"

"Yorick, I was charmed by you the minute we met. I love that you just up and bought a shop full of books in Paris. I love that you spent all your time moving the books around, from one shelf to another, and buying more books, before you even put a sign in your window. I love that you would spend half the day just sitting on the stairs in your shop, caught up in an old novel, blissfully unbothered, before you realized you hadn't even unlocked the shop door. And when you let me be a part of it all, I fell completely."

"Why did you spend so much time alone with Haze if it was me you wanted to be with?"

"He was the one who loved me." We sailed along in silence, our eyes on the ice glistening in the light of the torches and lamps. She then said, "And he wanted to take me away. Ever since I was a little girl, my hand in marriage has been a negotiation. Nothing was ever about love. What was I worth? And who might be worthy of me? But Haze wanted to be alone with me, to start over with nothing."

"The two of you were going to leave me, after all."

"I needed to stop seeing you. Every time I saw you, I just . . . I fell a little more. And I knew it was useless. I knew you couldn't love me back."

"Useless?"

She seemed heartened by my sad little *useless?* "Could you?" she asked.

"Could I what?"

Her eyes dropped from mine, down to my lips, then to my hands. She said, barely loud enough to hear: "Could you love me back?"

"You're in love with Haze," I said once again, insistent, though I knew that was no answer.

"Are you in love with him too?"

I said no, because I had no idea what it would mean to say yes. I was so used to lying about who I did and didn't love, it was the truth that felt dishonest.

She didn't believe me, anyway. I think I was counting on that. I didn't *want* to say yes, and I didn't *have* to say yes. I always liked to think I knew what went on inside her head, but clearly I was wrong. And now that my mind was casting back, looking for signs of her love for me, I could see it everywhere. She'd bought me things, took me out, dressed me up. She'd cut my hair, fed me champagne and snails. She'd kissed me. But I'd always been so convinced I was unlovable, I thought I was only a messenger. They only kept me around so I could bring them closer together.

"Tell me," she said. "You owe me that."

I changed my answer, but with a question this time. "Yes?" I said.

"I know," she said. "I always knew."

"You know me very, very well," I said.

But that wasn't what she wanted to hear, either. The driver of our sleigh was pushing us back to where we'd boarded, our ride almost over. She said, again without looking in my direction, "I can love you anyway."

"Zinnia—"

"I can make room for the disappointment . . . so long as you're with me." Her voice cracked, grew hoarse with the cold air. "Wouldn't it be better to be with someone who loves you so much rather than be alone?"

"I just think . . ."

"You don't have to be *in* love with me like you're in love with Haze. We could just be *together*. Like we were. That's more than enough."

I took both her hands in both of mine. "It's not that I can't be with *you*, Zinnia. I can't be with anyone . . . I love you, I love you with all my heart, but I can't love you the way you should be loved."

Her breath fogged the air between us. "I can be nothing to you," she said, her eyes on mine. "Let me be nothing."

"You could never be nothing . . . to anyone. You deserve . . ."

When the sleigh slowed, Zinnia took her hands from mine. "Stop," she said. "Never mind. Forget what I said. Don't say any more about it."

"I'm very . . . flattered . . ."

"I said *don't* say anything," she said. "Especially don't say *that*."

Zinnia stood and began to step off before the driver had even stopped at the edge of the pond. I took hold of her elbow, to make her wait. "Be careful," I said, but she pulled her arm away and gave her hand to a man who helped her from the sleigh. She left the paper cutter on the bench. I picked the box up and followed her.

"At least let me walk with you," I said. Even with the lanterns strung along the path, it was still too dark for her to walk alone.

"Please just let me go, Yorick," she said. I followed her, but several paces back, to escort her out of the park. I tapped the point of my cane against the path as loud as I could, so she would know I was with her.

Dear Titanic Survivors Book Club:

It's been too long. I never meant for so many weeks to go by. We last met in early winter, and now it's almost April. Would you please come to the shop again?

Let's meet on 4-14-14, which seems it'd be an auspicious date even if it wasn't the second anniversary of the Titanic striking the iceberg. It will be our shared birthday in a sense. We've had two years of survival.

It's also the first birthday of my bookshop. Some might think opening a business on an anniversary of disaster would summon bad luck, and maybe it did, but to my mind the date twisted my sense of my own destiny—after being dismissed by the White Star Line and fearing all was lost, the ship's sinking seemed to rescue me. (Of course I would never say that to anyone but you.)

I've sent along The Sea Lady, *a book I snuck into my library on the* Titanic, *and maybe it doomed the ship too. It's about a mermaid. Up on land, she describes her life down below, even describes a library underwater, made up of books found in sunken ships, and those blown overboard, or dropped by passengers napping in their deck chairs. She reads by the light of a phosphorescent fish, while reclining in a hammock of seaweed.*

Yorick
Proprietor, La Librairie Sirène

35

Only a few days after mailing out *The Sea Lady*, I glanced out my shopwindow and there sat Haze at Café Capucine.

I didn't know him at first, which made me wonder how often I'd missed him, if he'd been coming by for days. He sat at the sidewalk table nearest the café's wall, beneath its one window, a patchwork of broken bottles in many colors.

"You've lost your way, little lamb," I told him as I sat at his table. He'd shaved his head bald, which made his features cartoons of themselves, his lips fuller, his cheeks rounder. It was all the easier to stumble into his eyes, which, in the light of the afternoon sun, took on the wet chestnut brown of a violin's varnish.

"I've come for my book," he said. "I hear the club's getting together again." I furrowed my brow with question, and he said, "I see Rémy every now and then." We'd only ever referred to him as "the gambler," so I didn't recognize his name at first. "I finally returned his opera suit to him. I seem to have lost his *chapeau claque*, though."

I decided not to tell him that he'd left the hat at my shop. I sometimes toyed with it, popping it open, collapsing it again. I would put the hat on and check my reflection in the shop's only mirror, next to the section I marked *Portraits of Vanity* (autobiographies of war generals, infamous criminals, the handmaids of queens).

"It just so happens I've saved a copy of *The Sea Lady* for you," I said. "I just didn't know where to send it."

"I appreciate that, Yorick," he said. "I've kept all the books from the club. Someday I'll read them."

"Let me buy you lunch," I said, when the waiter came to the table. "They serve food here now."

"Ah," he said. "I leave, and the neighborhood improves." He ordered a bowl of soup, but I shook my head at the waiter. *"Perdrix,"* I corrected.

"It's horse soup they eat here," I said. "But he'll bring you a roasted partridge that'll taste like it was shot down from heaven."

Haze studied me for a bit, then said, "I've missed you."

"I've missed *you*," I said. "You look good, Haze."

He put his hand to his head and ran it along the baldness. "I fell into some bad habits," he said. "After Zinnia ended things. Not entirely my own fault, though."

"Can I ask . . . ?"

"Things are better now," he said, nodding. "Actually, Rémy would meet me at a . . . a low sort of place, a *bibine,* a wineshop where the ragpickers could snag a cheap lunch. But writers and journalists like to get drunk there. And he introduced me to some newspaper people. I've been taking photographs for them."

"I'm so glad to hear that."

He told me more about his work for the newspaper and as if summoned a newspaper arrived: the waiter brought us our roasted partridge torn limb from limb and served in a page of *L'Humanité,* the daily record for the Socialists.

War was still about five months off, and looking back, we might have seen our every day tumbling toward it. The headlines in the newspapers seemed to grow by inches, even as they took on fewer words, consuming the front pages with turmoil at a glance: LA GRÈVE, LA RÉVOLUTION, LE REVANCHISME. But it was easy to dismiss all the thick lines of ink as melodrama, the papers outshouting each other so you didn't dare pass a newsstand without dropping a coin—and there were hundreds of papers in Paris alone. Rumors of war were reliable theater. The papers were the boys who cried wolf, and the louder they cried, the more mythical it seemed.

There were elections ahead, and talk of revenge against the Germans—it was a blister that had been festering for decades, ever since the Germans bullied their way into Paris and knocked it over during the war of 1870. Many Parisians believed any war of revenge could be won by refusing to lose it. Pugnacity was a political stance. Meanwhile, pacifists threw bricks through windows, slashed tires, startled horses with fireworks. And workers from all walks of life sat down on the job, all of them knowing full well any war would impoverish the poor and make the rich richer.

Despite all the topsy-turvy, the only thing that mattered to me in that moment—the only spark of urgency—concerned all those lost days since Haze had left. As we drank our wine into the afternoon, one bottle, then another, he told me all he'd been through.

The mapmaker bought him suits, shoes, hats; he took him to the clubs of Montmartre. He carried cocaine around in a little enamel box that fit in his pocket. The first time he held it to Haze's nose, Haze didn't even know what it was, but once he did, he wanted more and more of the mood it put him in.

"You just buy it off the waiters until the cafés close," he said, "then you go to the street, looking for the windows that glow after two. But the thing is, the thing that gets you, is that you can get it cheap before dinner, but it keeps doubling in price every hour after. So a poor wretch thinks he's being frugal by getting an early start. But once you get your fix, and there's still hours and hours left in the night, you buy more and more and get poorer and poorer, and you get too slewed to even know you're happy."

I felt a rush in my stomach, like when you fall off an edge in a dream. "I hate that you had to go through all that," I said, my voice breaking. He was no longer mine, but I was terrified at the thought of losing him entirely.

"I thought he wanted me to be happy," Haze said of the mapmaker. "But he only wanted me weak." Haze now lived on the Rue

Brise-Miche—"which isn't quite as bad as it looks, but it looks pretty wretched." He had a room in a broken-down mansion, now a cheap hotel for six sous a night, the mold on the walls painted over with a rust-colored red, iron bars on the windows.

When we'd finished our wine, the waiter brought coffee. "I hope you can come to the book club," I said. "All of us will be there. Zinnia too."

"You've seen her?" he asked.

"Yes," I said. "I don't see her often. But yes, from time to time."

He nodded, then picked up his coffee. I meant to remind him: many of the café's cups had chips in them. You had to be careful not to cut your lip on the rim. But I was distracted; I was still watching for a reaction to Zinnia's name. Without seeming to even glance at the rim, he turned the cup to avoid the chip in it because, of course, Haze had a bat's sixth sense for all the city's damage.

36

I didn't tell Haze *everything*. I said nothing of my own collapse. I hadn't shaved my head or gone sniffing around Montmartre for midnight cocaine, but I'd been bad off.

Zinnia arrived one evening in early March, her arms overloaded with daffodils. I'd not seen her all winter, not since our night on the ice. "Delphine says you've fallen to pieces," she had said instead of hello. I had not even gone to see Delphine as Hamlet. I'd meant to, but the hour neared, then it passed, and it was over before I'd moved an inch from the divan.

I hadn't seen anyone else from the club, either, though they'd been by. I kept the shop closed most of the time, so I either ignored their knocks at the glass or opened the door a crack to tell them I was just fine, that I was getting the shop ready to sell. There was a buyer, I lied. I might be moving back to America. But still they came, leaving bottles of wine at the door, loaves of bread, boxes of chocolate. And then they started leaving books, oddly enough, most often books about booksellers and bookmakers, as if they might rouse me: *Princess Casamassima*, about a bookbinder; *The Typewriter Girl*, a romance about a young woman who goes to work in the office of a publisher.

But this was the first time Zinnia had come to my door, so I let her in. She passed the flowers over to me without even looking in my direction. She was transfixed by the bookshop. She even cowered at the sight of it, as if I had dropped a match after all, the rafters overhead still smoldering.

In the evenings, I kept the lights off to keep my bills low. I read by candlelight. As Zinnia stepped into the dark of the shop, she stumbled over a few books. "Oh, Yorick, it's positively gothic."

"I've maybe fallen behind a bit, but not to pieces," I said. "I need to catch up on my dusting, I guess." But as I followed her, limping along without my cane, the daffodils spilling from my arms flower by flower, she switched on every lamp she passed. Seeing the shop in Zinnia's light, I honestly wondered if I'd been ransacked. Books were strewn everywhere, and stepstools and ladders knocked over. A few of the toy ships that hung overhead—perhaps more than a few, perhaps six or seven, or ten—had snapped from their strings to crash to sticks on the floor and on the stairs.

The faint flapping I'd been hearing for days, which I'd thought was nothing more than the soft wings of a moth, became louder in the lamplight. Much louder. A bird was caught inside, or a bat, somewhere near the ceiling, and its frantic shadow was stretched thin and multiplied by the dim glow, making it seem I had a whole flock swarming in my belfry.

"Where's Alice?" she asked me.

"I had to let her go."

I'd let go my rented room too, and slept every night in Haze's barber chair. I still had the screen that separated the chair from the shop, but the clutter of my life was spilling out from behind it, and around it, my shirts and trousers draped over the backs of chairs, all my shoes stumbling across the rug. And my workbench was surrounded by broken books, with their pages torn out and scattered.

I stuck a jeweler's loupe in my eye every day and sat down to the task of repairing any battered books, but I most often ended up dismantling them, picking at their stitches, tenderly bending their spines.

"How long has it been like this, Yorick?"

I wanted to say it hadn't been long, that I'd barely noticed it happening. But the fact was, I wasn't sure.

"You need to fix this," she told me. "I'll be by every now and again to check on things." I began to cry. It came upon me fast, too fast for me to stop it, to keep from embarrassing myself, so I gave in to it, my shoulders shaking, all the daffodils falling to the floor. Zinnia took me in her arms, cooed in my ear. I hadn't realized how much I'd missed her perfume—the evergreen and rose—until I smelled it again just then. I kept breathing it in, until it faded away.

"It's been a long winter," she said, with a few tears of her own. "Now go to your barber and have him chop off that ugly beard."

She couldn't stop herself from taking charge. The very next day, she sent in an army of maids who cleaned and straightened with authority; they didn't ask where anything went, they just put it away. They were followed by carpenters who carried off my barber chair, despite my objections, and built in its place a Murphy bed that tucked up into the bookcase when not in use. On the underside of the bed, which would be part of the wall when the bed was put away, the carpenters screwed in picture frames. Zinnia had arranged for photographs to hang there, cleverly so, as I suspected she knew then I'd always be sure to put the bed up, to keep the photos on display.

Though I'd never seen the photos before, I knew they were Haze's. He projected his own vision outward, giving shape and light and shadow to the world on the other side of the lens.

Not only had I not seen them, I didn't know how he could have taken them—they were all of my shop, both inside and out. Somehow he'd managed to set up his camera in the daylight when I wasn't around. He knew I'd been superstitious about it, but now that they were in front of me, I knew I shouldn't have been. There were six of them, hung from the floor up, and I'd never seen a shop so inviting. These weren't like his other pictures, of a Paris on its last legs, but of a bookshop I'd always dreamed of owning: the dust motes shimmering in a slant of light, like stars in the firmament, the rows of books like cigar boxes. There wasn't a living soul in the shop, but the novels had lives of their own, all the narrators speaking at once.

Zinnia sent fresh flowers every day to put around the shop, vases of irises, tulips, lilies, and a basket of switches bright pink with cherry blossoms.

And she hired Alice back and paid her wage. "Zinnia feels guilty," Alice conjectured. "Love and guilt are always on opposite ends of a circus tightrope, playing tug-of-war."

"Who's the tightrope walker?" I said, trying to puzzle out the metaphor.

This caused Alice a moment's pause. She thought, then said, "The human heart," with a shrug, as if the answer were obvious.

Before the next meeting of the Titanic Survivors Book Club, a plot developed to dress as if for the ballroom of the last night of dancing on the *Titanic*. I wore the gambler's *chapeau claque*. Zinnia arrived in sea-green chiffon that seemed to float, all of it tethered to the bones of her bodice.

We didn't sit in our circle; we stood around like at a cocktail party. We didn't discuss the book at all.

Old Madame Petit of the vineyards had sent over a block of ice that had been chiseled into the shape of a ship, to lean her champagne bottles against to chill. Delphine Blanchet hired a quartet to play waltzes up above, in the upper gallery. And the toymaker brought us miniature life preservers—each one stamped *RMS Titanic*—that were big enough to slip onto our wrists like bracelets.

"Once upon a time," the toymaker said, "toys delighted. You could amuse children with a doll's fluttering eyelids. And now all the little boys—and even the girls—are building arsenals of war toys. Cannons with little lead balls. Rifles that pop and spark. It's the government. They train their armies young. Stir up tensions in the cradle."

But that was the only word of war all night. We chose to linger in our delusion: we convinced ourselves the *Titanic* would be the worst disaster we'd ever survive.

"There was a saloonkeeper in Liverpool," said Penny Dreadful's mister as he mixed some cocktails at my front desk, "who named a drink 'The Titanic' on the very first night there was news of the wreck. He claimed the ice in it was cut from the actual iceberg that sank the ship."

He handed around some glasses of it, explaining how the ship was built in Ireland and set sail from England, so he took some London gin and added a splash of Guinness.

"That's also a dog's nose," I said. "If you heat the stout and put in some sugar and nutmeg. It makes an appearance in Dickens. In *The Posthumous Papers of the Pickwick Club*."

"Ah, a book about a club," Zinnia said. "I love it. Let's read that one next. Can we?"

Dickens hadn't been part of my sunken library, so it didn't fit the theme of the club, but maybe that was just fine. Maybe it was time to steer the book club away from the *Titanic* entirely. We'd have our party, as the *Titanic* did, here on April 14, but on April 15 we could leave the ship at the bottom of the sea.

"Have you read every book in this shop?" the physician asked, glancing up and around.

"Oh no," I said. "No, that would take years, maybe lifetimes." Though in those winter weeks that I'd kept the shop locked up, letting it all fall apart around me, I'd lost myself in any number of them, waking before dawn to read by the light of a candle that sometimes singed a corner of the page when I got too caught up in the story.

"I've always wanted to ask," the gambler said. "Where'd you get the money to open the shop to begin with?"

And so I told him, and the others who gathered around, about Leopold, and how he worked in the wings of my father's theater when he wasn't off sailing the seas. I didn't tell them about the collapsible ship that crushed my leg—I wanted that part of me to always only belong to Haze. "He once gave me a key," I said, "and he told me if anything ever happened to him, I should find the lock it fit." When he didn't return from his last voyage, his ship having sailed off the edge of the map, I found a satchel of cash in the cabinet of his Victrola. *Rescue yourself someday,* he'd written on a note.

"How'd *he* come to have all that money?" the gambler asked.

"He worked hard. And he'd mastered an antique art—sailing those old clipper ships." But I liked to think he made most of it from his acting. Though Leopold never played Shakespeare in my father's theater, he did perform as Hamlet, and Shylock, and Iago, all of them, even Romeo, even Juliet, Desdemona, Gertrude, in his apartment in the theater's cellar, where I lay on his sofa, quiet and still, and listened to him read abbreviated versions of the plays into a horn that captured his dramatic recitations on a record. He was paid by a company that sold his beautiful voice to schools for the blind.

"He wanted to look after you," said the orphan. She had her arm intertwined with the fallen evangelist's.

All the racket in the room stopped. Even the quartet paused, rustling the sheets of music on their stands.

"Did he pity you?" Reverend Dew asked. "Because of your cracked-up drumstick?"

"Henry," the orphan scolded, giving him a slap on the wrist, even as she held his arm tighter.

I wondered about the two of them. Had at least one sensible romance blossomed from our club? She shined some vital light into his darkness; he cast a necessary shadow into her light.

"I'm just *genuinely* curious," Henry said. "Yorick's my friend."

It was only then, as everyone listened in, that I realized they were *all* curious, and probably always had been. With my leg the way it was, I'd gone through life feeling both invisible and conspicuous—people often wanted to stare, but without getting caught. In every room I entered, I was always there and not there at the same time.

"Nobody needs to pity me," I said. And I wasn't just saying it. I believed it to be true. How lucky was I to have all that I had? These were my friends and I was among them. My shop had endured for a year, despite my absent-mindedness and bewilderment. I knew love, and compassion, in a world too often driven by spite, bitterness, revenge. And I could find more love, more compassion, again and again in the hours and hours, the lifetimes of pages towering over me.

I think we'd convinced ourselves that all those battle chants of the newsmen, all that worst-is-yet-to-come, would come to nothing. The iceberg was miles off. None of this would end ever again; the club would meet, the shop would thrive. We were characters in a novel, enacting the same scene over and over.

I took a few steps up the staircase as I had on the night those soapy mermaids first appeared on the glass of my windows. I raised my Titanic cocktail—or my dog's nose. "Let's celebrate like it's the last night of the *Titanic*," I called out.

"April 14!" the evangelist shouted, raising his glass. *"April 14!"* they all cheered.

Among the voices I heard Haze's, which often seemed less a voice than the low hum of a fine foreign car. Then I saw him near the front window, his glass lifted. He'd somehow snuck in, though I'd been watching the door all night.

The music struck up again, and I walked to Haze. "So that's where the hat was," he said, taking it off me and putting it on. "On your head."

"I'm so glad you came," I said. Feeling tipsy already, I said, "Can we be friends, Haze?"

He clinked his glass against mine. "We can."

Zinnia came up to us then, and she clinked her own glass against both of ours. "Hansel," she said to Haze with a nod.

"Ma confiseuse," he said, with a slight bow and a tipping of the top hat he'd just put on.

She reached up to lift it. "What happened to your head?" she asked.

"Do you mean my hair?" he said. "I left it at the barbershop." He took the hat off and set it on the windowsill. "Do you like it?"

"It brings out your forehead," she said, which made him laugh. The band ended one number and began another, and she said, looking to both Haze and me, "They're playing our song."

"This is our song?" I asked.

"All of them are," she said as she took my glass from me and placed both hers and mine on a stack of books. She then took Haze's away too. She put one hand on my shoulder and one on Haze's, and she asked us to dance. And we did, but no dance in particular. We swayed in place, shuffling our feet, and I reached down to lift up the hem of Zinnia's dress, to keep us all from stepping on the bottom of it.

The dance was easygoing, tranquil, almost harmonious, and set the tone for the days and weeks after, when our friendship resumed. Not enough time had passed for much of anything to change: I was still infatuated with Haze, Haze with Zinnia, Zinnia with me. But I'd come to see my love for Haze as a luxury, not a deprivation. And all our confessions of love of weeks before were like polite ghosts sipping wine with us, none of them rattling their chains.

For now, the night had all the earmarks of a happy ending.

PART
TWO

April 14, 1915

Yorick,

Here I am, by the ocean.

I'm starting to think your fate has become mine.

You've always felt the ocean pulling you into it. But I've learned one sailor's philosophy: <u>The sea will always keep you afloat, until it doesn't.</u>

You don't know this handwriting. That sailor, with the philosophies, is taking down what I say, or so he says. But he seems to me a man of his word. You should see his mustache—he twists both tips of it fancy with a pinch of mutton fat. Is that the mustache of an honorable man? Seems it might be.

But he did steal this piece of paper. He jimmied the lock on a desk drawer. Did you faint dead away when you saw the <u>White Star</u> letterhead? And the ominous date at the top of the page? <u>Three years</u> since the <u>Titanic</u> struck ice. (And the second anniversary of our little bookshop. Pour a glass of champagne for me, my old friend.)

You would like my sailor. He has sad eyes but a smile that will lift your spirits if you're lucky enough to catch sight of it. The extravagant mustache is very fine, but it gets too much in the way of his face, if you ask me.

He just now told me he's not going to write down another word I say about him, but I can see that pretty smile as he says it (despite the mustache). <u>But this is the last I'll say of my sailor</u> (other than the fact that he's American): I've been taking his picture so maybe you'll see him with your own eyes at the newsstand. Some of the illustrated dailies only want the carnage and brutality—they figure if they give people only bad news, they'll keep buying the paper in hopes of seeing an end to it. But acts of war run afoul of the government censors. I have better luck getting into print with handsome soldiers being heroic with mustaches groomed.

We're in the <u>Cherbourg offices</u> of the <u>White Star Line</u>. Their ships have been requisitioned for war. My sailor attends to the hundreds of horses sent over from America on the SS <u>Georgic,</u> a cargo ship which has had many collisions in its history, he says, without going under. So is it doomed or charmed?

I've got pictures of my sailor soothing the beasts, leading them from the ship and onto dry land, their first steps on a brutal path.

<u>I miss you</u> and <u>I miss Zinnia</u> and I miss those days when it was only heartbreak that seemed like the end of the world.

These are my own words (but all the <u>underlining</u> is something the sailor did on his own).

À tout à l'heure,
Haze

May 23, 1915

Dear Zinnia,

Has Haze written? He sent me a letter he dictated to an American sailor, but I suspect the sailor's vanity put more of himself in it than Haze wanted. And the sailor was smitten with Haze, it seemed to me.

Nonetheless, I did hear Haze's voice in it, and I've read the letter so many times I could recite it without looking at it.

I worry about him. I worry about you.

I write you from the Paris censorship office. The letters of the censors are censored the most, because we know too much. We have to read everything before we can erase it all. But I've learned my way around the ins and outs of the office, so this letter should arrive to you with all its words in their rightful place.

This leg of mine has been my blessing, maybe even saving my life once again, keeping me out of the trenches. It was Delphine Blanchet who arranged my appointment here. All the theaters have to be less theatrical—the government gets nervous about crowds having emotions together. Even patriotism gets X'd out. You can't hate war, you can't love peace.

They were needing censors with an eye for nuance. Some

of the censors go at the words like they're at the front lines themselves, hacking their way in with a saber. I don't blame them—we have war secretaries looking over our shoulders, considering the depths of our blank spaces. They learn the language of our inkblots. A soldier's love letter with all its sentiments cut out fills them with desire.

So the more a war censor can silence, the less likely he'll be sent to war himself. It's a fitting punishment, I suspect, that he should be thrust into the terror that he's been robbing from the page. But we're already kept up at night from all that we silence.

As you might suspect, I sometimes want to rewrite the letters the soldiers send. Did you know "cliché" is a French printer's term? When the same phrases show up again and again on the pieces they set in type, the printer has the words soldered together in one piece, to save time when typesetting. I suspect if you've got that block of type at the ready, you probably use it even more than you would otherwise.

If you've heard from Haze, I hope you'll tell me what he tells you. Every time I get a letter from him, I want to open it right away, but I want to keep it closed too, to keep that moment for as long as I can, of anticipation, when I still have a new letter unread.

Please distract me. Tell me about your life in Japan.

Yorick

June 4, 1915

Anata,

*is how a woman might address someone she loves, in
Japanese, someone she adores, something like "darling," but
with more affection, more longing, more sweetness. No other
language has a word for it.*

*I've read the last letter you sent me at least a hundred times
and I'll read it a hundred times more. Haze, I know it's selfish
of me to want so much of your love, since I punished you so,
but you're always always always in my every thought, even
more so now that it's summer again.*

*The time we had alone together last June, in those feverish
days before you left Paris to take pictures of the war, those
secret days we stole, and the nights that were only ever ours
alone, I have no words for them, nobody does, in any language
that I know. It's more than love I feel for you, more than
passion, it's something no one's ever known but us.*

*If this letter arrives with all the words gone, all of it inked
over by some war censor, then you'll know better than I can
say how desperate I am without you. The censors only take
away what's worth reading, and my every expression feels
weak, feels cliché, compared to the feeling of it in my heart. A
few of your letters to me have arrived with phrases blacked*

out, and every last word before the censor's strike leaves me breathless. When it comes to you, Haze, I'm on the precipice of knowing everything, and I know what comes after the edge, you've brought me there, with your lips on my lips, up and below. Even once I'm there, once I know, it's still only mystery and I'm without words most of all.

Tonight I'll do as I always do, and I'll have two sips of gin from a tulip-shaped teacup, and I'll think of our nights at the Café Capucine last summer, when we would pretend we weren't lost in each other as we sat with our friends, and I would steal glances and a sip of your gin, and then you'd take a sip too, and put your lips to the cherry red of the rouge I left there. I only ever wore lipstick so that I could leave my mark when you kissed me.

Love letters in Japan were sometimes knotted, the paper folded up instead of tucked in an envelope, sometimes tied to a tree. One of the ways you tie the obi on your kimono is meant to look like a love letter tied shut.

When you've given up chasing this war around, and you're back in Paris to stay, send word. The world and its savagery won't stop me from finding my way back to you.

Zinnia

Oct 5, 1915

Zinnia,

I got your letters all of them I think and I'm sorry I've not sent much of anything of my own until now.

I'm <u>under</u> the war. I'm in the tunnels cut out centuries ago by the monks who pulled the chalk up to build a city of white steeples. Now the Germans have knocked those steeples down and the city falls back into the ground deeper and deeper to escape the rubble of its belfries and naves. We hide in the veins that might go for miles for all I know.

We've fled to cocoon like cicadas do, in the earth. Cicadas go under to hide from predators too.

I'm sorry my letters have grown shorter and shorter as the war has gone on and on.

Your letters somehow still find their way to me, intact, though the address I gave you might not exist anymore. Before I fell into this hole in the ground, I lived at a printing press we'd found abandoned. We put together our own newspaper. I got tired of the war censors, and the press office, and their demand for smiling soldiers, and I went to work publishing a paper for the soldiers themselves. They long to see truth on the page, as ugly as it is. I feel a part of something in this war, even if it's only a burning desire to end it. I want my pictures of all the wreckage to reach the streets of Paris. I've heard Paris goes on being Paris, even as it sends all its men into the maw.

I don't know what I'm saying half the time half done in by pain and half by drugs meant to soothe. I don't see through the same eyes anymore. But I don't know how your letters have found me at all, ever, because I'm not officially anyone. I was a child of the streets, and that's what's kept me from being sent to the front. I'm on no military lists. They read all my letters, but still I'm no one—it's as if my words dissolve before their eyes even before they blot them out.

And your voice has followed me all along from the seaside to the trenches. I'm dreaming of you.

I haven't always had someone I trust to read me your letters, but now I do. Somehow I'm wounded. I'm in a hospital bed underground. My nurse sits at my bedside with a lamp of her own and reads me all the letters you ever sent me—I've carried all of them always—and she reads them night after night over and over and doesn't seem shocked. She's a very forgiving nun, bless her heart.

(I shall make brief note here that when I am interjecting as myself, the nun, I will write in parentheses and I am only wanting to say here now that it would be perverse to be a war nurse shocked by acts of love.)

She told me she was going to write that above, so please know there are no secrets between me and Sister Céline. No secrets, but there is one mystery. I don't know why she won't keep me needled up to keep my fever dreams peaceful. If she loved me like she says she does she would. If night brings sleep at all it is sometimes sweet and sometimes poison and sometimes the horses swim gracefully away from the shipwreck like the gifted horses of a circus show. But other times they thrash and kick for footing they'll never find in the ocean's waves. I'll never not know their cries no matter how much morphine she feeds me.

(The pain often becomes so familiar to these men they still feel it even when they don't.)

Your voice is better than morphine in many ways, Zinnia. Sister Céline told me to tell you that. She is a poet though she doesn't like to tell people so. She wrote a poem about you and me that's about our love letters and a nightingale and notes tied around its leg.

A man in the bed next to me says people are jumping off the Eiffel Tower and that he'll do it too and the last thing he'll see in life is all of Paris becoming a rush of nothing before his eyes. His face was blown apart and it is held together only by bandages, but they won't let him stay because he still has two legs he can walk away with and the beds are for the men who can't stand up.

My own face still feels the same, but there aren't any mirrors down here.

(I tell Haze every day his wounds will heal. He doesn't remember how he came to be here. But I do believe he followed the soldiers too close. The last thing he remembers is looking through his camera and suddenly everything gone white, nothing but a cloud of chalk stirred up from the ground from the bombardments.)

Sister Céline tells lies to keep me in her care. She tells them I'm too broken to leave my bed, but I get up when no one's looking so I can take pictures by the light of a lantern of the wrecked faces of men who are dead even as they still live and breathe. There are American surgeons who have ways to put the men's faces back together again, Sister Céline tells me. Maybe if I take their pictures people will see what needs to be done. How can a war be won if there's too much that's broken for it to ever be fixed?

Here sits Sister Céline attending the beds of war despite being kicked out of her own bed only eight years ago. She was one of the nuns evicted from the Hôtel-Dieu which is not a hotel but the oldest hospital of Paris. When State separated from Church, the nuns who'd fed the living and shrouded the dead for centuries were marched out and away. No other French government in history has ever expelled the sisters of Hôtel-Dieu, not even during the Reign of Terror.

The only thing I know anymore is there's no way of knowing anything. But I'm drifting off into the mercy granted by Sister Céline who has finally blessed me with her dose. Other nuns play harpsichord like an angel but the heavenly music of mine comes from a glass syringe.

Please please please write me again of our love so that we might put sinful words on Sister Céline's rapturous tongue.

(Our patient often becomes rapturous himself as his pain takes wing. Haze has finally gone to sleep, so I will end his letter unsigned.)

October 24, 1915

Dear Yorick,

I don't know where to begin.

I start in the wrong place, cross every word out, start over. I should send you a letter full of inkblots.

I received just such a letter from Haze, just today, the war censor leaving a few words here and there to torment—<u>pain, forgiveness, broken, please please please.</u>

You work in the censorship office. Does it ever feel like cruelty? Stealing all those words away? (Forgive me, Yorick. I don't mean to accuse you of anything. I should cross out those sentences. Tear up the paper. Light it on fire.)

The artist of our candy wrappers offered to disentangle what she could from the muddle of black, but she said India ink on India ink obliterates. She could find none of Haze's words in that storm cloud on the page.

Yorick, I want to return to Paris. I want to return to you, and to Haze, and to those rapturous days that were so unlike anything else.

War has been good for our candy. We have endless supplies here in Japan. My father has let me in, finally. He actually likes my ideas. I arranged to buy the country's largest condensed-milk factories so we can serve the butter-and-

egg tastes of Westerners. I made a contract with the French military for an unending order of a peanut chew that keeps the boys strong and their jaws busy.

Our packaging has always been sophisticated—we've long had to account for Japan's humidity—which helps us send our candy everywhere. Keeps it from perishing in the pockets of military men.

With offices in America, Japan, Mexico, Paris, we can waltz around the duty fees, saving money on imports and exports. And that opens new markets—we're now breaking people's teeth in Manila and in the Virgin Islands.

And we're in people's hearts. My mother and I started a relief organization, and we send candy to the trenches, caramels that can be sucked for an hour or more. We sell the boys' sweethearts heart-shaped boxes of chocolate to send to their wounded soldiers. There's a wave of prohibition in America, so we've installed soda fountains in those towns, to serve up mugs of strawberry phosphates. We sell our candy at the cinema, where people gather to watch comedy and newsreels of military parades and enlisted men kissing their mothers goodbye.

I confess it feels like a victory, which is perverse, I know. But they've so often belittled us, the people of the West have. So here I am, the dragoness of the East, sprinkling sugar. We even sell the soldiers sweeter cigarettes, the tobacco dusted with crushed candy.

I'm glad to have the work, to keep my mind off things. I'm so worried about Haze. I'm so worried about you. How could we have ever been so clumsy, Yorick?

Maybe I'll carry this letter to you, so I can place it in your hands without a word lost.

Zinnia

I don't know what day it is.

I write this letter when I shouldn't.

I've had a swig or two too many of an old cognac you left behind.

When I touch my lips to the lip of the bottle, and breathe in its ether, I can taste your kiss again.

I've memorized all the letters you've sent me so that even if I were to lose them all I'd still always have them.

I don't deserve them.

J'ai caviardé. I have censored. All the words I scratch out catch in my throat to choke me.

I write you these sentiments with the same dark ink I use to blot sentiments out.

Does Sister Céline read to you every word I write? If so, how does my voice sound on her tongue?

Forgive me, Sister Céline, for I have sinned.

And thank you, Sister Céline, for caring for Haze. I don't know that Zinnia knows that Haze is underground in a hospital bed—the letters she gets have been severely redacted. I can't bear to break her heart even more, so I've written nothing of it to her.

My own letters from Haze have arrived untouched somehow, your beautiful penmanship pristine in violet ink.

Maybe it's not just the cognac that has me so sentimental— I'm at my workbench and I'm making a box for you, Haze.

I bought you a wristwatch that glows. The face is painted with radium so you can tell time in the dark. The strap is a piece of black moiré.

I'm going to put your new watch in a hollowed-out copy of a book on radioactivity. The cover is only a flimsy sheet of paper, like most books from Paris publishers, but I like it as it is with the title in French, <u>Traité de radioactivité,</u> with <u>Madame P. Curie</u> below it, but I want it to lift like a lid, so I treated the paper with Venice turpentine, a clear resin. It's a pale caramel color and smells like pine needles like your neck after a shave, and it has me dizzy.

But I won't send the box now, because it's not ready, and if I don't put this letter in the mail this very minute, I never will. I can only post it while I'm still under the influence of your cognac, and the taste of the cognac on your breath. This letter says too much.

Yorick

November 20, 1915

Dear Monsieur Yorick,

Please accept my deepest sympathies. Haze died in his sleep some nights ago.

And please accept my apologies as this is not an official letter of condolence. Haze's relationship with the military was somewhat covert—he moved about the war with identity cards picked from the pockets of dead soldiers. As you may or may not know, Haze has gone by many names.

But his were not acts of sedition. He believed deep in his heart that his pictures could change the ways of war. Only by moving freely along the sea and through the countryside could he find the stories he sought.

I ask that you write Zinnia.

Just as I read to Haze by candlelight so do I write this letter but that's all the light we have—the flicker of candles and lanterns. Every day is night here in the chalk quarry. We do our best to ready the worst of the wounded for transport to places where they can receive the care they need, but those places have too many wounded already.

The negotiations of war should be left to war nurses, not to men with medals.

This quarry that was gouged into the earth to build the

white city above might go on for miles or might be endless. As Haze died, he told me he could hear something far off. He could hear the echo of waves of water splashing against rock. He wondered if the monks dug a tunnel to the sea.

Sister Céline

PART
THREE

37

All we wanted was sleep. Some nights we could, some we couldn't. We spent every long evening in Zinnia's house, playing cards. We drank strong tea until well past dark—at our table we set a third cup, on a lotus-shaped saucer. The Japanese leave tea for the dead.

I had written to Zinnia immediately upon learning of Haze's death. I worried a telegram would be too abbreviated, but when I sat down to my typewriter, I could barely gather together a paragraph. I wanted to be consoling, but I was afraid of putting words to it all. It was all too dark. I couldn't offer her solace, because I couldn't find any myself.

When Zinnia didn't respond to my letter for days and days, I wrote another, or tried to, and I was at my typewriter in the bookshop when she walked in. She looked gaunt and pallid, her eyes bloodshot, as if she'd crossed mountains on foot. I stood from my chair and she began to weep, but without noise, without tears, her mouth open, her hands clutching the front of her coat. She wilted before me, practically falling against me when I went to her.

It was only then she began to wail, and I held her tightly to me, taking all her weight against me, and I cried too, terrified by how slight she was, how bone-thin.

"You're home," I said, my lips at her ear. I cradled her neck in my hand. "You're home now. You're home. I'm here." I realized that was what I should have written in my letter. *Come home.* I should have begged her.

When she put her arms around me and held me as tightly as

I held her, only then did I finally feel some of the solace I'd been longing for. I hadn't even known how to grieve Haze without her beside me.

Since returning to Paris from Tokyo, she had been especially devoted to Japanese customs. Some she learned from her mother and her mother's family during her months away, but just as many she learned from books in my shop—one on Japanese women by an American man; another on Japanese methods of worship by a British missionary. She read books on Buddhism, on etiquette and kimonos, on woodcuts and earthquakes. Her gowns were busy with Japanese motifs exaggerated by French designers—koi fish embroidered in gold thread; peonies in pink silk.

Every evening we played round after round of a centuries-old Japanese card game, based on the very short poems of a hundred poets. Half the cards had beginnings, half had endings. You're to scatter the endings across the table and read aloud from the beginnings. The first player to pluck up the ending to the poem's beginning wins the round.

We played with an English translation, and neither of us knew the poetry at all, so we'd often sit there speculating, attaching the wrong endings, reciting all the little collisions, composing discordant poems that nonetheless made a sort of sense in our state of despair—we sought meaning from the meaningless, and we loved when we could make something poetic of the mix-up. Even after we learned all the poems—which we adored for their melancholy, for their moonlight and clouds, for their blushing cheeks and loving hearts—we kept mismatching.

Every other poem I read, all those in the bookshop that I'd loved and relied upon, had ceased to make sense. I needed so much from them; they failed me. They'd become shallow and inarticulate.

We only once spoke of the specifics of Haze's death, when Zinnia first returned to Paris. We sat shivering at a table in front of Café Capucine; the place had closed early every evening—eight thirty or so—during the first year of the war, but was now inching later into the night. She told me that after Haze died, she abandoned Paper Crane Confectionery. Her father had finally allowed her a place in his company, and she no longer wanted it. And she'd become disgusted with herself, building wealth while the world burned down.

It was the candy itself that sickened her the most, all the new sweets inspired by the war. Toy soldiers made of marzipan. A wax artillery shell full of tiny pellets of candy shrapnel. Even the confections specifically for the military men worried her. One was a peppermint lozenge that would deaden your gums while you sucked it, for the temporary ease of toothaches.

We drank our watered-down gin slings hot as we read the letter about Haze's death, reading it aloud, once, twice, then again and again. I knew we had to stop. If we continued to read it, as an incantation to raise the dead, we were doomed.

In the nights after that, I would stand to leave our card game, to return to my bed in my bookshop, and Zinnia would stand too, to embrace me. It never felt like a farewell. She would say goodnight, but wouldn't let go. She pressed her cheek against my shoulder. I would begin to feel her shaking against me, shivering with her tears, sniffling softly. I'd hold her tighter, and she'd hold tighter to me, the only language that made sense anymore.

We would go to her bed—"Only stay with me until I fall asleep," she'd say, and either she would fall asleep or she wouldn't, but I never left. We'd lie atop her covers in our clothes. It was always such a relief to hear the soft puffs of her sleeping breath, to know she was at least having a moment's peace. But more often than not, just when I thought she might be drifting off, her trembling would begin again, and I'd hold her close, which only ever made the crying worse. She would clutch at my sleeves. She would press her forehead against my chest.

38

When Haze was alive, off taking photographs at the war front, I was forever composing letters to him in my head. It became the way I saw the world around me: everything was something to narrate to Haze. I was somehow often without a notebook, but always had my pen in my pocket, so I'd write the things I wanted to remember on a paper napkin stained with coffee rings or across a candy wrapper, or on the flap of an envelope, or even along my cuff and up my sleeve. After hours and days and weeks of inking out sentences in the war office, words came to seem fleeting, ephemeral. My brain took on the habits of my work, my own thoughts erased as quickly as they came to me. So I wrote everything down, sometimes returning to the shop at night with pocketfuls of sentences, on a matchbook, on a corner of a newspaper, even on the paper of a cigarette I'd torn apart.

After he died, I kept taking those notes, and even a few times I tried typing him a letter, thinking it might comfort me, but I got no further than *Dear Haze*. It seemed even if I typed for days, the page before me would stay blank.

And when Zinnia returned to Paris so unexpectedly, stepping right into my shop like she'd never left, I wanted to write Haze all about it, to tell him how her loss and loneliness clouded her eyes.

I began spending every evening at her house, and every night. We eventually stopped pretending I'd ever leave. After a day in the war office wielding my scissors, I would stop into the shop, which Alice kept open, then go sit in Zinnia's library on a sofa snow white from its pattern of egrets with outstretched wings.

"I think Haze got us drinking this when he was alive," Zinnia said of our nightly cocktails, always martinis of Haze's Holland gin, "because he knew it would rob us of sleep when he was dead."

The gin might make us drowsy in the evening, but it would spike later, keeping us up at two in the morning. We would always leave enough of a puddle of gin in the bottom of our glasses that we could drop our cigarettes in, as he always had, to extinguish them. Most often we didn't even smoke the cigarette . . . we just lit it so we could put it out and hear its hiss.

Though I'd been miserable before Zinnia returned to Paris, unable to think about anyone or anything but Haze and his death, I do think I'd have recovered in time. I was growing tired of my exhaustion, and not only was I busy in the war office, the shop was doing swift business—people had money to spend. The women of Paris had good jobs—war paid well and employed many, especially at the ammunition factories. In their hours off the assembly line, the workers longed to divert themselves from the weapons they built, to see, in the light of a lamp, a complicated life contained to the pages of a novel.

They longed for their tangled thoughts to be simplified. They wanted dramatic stories that followed simple rules—romances, mysteries, adventures. They wanted to follow paths to conclusions. If any of it was at all ambiguous, they asked for their money back. *It didn't end the way it should,* one woman said as she returned *Wuthering Heights.*

But Zinnia's despair fed mine. Her new devotion to old customs seemed less about consolation than it did about prolonging unhappiness. It became a kind of worship, our grief did, and we found comfort in being inconsolable.

"Why did you never have me to your house before?" I asked

her. A consequence of our being alone together every night was I tended to dwell on all the old things.

"When we *were* friends?" she asked. "We're not friends now?"

"We are," I said. "But we're different now too."

"I think I was embarrassed," she said. "You lived in that prison cell with the mean concierge. Haze slept in your shop, for god's sake. Meanwhile, I have a house full of rooms I never go in."

"But we knew you were rich," I said. "You paid for everything. Your generosity changed my life." I shrugged. "But I was never invited into your home. I thought maybe you were embarrassed of *me*."

"Oh, Yorick," she said. "We really didn't know each other at all, did we?"

I still didn't have my answer. But I knew that Zinnia liked to keep secrets. And I had more than a few of my own.

39

A massive armoire appeared suddenly in Zinnia's bedroom, and inside it were new suits for me. Zinnia's couturier still had my measurements from before the war, and though I'd changed some, he had anticipated my thinness, an inch or two gone from my waist, more poke to the bones of my shoulders. Somehow the clothes fit. Was there some kind of wartime conversion chart tailors used to calculate our diminishment?

She'd bought me only light-colored suits: a blond tweed, an ashen herringbone, a fox-colored houndstooth. In the drawers were linen shirts the color of clouds, and silk socks in all the milky shades of ice cream. I now had a newsboy cap in camel's hair, and a derby of moose-gray goatskin, and hatpins and tie clips with heads of teardrop pearl, of champagne diamond. Zinnia stepped up behind me to explain the subtle but hypnotic Japanese patterns of my new neckties, to run her fingers through them—one based on sharkskin, one on the fletching of arrows.

I was at first moved by it all, but then I wondered about the paleness, how these costumes seemed to be leading me away from the black serge suit I'd been wearing nearly every day and the rosebud of black silk I wore in the buttonhole of my lapel. I arrived at her house each morning and left each night in the black overcoat of an undertaker and a black felt hat with a black band.

"All the fashion magazines are scolding widows for wearing

black," Zinnia said. "Widows in black dampen the mood, they say. Isn't that tragic? To blame broken women for all the sadness?" She laid out for me pajamas the pink of the inside of an oyster shell and a robe with zebras galloping across the red silk. "We have to find quiet ways to carry on. Secret ways."

40

The hairdresser and the hairdresser's maid were the first outsiders invited into Zinnia's house. Zinnia wasn't just getting her hair done. She was getting it *constructed,* in a process that involved a Japanese *kamiyu* trained in the old traditions. The *kamiyu* only stepped in after her maid had washed Zinnia's hair with rosewater and perfumed it with a bamboo comb soaked in jasmine oil.

When the maid finished, she poured hot saké into pink cups. I sat back on the pillows of Zinnia's bed, my stocking feet crossed at the ankles, to watch the ceremony as I sipped. The *kamiyu,* in front of the vanity mirror, twisted and wove Zinnia's long tresses into a fat coiffure, installing little silk pillows to prop it all up.

"There's an old ghost story," Zinnia said to her hairdresser. "One my mother read to me. Maybe you know it? A ghost with long hair, all undone?"

I knew something of the *kaidan,* the old Japanese ghost stories, but not from Zinnia. At a bookstall on the quay, you can get a bundle of five for nothing at all. Printed on crepe paper as light as air but full of fright.

The *kamiyu,* all business, explained, "When her husband dies, a woman will cut off her own hair and drop it in his casket. Some widows saw it all off, every hank of it." She tilted Zinnia's head forward to attend to delicate mechanics, some little springs to make the heavy hairdo look light, make it all hover like a black cloud. "She might just drop her whole head of hair in the coffin. And then she lets it grow back to never be done again."

I didn't like the look in Zinnia's eyes when she brought her head back up. She was looking at herself in the mirror, but seeing a lost soul with long hair. She reached up to tug gently at a lock, pulling it loose from a pin. She took scissors from her vanity drawer and cut off a small piece from the end of her hair. She held the lock in her open palm as the *kamiyu* dressed her hair with paper twine and silk ribbons.

41

"I'm going to do something with this," Zinnia said, still holding the hair in her palm after the *kamiyu* and her maid had left the house. "I can't drop it in his coffin, of course, but maybe there's a way . . . to pretend."

I didn't even have to think about it: the grave of the aeronauts. I didn't suspect Zinnia knew anything about the memorial in bronze, the two pilots lying side by side, holding hands, naked beneath a blanket. On that night that we went to the cemetery looking for Oscar Wilde's tomb, when all of us barely knew each other, Zinnia had left before Haze led me to the grave, before he told me the story of their fallen balloon.

I worried she'd be offended if I suggested it. It was a moment Haze and I had had alone together. I realized I wanted our moment with the aeronauts all to myself. And it seemed like Zinnia wanted something to herself too—she wanted an intimate ritual of husband and wife.

It was probably time for us to stop sharing our grief.

But I couldn't help myself. "There's a tomb Haze admired in Père Lachaise," I said. I feared if I left her to her own grief, I'd lose her forever. And I might lose myself too.

We quickly devised our ritual. Zinnia had kept her unused *Titanic* ticket in a little see-through jewelry box that made me think of Snow White's glass coffin. She replaced the ticket with her lock of hair, and I helped her on with her coat—a heavy thing that was more like a blanket draped over her shoulders, black with a crisscrossing of gold vines, made from the silk velvet used for kimono sashes.

We decided to walk to the cemetery, in honor also of Zinnia's driver, Monsieur Toussaint. At the very start of the war, he'd joined the legion of drivers who drove soldiers to the front lines in taxicabs, five or six soldiers packed in each car. Zinnia's limousine fit seven. He ended up on a narrow road with a truck with no lamps, and he died in the crash. I'd hated hearing the news of his death, despite Monsieur Toussaint's distaste for Haze and me. His devotion to Zinnia had been sincere.

It had all been made even sadder by the way I learned of it; by the time Zinnia returned to Paris, Monsieur Toussaint had been dead for some time. She hadn't mentioned him, so when I asked if he'd be returning to his job, she seemed to forget, for just a flicker of a moment. At the sound of his name, Zinnia brightened, widened her eyes, nearly smiled, as if *I* was the one with news about him. But then the loss rushed back in, dropping its shadow.

As we walked in the cold autumn afternoon, Zinnia's lock of hair in the glass box, it began to rain. We'd forgotten umbrellas, but a seller of parasols appeared on a street corner, keeping dry under a giant parasol of his own, one covering his whole operation, allowing him his showmanship—he spun the parasols before himself, so fast the colors blurred, became animated, pink and blue and yellow dancing before us in the grayness of the day. "They're paper, but they won't turn to pulp in the rain," he promised. "They're shellacked with persimmon oil." It was as if he'd been summoned by Zinnia's ancestors. She was a widow in a Japanese fable, apparitions appearing in the path of her funeral march, to thwart the rain.

We bought a parasol big enough for the two of us to walk beneath, one painted with a purple-black panther so lithe it wound all around the top. I chose it in honor of Haze, thinking of the poem by Rilke about a panther in a menagerie in Paris. In the poem, the panther paces endlessly, so weary from the sight of the bars of the cage he can see nothing beyond them. *It seems to him there are a thousand bars; and behind the bars, no world.*

At the cemetery, it stopped raining and the clouds dissolved in the pale rays of sunlight. But the rain had kept people out and softened the earth, and with the handle of our cheap parasol I was able to covertly dig out a shallow grave for the jewelry box next to the tomb of the aeronauts. We recited no eulogy, no prayer.

As we stood at the tomb, I saw Zinnia's hair coming loose from its combs and ribbons, collapsing from the dampness in the air. She reached out to put her hand in the hand of one of the aeronauts. "Why did he bring you here, Yorick?" she asked.

"He was terrified of heights, but he longed more than anything to see Paris from above. And perhaps more than that, he wanted off these streets, to get as far away from them as he could. But he could never even bring himself to go to the top of the Eiffel Tower. He didn't even like crossing the bridge over the Seine."

"I don't think I even knew that about him," Zinnia said. "How could I have not known?"

"I'm sure you did know," I said. "You just forgot that you knew."

"That's worse, isn't it?" she said, looking up at me. "That I'm already forgetting?"

I put my hand to Zinnia's cheek. I brushed away a tear with my thumb.

"Zinnia," I said. "Tell me what I can do for you."

"You can't do anything, Yorick. You're devastated too."

I couldn't put my arm in hers, because her coat was like a shroud, consuming her, so I put my hand to her back and led her to the cemetery path. I was devastated, very much so, but, *It's different for me*, I didn't say. *I would never have let him go. You did.* But the last thing I wanted to do was compete with her in our widowhood. I needed our sleepless nights together.

And it wasn't quite true, the history I had in my head.

Secrets. Zinnia didn't know what I knew, but I didn't feel like I was betraying her this time. I wasn't lying to her. I just hadn't had a chance to tell her everything—at least not a chance to tell her everything the way she should be told.

42

In the last letter from Sister Céline about Haze's death, the nun made no mention of the leather satchel she'd sent along with it, the satchel he'd carried with him throughout the war, every letter of Zinnia's kept at his hip.

My secret wasn't just that I *had* the letters, but that I'd read them all, each and every one, and more than once. And I knew *her* secret, *their* secret. When we had reunited before the war, friends once again, they had rekindled their romance without telling me. Not only had it rekindled, it had intensified. I had thought the only time the two of them saw each other was when all three of us were together. But they were spending time without me, just as they had before—before *Frankenstein*, before everything fell apart for a while.

In those few months before the war, we would all say goodnight after an evening at Café Capucine, and Haze would go one way, and Zinnia another, and they would meet again somewhere else.

When I read the letters from Haze's satchel, I saw right off that the character of Zinnia's letters to Haze was so different from the character of those she'd sent me. Her letters to me were all business, all news, her day-to-day, but her letters to Haze swooned and caressed. They were dreamy and fanciful. She sent him snippets of love poems full of metaphors, and she made metaphors of her own. Her love for him was a wild fawn, the first bite of a summer peach, the leap of a ballerina, the smell of sage after a desert rain.

I learned, in her letters to Haze, about their stolen moments the summer before he left Paris for the front lines. She described their affair in detail. It seemed that Haze had asked her to reminisce in the letters she wrote to him. He longed for news of the past. He wanted to hear about the two of them, in her own words.

I licked honey off you, she wrote.

Zinnia had written to Haze that the perfume of the peony gardens in Japan reminded her of one summer afternoon they'd spent together. The two of them lay on a blanket among the white peonies in the Luxembourg Gardens. One of the flowers in the patch had broken apart, and he'd picked up a petal, which was the softest thing she'd ever felt against her skin. He'd touched it to her wrist, to her throat.

He'd unbuttoned her blouse, though anyone could have seen them. He touched the petal to her breast. He then kissed her there, and licked her nipple. He ran the petal along her neck, along the line of her chin. He'd brought along a bottle of red wine he'd been too proud of—he'd paid too much at an auction, a bottle decades old from the cellar of a fine restaurant, but it hadn't held up. *I can still smell the wine on your breath,* she wrote, a scent of clove and vinegar. And she could feel the heat of his breath on her cheek, as he whispered words she couldn't hear.

We rode those broken-down horses of the carousel, remember? she wrote. *You chipped off a little flake of pink paint from the one we rode. You gave it to me a few days later, in a heart-shaped locket, a locket I wear all the time now.*

That locket. When she returned to Paris, I saw her wearing it. I asked her about it, though I'd already read the letter, and already knew it was likely the one with the chip of paint from the pink horse. "It's nothing," she said, touching her finger to it.

"Then why do you wear it all the time?"

"It was caught up in a knot of necklaces in a drawer," she said. "I took so much time untangling them all, I can't bear to just put it back."

They drank wine near the apiary, near the hives in wooden boxes. First there was just one bee, buzzing around the lip of the wine bottle. Then another came along. And another. One got caught up in her hair. Haze and Zinnia fled, and as they fled, he told her they should keep running, they should run away. Once again, he wanted to take her miles from Paris, miles away from me, from us.

Reading the letters, I could feel all the hours I never had with Haze, even as his specter rose before me. Reading about him in Zinnia's letters, I could taste the cinnamon of his kiss. I could smell the eau de cologne he slapped on his neck, its scent of cedar and straw, of the oil lamps at Café Capucine, of his cigarettes that made me think of thyme, of pepper. I could smell the sting of the methylated spirit he used in developing his photographs.

I felt myself lose him all over again. Even if he'd not gone to the war front, he would have left, taking Zinnia away. And there was no mention of me in those letters, of how I might have felt if they'd left me behind.

I knew I had to be careful, so I told Zinnia nothing. I knew that my jealousy was coiled close to my skin, poised to stab its tongue at me at the slightest tap, to blind me with its venom.

43

When I got to the house one early winter night, I found Zinnia in the library smoking her pipe, her legs crossed, her foot tapping frantically at the air.

"I just the other day scolded Alice for smoking around the books," I said. When she said nothing in response, I said, "Is something wrong?"

She still said nothing, until finally: "I've been sitting here trying to think of what to say to you."

"Well," I said. "Here I am. What'd you come up with?"

"Don't be flippant, Yorick."

"I don't mean to be," I said. I went to the settee and sat down, still in my overcoat. "Just tell me what's wrong."

She put her pipe to her lips, but she didn't breathe in. She just bit the stem. She closed her eyes.

She lowered her pipe and looked at me. "Yorick," she said. "You've read the letters that I sent Haze."

"No," I said with a whimper, so taken aback, so unconvincing in my lie, I might as well have said yes. If I *hadn't* read her letters, I wouldn't have known to say no. I wouldn't have known what letters she was talking about. "What letters?" I said, too late.

"Why must you always lie?" she said.

"I don't," I said. But did I? When you have to hide who you are, you indeed have a different truth. But it's not a lie. Is it?

When she just continued to sit there, biting on her pipe, I cast about in my mind for something I'd said that I shouldn't know, some clue I'd left her. I knew the letters so well, I should have expected their sentiments to get entangled with my own.

But then I looked over to her desk beneath the window, and I saw the letters spread across the top of them, next to the leather satchel that I'd kept in a cabinet at the bookshop. *Alice.* Of course it was Alice. I'd only just that morning asked her if she'd gather some of my things and send them over to Zinnia's house. I needed belongings of my very own around me if I was to live there, no matter how inferior any of it was to what Zinnia had bought me. I needed my typewriter with its keys that stuck, a few pairs of old shoes, a half bottle of hair tonic, a wristwatch that ran slow. I had sent her a list that most certainly did not include the satchel.

Zinnia leaned forward to put her pipe atop an open book, then held her hands to her head. "I'm the fool for falling for it, again, after everything before. Why do I always have to learn the same lesson?" She dropped her hands to her lap.

I took Zinnia's hand and squeezed it, but she didn't squeeze back. "Zinnia, you know me better than anyone. The only time I've ever been truly myself is around you. And I've never lied to you; I've only ever just . . . just kept truth from you."

"You *just* lied," she said. She snatched her hand back from me. "When you said no. To my question. Just now."

"One little word," I said. "For one little moment. I'm telling the truth now. If I have lied, it's not to hurt anyone. The opposite. I've only ever lied so that I *won't* hurt anyone." I paused. When still she said nothing, I said softly, cautiously, "But you lied to me, just the same. You were back together, before he left. You didn't tell me."

"That's *not* the same," she said. "That was . . . private."

"You were going to run away together," I said. "Away from me."

She brought her hand up, and at first I flinched, but she was only reaching over to put her hand to my cheek. Her touch was such a relief. "He ran away from us both, Yorick," she said. "He didn't have to go to the front. No one was calling him up. His name wasn't anywhere on any official lists."

I put my hand to her hand, to hold it there. I spoke into her palm, my every word like a kiss against her skin. "He carried your letters around in his leather bag, with his camera," I said. "That's how much he loved you. He saved every one."

She took her hand back. "How did you get them?" she asked. "Did he send them to you?"

"Oh no no no, Zinnia, no. He would never have done that. He never meant for anyone else to see them. The nun, Sister Céline, she sent them with her letter."

"If he didn't want anyone else to read them," she said, "then why did you?"

"I didn't know if I'd ever see you again," I said. "And . . . I just couldn't help it. I missed you both so much."

"You wanted to know what we said to each other when we thought no one else would hear."

"Forgive me."

"Did he carry *your* letters around in his satchel?" she said, with what seemed to me a sour note of cruelty.

"No," I said. "He didn't keep my letters."

This seemed to both please her and fill her with pity. She returned her hand to my cheek.

I decided to stop by the shop on my way to the censorship office the next morning. I told Zinnia where I was going—I was now determined to be entirely honest with her—but I suspected she'd discourage me from scolding Alice. "I'll come with you," she said. We decided we would walk, despite the cold. I helped her on with her heavy cape of kimono sashes, which seemed to have grown a hood. She brought the hood up and over her head.

Just a few blocks into our walk, we turned a corner into such a rush of wind, she had to hold her hood to keep it over her head, and we leaned against each other to move forward. When we turned another corner, the wind vanished. And not only had we stepped into sudden sunshine and stillness, but we found a flower shop with its bouquets in baskets on the sidewalk, every petal unruffled.

It certainly wasn't unusual to find flowers in the winter months, but I didn't think I'd ever seen peonies at that time of year. Though they were deep pink, and not the white ones Zinnia referenced in her letter to Haze, it was enough to stop us. At first I wasn't sure I should buy them for her—I only knew about the peonies at all because I'd violated her privacy—but she seemed so touched by the sight of them, I couldn't just walk away. There were four of the flowers in the bucket, their stems tied together with string. I paid the florist and she wrapped them in tissue.

"You can't find that scent anywhere else," Zinnia said, leaning forward into the flowers I held out, breathing it in. "Nothing that's peony-scented is even close. Not the peony perfumes, not the soaps, not the bath salts."

"They smell like the month of June," I said, thinking of Haze—our June birthdays, days apart.

"I can't believe I'm just realizing this now . . . We all three have literary names. Hansel. Yorick. And I can't believe you've never asked me about mine."

"Haven't I?" I tried to think of a literary *Zinnia*.

"It's not taken so directly as yours," she said. "My mother had a favorite book in Japan. Hundreds of pages, hundreds of years old, full of women. One of them was named after a violet. Another after a hollyhock. There was no zinnia, but she liked the idea of it, of naming me after a flower."

"*Genji Monogatari*," I said. "I've got a few copies in my shop. In Japanese, in English."

"Have you read it?"

"I *will*," I said.

As we strolled along, she told me about how the book, in her memory, was full of romance, of moonlight, a zither with thirteen strings playing a winter song, crickets singing in the wall, carriages of woven bamboo. "Genji falls in love all the time, and I sort of adore that about him . . . mostly because all the women he loved were so lovable. He fell in love with one woman because of her handwriting." She nodded at me, as if that seemed something I would do. "She wrote him a note across her paper fan. She was named after the evening glories that wound up the walls of her house. This may sound very strange, and I'm not sure I can explain it, but . . . when I was a little girl, I somewhat believed I *was* a flower. I believed I'd been plucked from a garden. Maybe it was something someone told me once. Or maybe it was from other stories my mother read me. It seems there was one about a boy who was a peach. Or one about a family that raised a radish. And to be honest, I still believe it a little bit."

I adored her for this. I found myself composing her a letter in my mind, a love letter from Haze. I thought of that poem by Rimbaud in the book I read to Haze that night, the one we translated for Zinnia. Something about a summer dawn and "a flower which told me its name."

"I guess what I'm saying," she said after a moment more, "is that we can believe in these unlikely things, if we want to. Wouldn't the moon seem magical if there weren't so many people telling you it wasn't? The flight of a bird? The blood flowing in your own veins?" I wasn't sure what she was getting at, and I waited for her to say more, but she didn't. She didn't speak again until we approached the bookshop.

"Don't scold Alice," she said, just as I knew she would. "About sending the satchel."

"I'm not very good at scolding anyone, anyway," I said. "But she *should* be scolded. She knew what she was doing."

"You rely on her," she said.

"Doesn't it bother you that she probably read all those letters too? Before she sent the satchel?"

"It doesn't cost you much to allow her a few . . . indiscretions. It's hard for a young girl all alone."

Instead of going into the shop, we sat at a table at Café Capucine. We were the only ones there other than Capucine herself, the brown cat curled up in her chair. The waiter brought us coffee, and Zinnia shrugged her arms from her cape. She unwrapped the peonies and unknotted their string. When they fell across the tabletop, I saw that one of them was quite aged, about to collapse, the edges of its petals turning to rust. They brought to my mind a Renaissance painting, of flowers decaying next to a freshly shot pheasant.

"When you were a boy," she said, "did you hope you'd marry someday?"

"I assumed I would," I said. "That was my sense of how things went. I wanted to fall in love. And get married."

"Did you ever want children of your own? *Do* you want children?"

"I thought that's what it meant to be a man," I said. "To be a man was to be a father. I didn't think it mattered what a person *wanted*. It was just what you did. My own father wanted to be something else; he was never a father to me. But he was always happy to let people know he had a son."

"My mother never thought she was valued, as a girl," she said. "'They only want sons in Japan,' she told me when I was little. If you had daughters, you were being punished for a long list of sins left over from other lives you'd lived. And no one showed anyone any affection, son *or* daughter. She married an American to escape all that, she said. But, if you ask me, she just carried it all along with her. I was only ever held when I cried. And even then it was only to quiet me."

"You must have forgiven them," I said. "Your mother and father. You seem so close to them now."

"I don't know if a person forgives, really," she said. "You just . . . overlook."

I put my elbow on the table and my chin in my hand. Her hair was down, her tresses fallen from the wind and the hood, strands of her hair dangling in her face.

Looking in her eyes, and feeling sentimental, and dreamy, so near my shop again, with the scent of the peonies and her story of the flowers, I said, "Will *you* marry?"

I seemed to startle her with my question. She looked down into her coffee.

"Marry?" she said, sharp. "Who'd want to marry, with all that's going on? Or have children? Bring up a son, just to send him into such agony? To his own death?"

I'd upset her somehow. I picked up a peony and held it to my nose. After a few more sips of her coffee, Zinnia calmed. "I did hear about a special hospital the Red Cross wants to start in Paris," she said. "To rebuild faces. The soldiers whose lives are saved but whose faces are mutilated get kicked out of the hospitals in France, because the doctors need the beds for all the wounded. Millions of them. Millions of wounded men. And just to maintain one bed costs twenty thousand dollars. They want at least a hundred beds, but they need hundreds more."

"That would be remarkable," I said.

"I would do it in honor of Haze, of course," she said. "Maybe a wing could be named after him."

"A building in Paris, named for Haze," I said. "He would never believe that."

"Before, when you asked, 'Will you marry?' . . . I thought you were saying, 'Will you marry *me*?'"

"Oh, Zinnia, I—"

"No, no, I know," she said. "We don't have to go through all this again. I understand. I don't know I'd even say yes to such a thing." She paused. "And who knows? Maybe the world will change after the war. Maybe people will be allowed to live how they want to live. You can take in a wounded soldier of your own."

My first instinct was to roll my eyes, to harrumph, to deny that I could ever find romance with anyone. Instead, I smiled and nodded. I wanted more than anything to be completely honest with Zinnia from now on. I wanted her to know me like no one else.

Dear Titanic Survivors Book Club:

"The murmur of winds, the music of insects, now only served to cause him melancholy."

 I've become captivated by the handwriting I've read in my work as a censor. A handwritten letter holds the very soul of the writer. Even if you don't read the words, you feel like you know something about the person from their penmanship. And not only that, you know something of their state of mind as they wrote. You might choose your words very carefully, but if you write by hand, you reveal much more than you realize.

 Handwriting is an art in Japan, so much so that many of the stories of hundreds of years ago are said to have just flowed from the brush, the tale a mere consequence of the calligraphy.

Zinnia has returned to Paris, and she longs to see you all, so I'm reviving our little club. I've sent you her favorite book, Genji Monogatari, the first novel ever written (or so say some historians), and it was written by a woman, and while many scholars credit her with having written the first novel in the history of the world, there are others who would deny her that, for not conforming to the conventions of the form she'd invented, a form that hadn't even existed until she put ink to scroll.

Even the novel's translator writes in his introduction that she had more imagination than skill, criticizing the book as disjointed. He never refers to it as a novel, only a story, a work, a romance. And though our hero never settles for only one woman, having many wives and mistresses, liaisons, infatuations, we fall in love with each and every one too.

Yours,
Yorick

44

The club's revival seemed exactly what we needed. I sent no candy with the book, because Zinnia wanted to create fresh confections for us all—she spent days in the kitchen rehearsing, practicing, and perfecting old family recipes. Ingredients for baking had become difficult to come by with the wartime rations, but Zinnia didn't need much of any of it; her sweets called for millet, rice, seaweed, black sesame, green tea, soybeans.

The house, which Zinnia kept so cold in those winter weeks, was warmed by the kitchen and the scents that drifted from it, of roasted chestnuts and baked sweet potatoes.

The Japanese saw eating their unsweet sweets as a moral act, their ornamental desserts innocent of any animal abuse that might haunt them later. "We use plants grown in the fields," she said, "not milk and eggs robbed from the barn."

Nonetheless, the delicate confections took the shape of gentle creatures.

"What's your favorite animal?" she asked me one night when I got home.

I shrugged. "I don't have a favorite," I said.

"That's the least interesting answer you could possibly give me."

"What would be the *most* interesting answer?"

"I don't want that, either," she said.

"A flamingo, then," I said.

"Too interesting," she said.

"A dog," I said.

She turned her back to me as she stood at the counter, snipping at something with a pair of scissors. She turned around with a treat made of barley in her open palm. "I've made you a rabbit," she said, and from a certain angle I could see it—she'd given the plum-shaped lump a few clips to make long ears resting back along its body.

Her grandmother, who'd been a candy seller with a street cart in Tokyo, had been able to fashion, on demand, with a few twists of her knife, sweets shaped as cats, elephants, pigs, whatever the child wanted. She'd also made candy with a straw, like blowing glass, and though Zinnia hadn't quite mastered it in time for our book club, she was able to hang some lopsided goldfish in the shopwindow, to catch the light in its delicate fins. She made a sugar-glass octopus too, with twisty legs, and a fire-red sea dragon shaped like the letter *S*. They all dangled from fishing line.

The fish fit with the window's theme, not only because of the mermaids, but also the paper tape Alice had strapped across the glass. The tape was to keep the window from shattering everywhere should a bomb drop, and shopkeepers had become creative with designs and patterns abstract and otherwise. Alice had taped ocean waves to the bottom of the window, with little sailboats atop them.

On the night of the book club's reunion, Zinnia followed the nautical theme in a snugly fit dress she'd had her seamstress fashion from an old kimono, the fabric patterned with midnight-blue ocean waves crashing with silky white froth. Her hair was impeccably piled up to appear windblown, staying on the very verge of collapse all evening long.

She received the Titanic Survivors Book Club like the widow of a funeral would, taking one hand in both of hers, thanking everyone for coming, putting her cheek forth for a peck of sympathy. "'The pleasant persuasion of saké,'" she said, quoting from *Genji Monogatari* as she handed out cups of the liquor she'd warmed in a teapot on the shop's stove.

Atop the front desk were the desserts she'd made—*sakura-mochi*—beautiful rounds of *omochi* she'd colored pink with strawberry powder and wrapped in the pickled leaves of the cherry blossom tree.

"To Haze?" I said when we sat, though I didn't mean for the question mark at the end. But ever since Haze's death, it seemed I always ended everything with that inquisitive lift to my voice. I raised my cup of saké. They raised theirs.

"To Haze," they said, as if to answer me.

Alice had kept the shop stocked in new books, so we were all surrounded by war, which was proving profitable for publishers despite paper shortages. Essays, philosophies, admonitions. They'd sell you one book that explained the war, then another that explained it as unexplainable. They sold romances about soldiers and their ladyloves, and comical war cartoons, and recipe books for patriotic cocktails.

I wasn't the only one among us peddling war. Paper Crane Confectionery sold Zigzag, named after soldiers' slang for stumbling drunk. It tasted of molasses and whiskey, and it was said to be sobering. The toymaker, despite once being so troubled by war toys, now sold military maps, and fields of green felt, and infantrymen made of lead, everything tucked into cases with handles so boys could carry the war around. His bestsellers were little German soldiers, the children of France keen to assassinate them by the handful. "And look at this," he told me when he arrived, showing me one of the windup *Titanic*s, intended for the bathtub, that had cluttered his warehouse but had now been repainted, renamed. Because all the White Star ships had been armed and decked out for war, his *Titanic*s were now *Oceanic*s, *Britannic*s, *Laurentic*s.

I wound it up and listened to its motor spin. I thought of the letter Haze sent me from the White Star offices, about the mustachioed sailor and the horses he soothed.

When Delphine had first arrived, she insisted we touch her

sleeve. "Not linen at all," she'd boasted. "It is 'linetta.'" With the flax fields of the north occupied by the Germans, fashion had lost linen, along with piqué and tricot and other fabrics and weaves manufactured in the overtaken towns.

Otherwise, the people of Paris pretended that nothing much was amiss, as if the war was taking place in distant lands.

But those of us who'd lost someone—and thousands had been lost already—saw their absence everywhere we looked. Haze sat in every empty bistro chair in every café I passed. And our club that night was short not only Haze but also the evangelist, still at the western front, and the physician, who was serving in a military hospital. In each brief silence that fell, we could hear them not talking.

We listened now. We said nothing of the book. The evening had cast a spell, and we knew why: the book club was a habit we'd had before the war. It was genuine linen, serge, gabardine—it was everything silken we'd lost.

"There will be no words to define these times," said Old Madame Petit. She didn't have *Genji Monogatari* open in her lap; she'd plucked from a nearby shelf a memoir by a soldier that sold particularly well for the shop, the battles it described still smoldering. I think it actually helped sales that so many of its pages were blank, all the blocks of missing type replaced with a single phrase: *"Supprimé par la censure." Suppressed by the censor.* There was something provocative about the absence, but also frightening—what was missing might be something unspeakable. Or unimaginable.

I started to say something, to bring the discussion around to the book I'd assigned, but Old Madame Petit was not done. "The war won't end," she said. "It will just lead to another one, and then one after that. How can something like poetry survive? Art? Truth? Beauty? What chance does any fragile thing have?" I'd never seen her so impassioned, none of us had, and I think we all wanted her to go on and on. And it seemed she might. "All the fathers of soldiers should be ashamed," she said. "They had their lives, and now they sacrifice their children so that they themselves can just go on. The old men should be the first at the front line, whenever a war kicks up. Let the enemy armies spend their bullets on *them* before they can touch a hair on their sons' heads."

When there was a moment's quiet, Mr. Penny Dreadful spoke up, in that gruff singsong of his. "I'm one of those old men, I guess," he said. "I have no sons, but I have a son-in-law. He left his family to fight."

"Our daughter lives in St. Ives," Penny Dreadful explained, "raising boys of her own. Three of them. I can tell you, I wake every morning relieved that the phone didn't ring in the night. And then I remember that terrible news can come at any minute of any day. Any second. There's no calm in the quiet of things."

"I never knew you were a grandmother," I said. "Or even someone's mother, for that matter." The bookshop suddenly filled with the children, the grandchildren, the husbands, wives, lovers, all the lives of these people I thought I knew so well.

"I have children also, two boys," the toymaker said. "Little boys. But not that little. Hopefully the war will be won before they have to go fight in it. But they'll *finish* that fight if they do go, I'll tell you that much. They're a couple of devils." He smiled as he spoke, but I could see a trembling of his chin. "The war will have met its match in them."

"I have a boy in the trenches myself," the gambler said, dressed to the nines as always before, but all in black and dark blue. His legs were crossed, showing off a black tweed boot with an absurdly high heel. "We've been estranged for most of his life. I married when I was too young, and she was too, and she threw me out when the boy was a baby. But she says she *didn't* throw me out, that I left on my own. She says I abandoned them both. That's not how I remember it, but she's as sure of her version of events as I am of mine."

"But you've heard from him?" the orphan asked the gambler.

The gambler nodded a nod that moved his whole body, and for the first time ever I saw a kind of pride bubble up in the man. He uncrossed his legs, leaned forward, folded his hands between his knees. "I have heard from him," he said. "I thought the first letter was a mistake, because he talked to me like he'd just talked to me days ago. I thought the letter was meant for someone else. But no, the letter was mine. All mine. I wrote him back, and he wrote again. Back and forth, back and forth. And not a word in his letters of recrimination, or rebuke, or shaming. His letters are warm. Kind. And when you get a letter from the war front, it's not just a letter you're getting. It's a ray of light. And whoever's right—his mother or me—about how things happened twenty years ago—that takes quite a man, I'd say. To forgive me. To invite me in like that."

The orphan said, "It must mean quite a lot to him too."

"I hope so," he said. "Couldn't possibly mean more to him than it does to me, though."

"Are the letters full of holes when they arrive?" asked Old Madame Petit, still poised for protest. "Has the censor spilled his ink across the page?"

"Most are intact, Madame Petit," he said.

And then came the question I was dreading. "What do you censor, Yorick?" Old Madame Petit asked me.

"What *do* you censor?" asked Penny Dreadful, softening the question. Unlike Old Madame Petit, she wasn't accusing, she was curious. She was plotting another murder, maybe. *A Loss for Words,* a censor gone mad, cutting out tongues.

"Whatever comes to the censorship office," I said, a feint and dodge. I didn't want to talk about it. I didn't want to talk about all the personal letters I shot full of holes. I didn't want to talk about letters at all, especially not with Zinnia at my side.

"I sometimes imagine it's the same censor reading all the letters Henry sends me," the orphan said. It took me a moment to realize the Henry she spoke of was *our* Henry, the evangelist. "This censor doesn't use ink. He cuts holes in the paper in a very . . . *specific* way, a very *intentional* way, it seems to me. Henry and I write to each other all the time, and I sense a kind of . . . well, a *rhythm,* I guess, to all the parts ripped out. Like Morse code. Or a message sent with mirrors and sunlight. I have no idea what the censor is censoring, but I don't know that it matters to him either. He's making patterns." Even she, the goodly little teetotaler, was drinking the saké by the gulpful. She took a swig and continued. "I sometimes include messages for the censor in my letters to Henry. The last letter I sent was *all* about the censor. I want the censor to know that I know who he is. He's not nobody. His own story, his own life, his own silences, he leaves all of that behind in the letters he takes his scissors to." Another swig. "Yorick," she said, slurring now, "are you ever haunted by the words you cut out?"

I didn't know if she meant for it to sound so accusing, but it certainly felt that way. Of course I was haunted. There was hardly anything I'd ever done in my life that didn't haunt me. Everyone looked my way, waiting. "I let too much get by, probably," I said. Maybe if they thought I was *bad* at my work, it wouldn't seem so egregious. And it was true: it was difficult to gauge the verboten. In the censorship office, we had to attend not only to letters but to the scripts for plays, to the programs for concerts. We were sent sheet music, and we had to censor songs that were too passionate. We had to flatten everything out, good *and* bad.

"The hero dies eventually," Zinnia said, "and when he does, the page is blank." She was coming to my rescue, leading us toward the book. "This volume we have is only the first twenty-some chapters. There are fifty-some altogether. But this is all that's been translated into English in the nine hundred years since it was written. My mother read it to me when I was a little girl, translating from the Japanese. She had the whole novel, all the chapters, in a series of books printed from woodblock. When she got to Genji's death, to the blank page, she held it out to me, and I don't think I've ever been more moved by a page in a book. Some scholars suspect that the chapter might just be missing, but I don't believe that. I can't. The author knew what that blank page would do when you came across it."

When the young companion of Old Madame Petit read a passage from the book aloud just then, I realized I barely knew her voice at all. She almost never spoke, but now she spoke with great passion, great emotion, about one of the women in the story. "'There,'" she read, "'in an uninviting room, she lives, full of delicacy and sentiment, and fairly skilled in the arts of poetry and music, which she may have acquired by her own exertions alone, unaided . . . surely she deserves our attention . . .'" She looked up at us all. "'Surely she deserves our attention,'" she repeated. She sighed and hugged the book to her chest.

I looked to Zinnia, who would have more to say on the subject of the women in the book—but when she met my eyes, I knew she was up to something else. She was contemplating, considering the tenor and tone of the room. She opened her mouth to speak, but said nothing. A few others made comments, the conversation took a few turns, and finally Zinnia stepped in.

"What did you all make of the spiritual possessions?" she asked. Before all the words were even out of her mouth, I knew this was what she'd been getting at that day she'd talked about being a flower, about the moon being magic, about birds flying and blood flowing. What she really wanted with her recommendation of this book was to stir up ghosts.

And there was indeed something to make of the possessions in *Genji Monogatari*. There were ceremonies of exorcism, the burning of sacred perfume, spirit work. There were footnotes that explained Buddhist doctrine on the souls of the dead.

"There's a word for it," Zinnia continued. "*Shiryō*. A dead person that possesses a living person. And there are whole other words for other kinds of possessions. In Japan, we have this . . . this vocabulary for all the ways the dead live among us. We don't have words in English, not even in French, for all the ways. And words let us in, don't you think? When you don't have words for something, it doesn't mean it doesn't exist. It means it doesn't exist because you don't have words for it."

"Sometimes the characters I play onstage don't leave me willingly," Delphine said.

"So you agree with me," Zinnia said, but I suspected she would say that in response to anything anyone said just then. "There's so much we don't know," she said. "Maybe that's something that will come of this war; maybe we'll learn how to summon the dead. By necessity."

Old Madame Petit said, "There are spiritualists already making a killing off this war."

"Yes, darling, you have to be careful," Delphine told Zinnia. "There are any number of failed actresses who find steady work as clairvoyants."

"Is this about Haze, Zinnia?" I said.

She thought for a moment. "I should have begged him to stay with me," she said. "Why didn't I? I should have insisted he come with me to Tokyo. I could have saved his life."

"You can't let yourself get caught up in all of that," I said.

"The Buddhists say that the souls of the dead wander in an intermediate state," she said, "before their fate is finally decided. If that's so, if there's a way to . . ."

"Opal Havely." It was the gambler who said it.

"Who?" Zinnia said.

"You don't know about her?" he said. "What kind of *Titanic* survivor are you?"

"I've spent years avoiding news of the *Titanic*," she said. We all had, outside of the confines of our little club.

He waved his saké cup in Alice's direction. She went to him with the teapot, and after he'd had a drink, he began his soliloquy: "In my work, you get to know the grifters. There's a gentlemen's agreement among bandits. We're careful not to get in each other's way. We keep track of each other. And that's the real reason I didn't get on the *Titanic*—because there were other crooks booked on it too. The Havelys, in second class: a husband, a wife, and a girl, the daughter, Opal, seventeen or so. The husband and the wife—they were cutthroat. They did the usual—fleecing folks at cards, like I do—but everything they did was a cheat. Now I'm not saying I'm a saint, but I do thieve honestly. My real talent at cards is that I have a keen eye for amateurs. I slip into their ranks and intimidate. Ships are the place for that. Travelers are friendlier when they're all stuck together. And they tend to be carrying all their money on them. So you watch, and you study, and you learn all their habits. You learn their sensibility. But the Havelys—there was no art to it. Their cards were doctored. They rigged their faro box. Their dice had weights in them.

"And they went down with the ship. The mister and missus did, anyway. The girl lived. Her cheat wasn't cards—she'd tell your fortune, or read the bumps on your head or the lines in your palm. Or she'd flutter her eyelashes and flirt with your ghosts. And when the ship sank, she saw her shot. From the very second she survived, she's been dragging up ghosts from the bottom of the sea; some say she was channeling souls while she was even still in the lifeboat. She became a mascot for the rich who lost people on the *Titanic*—a very exclusive parlor game—the *Titanic* survivor as a vessel for your dead. And then along came the war, and she became an industry of her own. She can afford first class herself now."

"You're suggesting Zinnia consult with a swindler?" I said.

"All I'm saying is Opal has convinced a lot of people that she talks with the dead."

"Shouldn't the dead have told her not to get on the boat?" I said.

"Maybe they told her *to* get on the boat," the gambler said. "If she didn't get on the boat, she wouldn't have got rich off it."

We heard a *pop*. Though it wasn't loud, it was sharp and sudden enough that we all jumped. We looked around, and at each other, and we heard yet another *pop*, and we all imagined the worst: it was the shot of a distant rifle, or a bomb gone off a few blocks away, or a low-flying enemy plane backfiring, or the fall of the chandelier in the Paris Opera House, the tumbling over of the Eiffel Tower, Notre-Dame falling into the Seine.

"The candy exploded," said Penny Dreadful's mister, nodding toward the front window. "The temperature drops sharp at nightfall. And you keep it too warm in here."

We walked over to where Zinnia had hung the blown-sugar goldfish. Dangling above were a few pieces of fishing wire with just a little bit of glass candy at the end of each one. A fish and the octopus had shattered. Zinnia looked at me as if this meant something.

Alice squatted down to pick up the shards of sugar from the floor. She popped the tail of the goldfish in her mouth and bit down on it, cracking it apart with her teeth.

45

The *Titanic* spiritualist had told us by telegraph: *I'll be the one with the white fox.*

We wouldn't have been surprised to see her with a fox on a leash, but she was only wearing it, a fox-fur scarf draped over her shoulders, the pelts of *two* foxes, actually, still with both their heads and all their paws. "It's like they curled up on my shoulders and fell asleep," she said.

We already knew something of her extravagance by her demands. Only an hour before she was to arrive at the train station, Alice told us we needed to go meet her. "I was too nervous to tell you all I agreed to," she said. She had coerced Opal to Paris by promising to attend to her demands: a top-notch hotel room, tips included, with a daily budget for Parisian chocolates, Parisian fashion, Parisian cigarettes. *It's my first time in Paris,* Opal wrote Alice. It seemed the list a twelve-year-old girl would make when imagining her life as a fine lady.

And she certainly didn't seem much older than twelve—she couldn't have been more than twenty.

"I made an appeal," Alice told us, "working girl to working girl. But then I ended up saying yes to everything."

We owed Opal Havely for her boat ride from London, and we owed her for her recovery from that ride, a few days at a beachside hotel in Saint-Malo.

But Zinnia would have paid anything. She feared we were missing messages that were everywhere around us.

The only sign of Haze's ghost we could put our finger on: books falling off shelves. But it only happened every now and again, and though we studied each fallen book for something meaningful—*Parasites of North American Butterflies; The Proceedings of the Helminthological Society; Characteristics of Volcanoes*—we could draw no connections. We now spent our evenings in the bookshop, playing our poetry card game, flipping the cards atop the chessboard, listening. The act of the books falling, sometimes plummeting from the upper gallery, and that *thump* of its landing—*that* was what felt ghostly to us. We didn't even go looking for the books anymore. We would hear a book land and exchange a look.

Mr. Penny Dreadful tried to offer a practical explanation: the shop and its shelves, and even the books, were all still warping and buckling from the flood of 1910, from a dampness that would never dry.

I never told Zinnia about the night Haze teased me, when he stumbled through the shop lovestruck after an evening with her. He strolled among the shelves, sometimes walking backward, reaching up here and there to tug at a book's spine, to send it to the floor. I followed after him, scolding him for his childishness, for being careless with my books, shaking my head, falling in love. I would pick up each book and return it to its place.

When Zinnia, Alice, and I reached the Gare de l'Est station, I was doubtful we'd ever be able to find Opal. The station was hectic and packed, overwhelming, full of soldiers on leave, or leaving from their leave, or leaving the war altogether with their injuries, on their crutches, in their wheelchairs. Alongside them was everybody else from eastern France escaping into the safety of the city.

"You found me," Opal said, though we hadn't found her at all—she'd found us, though we'd offered her no descriptions of ourselves; Alice hadn't even mentioned my cane.

"I'm Alice," she said, stepping forward to take the little vanity case Opal was carrying.

"Won't you rummage around in there for one of my cigarettes? I have to get the taste of that train off my tongue."

Alice pulled out a box labeled *Haidee Cigarettes Parfumées*. "I have so many beautiful cigarette cases," Opal told us, her foxes seeming to grimace with her every shift of her shoulders, "but I just love the paper box these come in. It has a little mirror in it," her voice lifting in a girlish lilt, "I can check my lipstick after I've smoked one. And I think they stay perfumed better in their own box. Oh, and, Alice, look for the case with my cigarette holders." When Alice plucked out the case and opened it, Opal selected the longest one. "Opera length," she explained. "My ciggie may be perfumed, but I like to keep the smoke as far from my hair as I can."

And *such* hair it was. "Such hair," Zinnia said, reading my mind.

"Do you like it?" she said, and she twisted a finger up in a curl. "I got it dyed gold on the beach. Henna and peroxide." It was a cloud atop her head, not a single curl drooping below her jaw. The latest styles followed those of the women in factories keen to keep their hair cut short so as not to get strands caught in the gears and pulleys.

She talked and talked as we walked away from the station. Not only had she gotten her hair *revivified*, as she put it, but she'd got her nose riddled with a number of minuscule gems. She scrunched her nose up and down, like sniffing at the air, to make the gems glisten. "My snout got pierced by the wives of the pearl merchants," she said.

Alice and Zinnia leaned in, squinted, studying, wrinkling up their own noses. Opal then pushed at the neck of her dress, pushing it away from her naked shoulder, to show us her skin pink and patterned with the lace she'd been wearing when she got burnt by the sun.

"We'll have to take the Metro, I'm afraid," I told her, clearing my throat, getting everyone's attention. Zinnia had never replaced the limousine after Monsieur Toussaint's death. "Would you like to go to the bookshop first? Seems the most likely place to begin."

"Heavens, no," she said. "I need a hot bath. Do they even have hot baths in Paris? I've heard terrible things about the hotels. I read in a book that I should only stay where the Americans stay. Otherwise, they'll bring up your bathwater in a bucket."

"We'll put you up at Claridge's," Zinnia said. "The rooms have baths. And there's a Turkish steam, too."

I was already skeptical of the clairvoyant. I had planned to suggest the Hôtel d'Alsace, where Oscar Wilde died in the arms of the hotel's landlord on a sofa the scabby brown of spilt wine. After, to help settle the outstanding hotel bill, the landlord sold Wilde's China ink bottle, which I wish I'd been there to buy. But the discussion of the hotel had already carried away from me as we walked along. As Opal talked more and more—and she did talk and talk—our names lost most of their letters: Alice became *Al*, Zinnia *Z*, I was *Y*.

46

After checking Opal into Claridge's, we saw little of her over the next few days. She needed a sense of the city, she insisted—she needed to get lost before she could find her way. "If Haze came up from the streets," she'd said, "I need to stumble down a few alley-ways myself." But she seemed only interested in a Paris that Haze could never afford. The bills and receipts Zinnia received—the paths Opal cut through the city's best restaurants and cabarets— seemed to follow more closely the recommendations in a rich American's handbook.

In the shop, I had two whole shelves labeled *Flimflam and Humbuggery,* and there was no reason to think she wasn't lurk-ing already in one of those chapters.

The censor's office received tickets to all the city's newest enter-tainments, for us to assure all the plots were properly riddled with holes, that all the tunes were sufficiently tone-deaf, that every-thing only distracted and distorted. I gave those to Alice, who took Opal out in the evenings.

"She'd love to see the opera," Alice said.

"What opera are they staging?" I asked.

"Oh, she doesn't care so much about the opera itself, but she doesn't want to leave Paris without sitting in the Palais Garnier and seeing the chandelier. But since it just opened back up, there's not a ticket to be had. Is there anything you can do?"

Not only was Alice looking after Opal, Opal negotiated for Alice too. "In my experience, most workers get a weekly wine allowance," Opal had told her to tell me. "Three bottles a week."

"I can arrange for the wine," Zinnia said when she and I were alone.

"There's no wine to be had," I said. "They need it for the soldiers. We're even supposed to be emptying our own cellars to send to the front."

But we both knew that rations and restrictions were easily violated via the black market.

"And what if they're conspiring?" I said. "Alice and Opal? Alice gets these ideas in her head from all the dime novels she reads. The ghost stories. The tawdry romances."

"You're starting to sound like one of your book-burning preachers," Zinnia told me. "You're finally going to drop that match, aren't you, on the whole works." We were having our Holland gin, just the two of us, at Café Capucine. She twisted up a paper doily into the shape of a ghost in a sheet, then touched its edge to the candle flame, sending up a tall lick of orange fire.

She dropped her ghost into the ashtray, and the flame made one last lick at the air before burning away into a wisp. She then leaned toward the candle to light one of those perfumed cigarettes that Opal smoked. When she breathed out, the scent of fire and rose stirred up all that I felt when I first sat with Opal, an interlacing of disbelief and hope.

"We don't even know if she was on the *Titanic* at all," I said.

"Her name is on the list of survivors," Zinnia said.

My name was on the list of the dead, I didn't say, because what did it matter? "She could have just lifted any name she wanted, any of the names that aren't known."

She gave me that look that said, *I know you better than you know yourself.* "You're worried I'm too gullible," she said. "Because I fell for all those love letters you sent me as Haze." But she reached over to put her hand on mine.

47

Another week went by with nothing ghostly. While Zinnia wouldn't entertain for a moment the possibility of fraud, I could tell it was all taking its toll. She was both disappointed and afraid of that disappointment, afraid of any possibility that Haze's spirit could be stifled by her own doubt.

Opal still wasn't ready to meet us at the shop ("We have to sneak up on it," she said), but she did consent to meet us in the restaurant of her hotel. It was late morning, but it looked like she'd had a long night. She dropped hard into the bench of the banquette, stirring up a gust of perfume she must have poured over her head, something so flowery it made my eyes water.

She'd swapped out her white foxes for a thick fur coat of mouse brown. She shrugged it off halfway and she was still in her night's negligee, it seemed, something slight and pale ("cloudy amethyst," she told Zinnia when she asked), with two satin bows tied at each shoulder. She stretched her legs out from under the table, and though she wore a long skirt, it was unbuttoned along the side, showing off her long, clocked silk stockings and a pair of white buckskin boots, both unbuckled.

She wore yellow-tinted lenses for no reason that I could tell; they seemed to be built for the desert, with little bits of canvas on either side of them, to keep the sand from blowing in your eyes. She was brusque with us but very sweet to the waiter, asking for ice in her coffee and "just a nip of curaçao." She held out to us a map of Paris on onionskin so brittle it seemed it might all fall apart as we unfolded it. "Put *X*'s on the places Haze would go," she said.

Zinnia had brought a portfolio of Haze's photographs of the old shops and cafés. "Many of them are gone," Zinnia explained, "but the photographs will give you a sense of how he saw the city."

"Thanks, Z," she said, and she seemed sincere.

"And there's these," Zinnia said as she took from her pocket a handful of the cinnamon whistles we'd sucked on that night we all kissed. The candy had been off the market since fall—Zinnia had discontinued it the moment she learned of Haze's death. "It's a candy we shared" was all she said of it.

"What's the candy called that changes color when you suck it?" Opal asked Zinnia. "That's one of yours, isn't it?"

"Smickets," she said.

"Smickets! Believe it or not, that was my first cheat. I'd make the kids with money in their pockets buy me a piece, then I'd suck on it and stick out my tongue. Whatever color it was meant something. I told their fortunes that way. One little boy always wanted his fortune told, even though I always predicted he'd be dead in a month."

Cheat, I thought. Was she under the impression we'd hired her to put on a show?

I said, "Wouldn't it make more sense for *the boy* to suck on the candy, to see what color it turned?"

"None of this hinges on *sense*, Y," she said. "And I didn't want to give my candy away." She gave me a wink. "Most people don't have imagination. They believe what you tell them to believe."

I reached over to take Zinnia's hand, to hold it. "Opal," I said, "we might need to clarify a few things—"

Zinnia squeezed my hand tight. She leaned toward me to whisper, *No*. She then said, to both Opal and me, "It's best to respect the mystery of it, isn't it?"

"I don't know that it's a matter of respect," she said. "You have to meet it all eye to eye. Stare it down. In the spirit world, nobody's better than anybody else." She smiled brightly at the waiter when he set down her cup of coffee and glass of curaçao. After he left, as she poured the curaçao into the coffee, she said, without looking at us, "Don't matter how much money you got when it comes to finding the dead."

"Did your fortunes ever come true?" I asked. "When the candy changed colors?"

"That little boy did eventually die," she said. "But not until the war did him in."

A few more days went by, with nothing to report but the receipts that came in.

I stopped into the bookshop. "What do you two talk about on your evenings out?" I asked Alice as she put on her coat to leave.

"She's been everywhere," Alice said. "I've been nowhere."

I decided I'd follow her, even going so far as to kick off my shoe, pull off a sock, and put the shoe back on, while I tied the sock to the end of my walking stick so she wouldn't hear the *tap* of it behind her.

I never quite realized how vital a sock was to walking comfortably in stiff shoes—in cold weather, no less—until Alice led me down street after street without end. But when she ducked into Entrée Interdite, our saloon with the incense lamps and café glorias, I was actually pleased. At least Opal was following the fragile map we'd marked up.

When I approached their sofa, where they sat slumped in silk pillows, Opal seemed entirely unbothered to see me—unsurprised. Alice even seemed pleased. I wondered if she'd noticed me following her. The first thing I did when I sat down at the marble-top table was to remove my sock from the walking stick and return it to my foot. While I was doing so, I noticed Opal was wearing baggy silk pants, gathered at the ankles with little tasseled ropes. "Trousers," I said.

"Lounging pajamas," she said. "But yes, to get a better sense of Haze's stride through the city."

"Is that so?" I said. I then told her, "You know, it's illegal for a woman to wear trousers," thinking back to *Monsieur Vénus*, one of the first books of the book club, "unless you're disguising an infirmity."

"How would a policeman even know if I had an infirmity, unless he undressed me?" She smiled with half her mouth and winked— one wink for me, one for Alice.

"I'm just going to tell you what I've come to tell you," I said, afraid I'd lose my sense of doubt in the face of all her confidence. The scent of the incense—of smoke and moss and ginger—made me sneeze.

"I've not been ticketed yet," she said, moving on along. "And the policemen have been helping me stay lost. I've heard that when you ask for directions in English, they often send you the wrong way on purpose."

"Opal," I said, tucking away my handkerchief, "I want to thank you for taking time to consider our . . . our predicament, if that's what you'd call it . . . but I think we should discontinue this. I think it's hurting Zinnia."

"Hurting her?" Her voice took on the gentle notes of concern and curiosity.

"I'll assure that you're paid," I said, "whatever you feel you're owed."

"Does Z know you're here?" she asked.

I shook my head no. The waiter came along to prepare our usual—three café glorias—as if Opal had been expecting me all along. I wanted to ask how she knew about the drinks, but I didn't want to hear some flight of fancy. It seemed likely there'd been some mention of the drinks somewhere in all the various letters Alice had invaded over the years.

The waiter dropped in the sugar candy, poured the cognac over the back of the spoon, set the whole thing on fire.

After Opal blew out the flame, she said, "You don't believe in me. You don't think I know what I'm doing. Or, worse yet, you think I know very well what I'm doing, but you think I'm fake."

"I'm only asking for some sympathy," I said.

"If I didn't have sympathy for the dead, they wouldn't talk to me at all. Sympathy is my forte."

"Sympathy for the *living*, I mean."

"I know what you mean," she said.

"You haven't even been to the bookshop," I said. I turned to Alice. "Has she?"

Alice just leaned forward to sip at her hot drink.

"I told you," Opal said. "The timing has to be right."

"I think the time *is* right."

"If you know so much about how this should be done, what do you need me for?"

"I just think it's peculiar you haven't been there yet," I said.

Opal looked at me as she clinked the cognac spoon around, stirring her coffee. "You want that shop to have meant everything to him," she said, her voice soft, kind, convincing. Maybe she was hypnotizing me with the rhythm of the spoon in the glass. "And if that's true, and if it did, then I have to be careful. A spiritualist can bring a spirit close or chase it away. It's a delicate balance."

In the silence that fell between us, I realized all I didn't know about the particulars of Opal's own survival.

"Some of us have questioned why," I said, "if you truly do have supernatural connections, you would have gotten on the *Titanic* to begin with."

She flinched at that, and glanced over at Alice, who shook her head with disappointment.

"A word of advice," Opal said to me. "Or, really, some etiquette to follow. If you ever should happen to meet another *Titanic* survivor, don't ask her how her trip went."

I felt a tingling in my cheeks, blushing hot. I swallowed. "I'm sorry," I said. "I'm just very worried about Zinnia. That's all."

Opal leaned forward. She waited for me to look up and meet her eyes. Again, her voice was kind. "I was deathly ill," she said. "I was sicker than a dog. But my mother wouldn't take me to the doctor *before* we boarded the *Titanic*, because if I got *on* sick, we'd be charged for any visit to the ship's doctor. But if you get sick *from* the ship, they'll treat you for free. So we rouged up my cheeks, I leaned on my father, and we climbed on board." She took a drink of the café gloria, then leaned back into the pillows. "But I ended up not even going to the doctor. A few days of sea air in my lungs, and I was good as new. My father even splurged on renting me a lounge chair, so I could recline on deck."

She nodded in Alice's direction, and Alice stooped over to pull a box of cigarettes from her bag. Alice put three of them between her own lips, lighting them all at once, one for each of us. "Yorick, I'm in business the same as you," Opal said. She paused, looked off in thought, forming her question. "If your shop was on fire, and you could save one book, which one would it be? What book is most valuable?"

"There's a difference between a book I value and one that's valuable," I said.

I thought of my volume of Rimbaud's poetry, the one I used as my diary of my days with Haze, composing all my lovelorn notes in the margins. And I thought of the memoirs of the great actor Ira Aldridge, with Leopold's signature on the inside cover. *Those* I would absolutely pluck from the fire first, but I wouldn't get much money for either of them.

"The book that would cost the most," she said.

"My copy of *Il Divortio celeste* is quite rare," I said, smoking the perfumed cigarette Alice handed me. "*The Celestial Divorce*. Almost three hundred years old. Zinnia once asked me if a book could kill its author, and I think you could say this one did. It's just a small thing—it would fit in your palm, you could hide it in your pocket. Booksellers could only sell it secretly. But it was a satire of the church so blasphemous, it led to the papal authorities beheading the author."

Since becoming a censor, I read every book I could find on the subject of censorship. The cartoonists in the satirical French press called the censors "Anastasie," named for a pope.

Just this discussion of books—even the death of this author—made me feel more alive than I had in some time. And I couldn't keep from tossing glances back at the booth where I'd first sat with Haze and Zinnia.

More than anything, I wanted to be out of the censor's office and back in my shop where I belonged, among all those ghosts of authors, among all the flimflam and blasphemy. I wanted my own soul back.

"Let's say someone wants to buy your *Il Divortio celeste*," Opal said. "They're willing to pay the price you've put on it. Does it matter to you if the book is actually worth to them the price they paid?"

"That's not the same," I said, sensing she meant for me to align my bookselling with her hotel bills.

"And if they buy a book from you, any book, and they read the whole thing, and it doesn't move them at all, do you give them their money back? Or if the book troubles them, or gives them nightmares, or breaks their heart? Don't pretend your own livelihood doesn't hinge on emotion."

Alice finally spoke up. She said to Opal, "What would you do, though? Let's say you *were* corrupt. How would you convince us?"

Opal looked up and off again, but I had a feeling she'd given this some thought already. "Y, here, would write a letter," she said. "Like he did before . . . he would write a letter to Zinnia, as Haze."

Of course Alice had told her all about the letters I wrote.

"There's a spy book in the shop," Alice said, "with a recipe for invisible ink. The words show up with lemon juice, I think."

"Yes, a blank page," Opal said, "suddenly covered in words.

Actually, I can picture the whole haunting, all words and books. Words suddenly crawling across my tongue. Or in the whites of my eyes."

I felt that tingling of a blush again, something akin to desire, and it was dangerous to let it lead me, I knew. I loved the idea of it. I lusted after it. I wanted to write as Haze again. I could even feel his words rolling across my own tongue. I could feel his deep voice rumbling in my throat.

But Opal put an end to it. "*That* would be the cruel thing, Yorick," she said. "Nothing I could do to Zinnia would be worse than that."

"I'm not the one who suggested it," I said, sheepish, but I was already curious about what book Haze would send from the grave.

Opal said, "To be honest, Y, maybe I *should* leave. Maybe that's best. Because I might never reach Haze. Not the way things are."

"I don't know what you mean."

"You're both holding back on me, you and Z. You're not telling me everything."

"What is it you think I'm not telling?"

"There's a secret diary, for one thing," she said.

"That's a pretty safe speculation, isn't it?" I said. "If you were looking to dupe someone into believing you. You can probably always count on someone having a diary stashed someplace."

"The diary is yours. You wrote about Haze in it. You were in love with him."

I glanced at Alice, who glanced away. Had she read it? Or had Opal read my mind about my book of Rimbaud's poetry?

"No, *Zinnia* was in love with him," I said. "That's what you're sensing."

"Zinnia's in love with you, though."

"No."

Opal sighed and shook her head. She then lifted her foot so that she could hook her ankle around my walking stick, which I'd leaned against the table. She pulled it toward her and picked it up. She tapped the end of it at my chest, poking at me, until I grabbed it and held on to it until she let go.

"This isn't fun for me anymore, Yorick," she said. "Haze *might* show up at some point, under different circumstances. But he doesn't want to wallow in your grief. So I'll leave, like you want me to. And if you ever suddenly become honest with yourself, you can write me, and maybe I'll come back."

This was what I'd wanted, to convince Opal to leave, but it seemed to be happening so quickly, I suddenly regretted it. I tried to object, to think of something to say, to take it all back. Zinnia would be furious with me.

I heard that hiss of Haze's. Alice had dropped her cigarette in her café gloria. When I looked over, she was scowling at me. "The least you can do is take her to the Palais Garnier before she leaves Paris," Alice said, pouting. "The opera is all she's talked about."

"Yes," Opal said softly, almost soothingly. "You can at least do that. I've been dying to go there ever since I read *The Phantom of the Opera*." She gave me a wink.

48

We didn't even know what the opera was when we went. And the program, mostly advertisements for perfume, told us little more than the title and cast—*Castor et Pollux,* "by Rameau, the first great French composer," Delphine said, holding out her glass for me to pour her more champagne.

Zinnia and Opal sat on the other side of Delphine and me.

I didn't tell Zinnia that Opal was leaving, and I begged Opal not to say anything either. Delphine had made the night's arrangements, using her theater connections to reserve the box that hovered just above the orchestra pit. We all sat in that fateful balcony where Zinnia had sat with Haze, that night I watched them through opera glasses.

"Opal's story would make a great piece of theater," Delphine said to me, her voice lowered. "I'd like to introduce her to a playwright I know. I've been looking for just such a character."

"She was only eighteen when she was on the *Titanic,*" I said.

"I can play eighteen," she said, defending her own honor. "I've played *eleven,* for god's sake." I was actually glad she was seeing herself as ageless again. Delphine then turned her attention to Opal and Zinnia. "This is the last opera Marie Antoinette saw before being dragged off to prison by revolutionaries," she said, with a patriotic upswing—but I wasn't sure whose side she was on. "They won't do Wagner here anymore, no Mozart, no Bach, no Beethoven, nothing with a note of German to it. Perhaps they never will again."

Zinnia and I had decided early on to keep Opal all to ourselves; we didn't want to introduce her to the Titanic Survivors Book Club. But the opera house had only just opened back up, having shut down at the start of the war, and it took Delphine some doing to get the exact balcony we needed—every seat in the house was sold out. I told Zinnia that Opal insisted on the balcony, that she was certain she could find Haze even just by keeping her eyes on us. *We need to surround ourselves with the lights and shadows of the nights you've lost,* Opal said, politely playing along.

Opal would see, if she looked, echoes of that long-lost night. I saw Zinnia arch her neck as she had when Haze kissed her there, kissed her throat, the line of her jaw, the lobe of her ear. It all came back to me as it came back to her. I could see her with Haze as vividly as if magnified by my binoculars.

But Opal didn't see any of it. All her attention was cast out and down into the crowd. I half suspected she was simply looking to see if anyone was looking back at her, to catch the eye of those who noticed her so high up. She wore a satin gown of pastel pink, or *cerise vapeur* as she called it, cherry mist, and in the balcony lamps it looked as oil-slick as a wet cat.

It seemed that Haze's ghost might be everywhere she wasn't looking, even in the opera itself. I'd read some mythology over the years, but not much, so I was startled to learn that *Castor et Pollux* was not only about brothers, and not only about a triangle, and unrequited love, but also about war, about death.

"*Twin* brothers," Delphine explained, "one mortal, one immortal, are in love with the same woman. The mortal brother—the one the woman loves the most—dies in battle. The immortal brother goes to the Underworld to take his brother's place among the dead, but the mortal brother won't allow the sacrifice."

Opal and Zinnia paid no notice, leaning into each other, their voices low and lilting, like they were mumbling gossip. Zinnia examined Opal's many necklaces, entangling her fingers in all the strings of gold and silver.

Even just the plot was enough to put a catch in my throat, but when Castor died, Télaïre, his love, sang an aria so anguished I cried my eyes out. *Et je renonce à ta lumière,* she sang at the end of it. *And I renounce the light.* I renounce the light. *Lumière,* such a finer word than *light* for all that light can be. I brought the crook of my arm to my face, to press my wet cheeks into my coat sleeve.

I wasn't alone. When the curtain dropped, it seemed like all of Paris was there to weep together, to mourn and applaud, and we didn't give it a thought—we didn't just stand from our seats, we were lifted, and our ovation thundered, rising up to rattle the crystals of the chandelier.

It was so loud, so spirited, I didn't at first notice all the collapse around me. My eyes were on the stage, on the opera singers taking their bows, tapping their toes at the roses tossed at their feet. But then I heard Opal's wails for what they were. When I looked to my side, she was cowering and moaning, keening, really, and Zinnia had her arms around her, trying to keep her from falling to the floor. I stepped over to help, lowering myself to her side as she slipped down farther and farther, until she was on her knees, her head in her hands. This was not a fake conniption—this was real terror, real tears. She would not be consoled.

49

None of us said a word until we were at Café Capucine an hour or so later—just Zinnia, Opal, and me, after putting a bewildered Delphine in a taxi. "Cinzano and water," Opal told the waiter.

"L'eau plate ou l'eau gazeuse?" he said.

She sighed and looked to me.

"Still or charged," I translated.

"Absolutely still," she said. "If I see one bubble pop, I'm falling down dizzy."

Some rain fell, but lightly, and the café had opened its umbrellas and unrolled its awning. We bundled up in our coats, and they brought us blankets for our laps. The waiter had lit a few braziers, filling the air with the fumes of charcoal.

"Sometimes music snakes its way into your soul in unexpected ways," Zinnia said.

"It wasn't the music that did me in," Opal said.

She said nothing more, so I prodded. "Is it Haze? Did you find him?" If her collapse was because she sensed she should get theatrical about her grave-rattling, for Zinnia's sake, I needed to play along.

She looked at me puzzled, perhaps exasperated, as if I was being frivolous. She said nothing more until after the waiter had brought us our drinks and she'd had a sip of the Cinzano.

"It was the sound of the crowd," she said.

"The architect of the opera house wrote a book about it," I said, and when I said the word *book,* I could swear Zinnia rolled her eyes ever so slightly. I continued, but half under my breath: "He said that acoustics are a bizarre science."

"And it does get noisy at the end of a thing," Zinnia said. "The French have a long history of professional applauders. They're hired by the theaters, and they know exactly where to sit to make the most racket. You can hire people to clap, to laugh at jokes, to weep at endings."

"Professional weepers," Opal said with a mirthless laugh.

"*Les pleureuses,*" Zinnia said. "You can hire them for funeral processions too."

I wondered if we'd soon be suppressing the tears and laughter of these professionals. As censors, we were supposed to be troubled by the crowds and their emotions. Our goal was to stifle passion.

Opal put her elbow on the table, her chin on her hand, and looked away, down the street. "I have been to the theater . . . since. To symphonies and plays. But . . . I didn't think I'd ever hear anything like it again." She took another drink. "They were all crying out as they died," she said. "We'd paddled our lifeboat away, for what seemed like miles into the night, but we could hear them, all those voices. Those cries weren't cries for help. They knew they wouldn't be saved. They were crying because they knew there would be only cold and darkness until their lives faded away to nothing. And we were crying too. For them, for ourselves. If the *Titanic* could sink, what chance did our little lifeboat have?"

In that little boat, they were in between, entirely untethered, still alive but not yet survivors. I'd never experienced anything like it, no matter how you looked at my time with the *Titanic*. Opal could only sit and wait for whatever was inevitable.

"I'm so sorry, Opal," I said.

"I can't imagine what it must have been like," Zinnia said, but I could tell she *wanted* to imagine it. She wanted Opal to tell her everything.

"I was in and out of trouble growing up," Opal said. "Sometimes something awful would happen, or maybe I'd go someplace I shouldn't, and I'd think, 'Ah, this is how I'm going to die.' And then when I didn't, I was immortal all over again." She took out her box of perfumed cigarettes and checked her eyes in the mirror, touching a fingertip to her lashes. "But that night in the ocean . . . it got in my bones. Yes, I survived, but there's this sense that it did a kind of damage." She tapped a finger against her temple. "Not just in my head, but in my body. My blood. That night is in me like a sickness. It will do me in eventually." We were quiet together. We each of us smoked one of Opal's cigarettes.

"There was a sheet of glass to keep the wind off you," Opal said. I was still picturing the lifeboat, so I had to shift, putting her back on the deck of the *Titanic*. "On the first day I was so feverish that I was delusional. It didn't seem like I was behind glass; the ocean was. And now when I think about everything before the *Titanic*, my whole life before the ship sank, it's all behind that glass. Or encased in ice, really, clouded over with frost. All my memories. Befogged."

Opal reached past our cocktails to take Zinnia's hand.

"Why do you need this, Z?" Opal asked. "What do you need me for?"

"I can't sleep."

"Nobody can," she said. "I can give you something to sleep, if that's all this is."

"That's not all it is," she admitted.

"If we're going to continue with this," Opal said, "there are a few things you need to know. I don't much go in for the show of it. The levitating table. The flickering lights. That's all theater. I'd make more money doing it that way, for sure; I could do ten séances a day. There are that many ghosts in a city like this, every street full of windows with lights on, and for every light, there's a whole life you can't possibly fathom. But I . . . *I* counsel the grief-stricken."

"Yes," Zinnia said. "That's what I want."

"Then you have to be honest. With me. With each other. If you have any hesitance to reveal something, then that's an indication that you absolutely must tell me about it."

Zinnia brought her fingers to her locket. She looked down at the table as she spoke. "I'm afraid that Haze knew . . ." she said. She stopped. We waited. "That I wanted him to be more than he was."

"How did he disappoint you?"

Zinnia looked up, surprised. "Disappoint?" she said. "*I'm* the disappointment. I wish he knew how much I needed him. But even I didn't realize it myself. Until he left. Is that *why* he left? Because I didn't love him enough?"

When Opal said, "You'll never know," and shot back the rest of her drink, I was miffed with her again. Wasn't Zinnia paying her a mint for answers to these questions? *You'll never know.* That was nothing more than we ever knew.

"I just . . . I think he always thought I could only love Yorick," Zinnia said. "But I did love them both."

"Z," Opal said, shaking her head, "if you forgive yourself, you're not denying Haze anything. You can let it all go, everything, everything in your past, and it won't hurt a soul. You're not saving anyone by punishing yourself."

She then turned her attention to me. "And what did *you* want from Haze?"

"Want?" I said. "Well, he was my friend." This was somehow the truth, but completely dishonest at the same time. And then I felt a tap at my ankle, like how Haze's jittery foot would forever knock into my leg. I didn't dare tell them what I truly wanted. If Haze was a ghost, I wanted him to haunt me with regret. I wanted him to wish he had loved me more.

50

Though I'd been in the same cramped office since the beginning of the war, among the same four censors, we kept getting transferred, in theory, to serve under different authorities. We'd begun under the eye of the Ministry of War, and for a while we belonged to the Mayor of Paris, who moved us among three different units, until we'd most recently landed with the Prefect of Police. And within the prefect, we'd been assigned to an ever-shifting glut of special commissions. All the while, I sat at the same desk, with the same drawers too warped to open.

Our expertise was also always being bureaucratized. I started as a censor of foreign correspondents filing stories with the American press, and then I was attending to personal letters sent to and from the front, and next I was scrutinizing the French newspapers and magazines. My favorite responsibility was a satirical weekly that would entangle its rumor and sedition in word puzzles designed to thwart censorship. It might take me hours to unlock all its riddles, which spared me from cutting into other things. It was a merciful waste of time.

Despite all our days together, I didn't get to know the other censors. We'd developed a complicated relationship to communication. But the one who sat across from me I grew to like for the way he seemed to wear his reticence. There was something about the way he read—the slant of a shoulder, his fussing with his spectacles (pushing them down the bridge of his nose or up onto his forehead), the chewing on the end of his pencil.

But it was that pencil that did him in, I suspected. He seemed to be growing sluggish, leaning against the wall as he read or even dropping his head to his desk to rest a minute. He was losing weight, growing slighter and slighter until he shrunk away to nothing. His desk was empty for a few days, and then we all received an addendum to the censorship instruction booklet, which was hardly a booklet at all, as it had grown to hundreds of pages of microscopic print. *On Aniline Pencils,* was the title of the new chapter. All us censors used them, for the ink was indelible. When we obliterated paragraphs on the page, those words were irretrievably lost. But the tips of the pencils needed frequent wetting, and those who tapped it at the tips of their tongues were making themselves sick. Censors sometimes got the stuff in their ears too, or up their noses, or a fleck of lead in their eyes, sending into the whites of them a splatter of blue wash, like the rose on a Delft teacup.

The day after our night at the opera with Opal, my quiet censor was replaced with a boisterous one, a man who seemed not to understand the vow of silence we'd all taken wordlessly. He talked and talked to us despite our not talking back. He did manage to eke out a little information from us on his first day there, and once he discovered I was a bookseller, he became even more animated. This censor, unfortunately, had ambitions. "You're just the man I need to make this work," he told me. "I've been wanting to form a committee. A special commission . . . a way for us censors to take some authority of our own. I don't think it's enough to censor the books being published now—they *all* need revision, even the ones a hundred years old. We need special lists of condemnation. We need an army of librarians and professors of literature and booksellers such as yourself, people with some say in the world, professionals with a keen intuition into the psychic influence of profligate material."

"Profligate?"

"Yes!" he said, as if he hadn't first said the word himself.

"Exactly. Writers lead you along, dressing everything up in story and extravagance, slipping in *ideas* when you think all you're doing is reading a poem about a lilac bush."

"Lilac," I said. "A sinister metaphor." I slid the new chapter for the instruction booklet across my desk to his. It listed the censoring pencils' ingredients, which seemed to give all its colors a touch of poison: crystal violet, lampblack, malachite green, Victoria blue. "The censor who sat there before you got very sick," I said, returning to my work.

I went to Zinnia's that night preoccupied by the new censor's scheme. It seemed somehow inevitable, this notion that we'd eventually spill all our venomous ink over every page ever written. One of the books in my own forbidden library, now rotting at the bottom of the Atlantic, a prerevolutionary French novel set in the year 2440, included a group of librarians whose job it was to destroy all the books that didn't fit in one little room.

I was exhausted, and the last thing I wanted to think about was Opal. So when Zinnia called out from the kitchen that I'd just missed her, I was relieved. But that relief was short-lived when I saw the condition of the dining room table. Across the top of it were letters so full of holes they looked like lacework.

"What do you think?" Zinnia said, stepping in, hair shorn shorter even than Opal's, just a mere inch or two longer than what could be considered "boyish."

"What . . . what happened?" I said, dropping into a chair at the table.

She hesitantly brought her hand to the top of her head. "I kind of like it," she said.

"I just mean . . . why did you do it?"

"Some of my hair got into the hot sugar," she said. "Opal cut the sugar out for me, and then said she could fix it. And I just let her keep cutting away." She brought her other hand to the top of her head. "It's not so bad, is it?"

"No, no," I said. "I'm sorry, Zinnia. It's been a long day."

"Opal says that you work in the censorship office to punish your-self for something," she said with a spark of enthusiasm, sitting in the chair beside me. "And I think she might be right."

"Opal says that, does she?" I muttered. "What is it I'm-punishing myself for?"

"That's my question too. Opal says you shouldn't go in any-more, and I agree. I'll find a doctor to write you a note. You're going blind, we'll say. From years of reading."

"It's probably not so far from the truth," I said. *Opal says . . .* How many times was I going to hear that before Opal finally stopped saying things? I gestured toward the letters across the table. "Is all this to taunt me?"

I knew without her telling me that these were the letters Haze had sent her from the front. All of them had been cut up by censors to a perverse degree. I knew there'd been no reason for so much to be scissored out—it seemed unlikely he was sending Zinnia anything that could be useful to the enemy. I wondered if it was jealousy that provoked the censor, if it was reading about the love affair that made him want to erase it all.

"Opal asked to see them," she said. "She wanted to . . . *intuit* something from them. She likes to work by candlelight. And as I held up the paper and the light shone through all the holes in it, the shadows flickered, they moved, fluttering, and I felt he was . . . speaking to me, in a way."

Opal had then gotten a pen from the drawer. Zinnia held the letter and Opal wrote, following the lines of the cursive, tracing the letters onto the tablecloth.

Zinnia now tapped her finger against the words written there, which I hadn't yet noticed.

"That's something he said to me once," Zinnia said. "I'd asked him about his photographs. I asked him how he could take a building that I thought I knew, that I'd passed several times, and make it look unlike it ever looked before. He said it wasn't any-thing *he* did." She tapped her finger again on the cloth: *The light bends for me. The shadows fall just so.* "Paris posed for him," she said.

I lifted the letter slightly. The shadows it cast were as pale and faint as dust. I wanted to tell Zinnia that this was exactly what Opal herself said would be the best method of fraud. I'd practically put the idea of it in her head when I confronted her that evening over café glorias.

"Yorick," she said, "Opal is helping. I think she's brought him close. I don't want to beg you to believe me. But I do want you to believe that *I* believe. I don't want you to think I'm lying to you."

I lifted her hand and kissed the back of it. I asked if we could have some gin and play our card game of the hundred poets. I was already nostalgic for our nights before we knew the difference between the beginnings and the endings.

51

Whether it was Zinnia's suggestion that I feign blindness or that all those nights reading by dim light had finally taken their toll, I felt my vision clouding every midafternoon, the words on the page beginning to fade to a blur before I could take my ink to them. Opal and Zinnia spent every hour together, even late into the night, so I moved back to my bookshop, returning to my own bed after every long day of shoving everyone's words back into their mouths. Alice felt left out too, after having had Opal all to herself, so the two of us would sit at Café Capucine and share a bottle of wine, a burgundy so dark it was as black as an iris.

Zinnia described her time with Opal as a kind of hallucination—which made sense, as she hadn't eaten much, or so she said. It was a tradition with a Japanese word of its own, one we learned from a footnote in *Genji Monogatari:* it was the fasting that followed a supernatural occurrence.

"They're not completely starved," Alice told me. Alice and I sat close enough to the bookshop that the light from its windows fell across the tabletop. "They spend all their time in Zinnia's kitchen, tasting all those cakes and cookies she makes. Opal brought me a pretty white biscuit that looked like a bar of soap and tasted like paper that's been pressed together wet."

"You're used to all the creams and custards of French desserts," I said.

"Oh, am I?" she said, looking askance. "I seem like a girl who's been spoiled by fine French pastry, do I?"

Zinnia did stop by my office once to take me out for a stroll. Even a leafless tree took on life when she pointed out the flock of blackbirds and the fluttering of their wings, how they made the sunlight glisten through the branches like a string of lights.

"You have to eat something," I said. With Zinnia at my side, every chill breeze brought the warm scent of roasting chestnuts and pipe tobacco.

"I boiled red beans in sugar water," she said, "and I could see Haze's spirit in the steam of it. Opal doesn't summon ghosts . . . she helps us find where they are."

"I'm happy you've found some peace." *Peace.* Some of the strangest rules in my censorship instruction booklet involved peace and the erasure of it. We weren't to allow any discussion of it in the newspaper editorials or to even permit the very word itself. The authorities feared that a pursuit of peace would lose the war.

"It's not been about finding peace," she said. "It's about a way of seeing the world. That's what I've learned from Opal. Our lives don't have to be shaped by the inhumanity around us. We don't have to lose our own souls to the soulless. Survival can be a way of seeing. 'All looks yellow to the jaundiced eye.' Isn't that Shakespeare?"

"Alexander Pope," I said.

"Are you sure?"

"'All seems infected that the infected spy / As all looks yellow to the jaundiced eye.'"

"That brain of yours," she said. "It's like an apothecary cabinet . . . all those little drawers." I thought of my desk in the office, all its drawers stuck closed. My whole life was that lopsided swivel chair, the windows that wouldn't open a crack, pencils of a deadly violet.

"And that's what I've always loved about you," she said. "You've given yourself over entirely to your books."

"I'm afraid that's so," I said. We walked for a bit without another word, the melancholy of it all seeping its tint of blue over the afternoon. But then she said, "I just mean: the life you have is the life you pictured for yourself."

"The life I *had*, I suppose," I said.

"On the first day I visited the shop, you talked about synchronicity. You saw coincidence as a kind of harmony. Do you remember that?"

"I don't know that I do," I said.

"I knew I'd never forget it."

I didn't quite remember what I might have said about synchronicity, but I remembered her standing there in my shop. I'd been nearly giddy from the attention of such an elegant woman, so it was likely I tried to stitch together some theory that would bind us. I wanted our meeting that day to be another example of our uncanny luck. Fate had plucked us all from the *Titanic* and tossed us into each other's arms.

It hadn't been so long since the club met to discuss *Genji Monogatari*—perhaps only a few weeks—but it seemed months and months had passed. No sooner had the gambler evoked Opal's name than she appeared in our midst, and no sooner had she appeared in our midst than she'd begun dragging her feet. We were waiting, in vain, for any spark of coincidence, synchronicity, harmony, for even the slightest hint of a haunting. It seemed the only magical spell Opal had cast had lengthened our days, filling them with Haze's absence.

I wondered if I'd even been cruel in leaving the club out of Opal's visit. I'd told Zinnia I was protecting her from their scrutiny, that I wanted to keep them from troubling Haze's spirit. But I knew my reasons had more to do with my own sadness. When we'd all last met, and they'd riddled me with questions about the censor's office, I took it all to heart. I'd felt like a bureaucrat or, worse yet, one of the very engineers of war.

Haze had died on the fields of battle, fighting to tell the true stories of the soldiers, while I sat in an office touching a match to the love letters of the soldiers' sweethearts.

But whatever they might have thought about my efforts, I missed the misfits of my club. And I missed Haze especially, and I hated more than anything not seeing him among us. He would sit there drinking it all in, every word, getting to know all about us by the way we gossiped about the loves and losses of fictional people. There had been times when weeks and weeks had gone by without the club meeting, but I always knew eventually we'd be back in my shop to entangle with the imaginary. We were a family more constant than the families we'd been saddled with.

Before Zinnia and I parted ways at the edge of the park, we kissed goodbye and she said, "Opal is finally ready to see the bookshop." I wanted to hold on to her, to beg her to keep Opal away from me. It was too dark, this necromancy. I wasn't afraid of Haze's ghost; I was afraid I'd see no ghosts at all.

52

After leaving Zinnia, I went to the nearest barber for a haircut and shave. I also bought new shoes and a necktie that was so thin it barely had room for the one stripe down the middle of it. Its skinniness seemed fashionable to me.

I sent Alice home, locked the door, and went to the cellar for a bath. I slapped on some citronella oil—I'd never smelled it on Haze myself, but Zinnia had mentioned it in one of the letters she sent him, about the scent of it on his wrist.

I brought out a bottle of old cognac, Renault, one I'd stolen from Haze's collection before he had his trunks carried away. I never really knew what I was saving it for, but it seemed it might very well be this. I set it on the table in front of the divan, and two glasses.

I also brought out my book of poetry with my notes about Haze in the margins. I'd read and reread those notes so many times, they were beginning to lose their magic, fading away into the pulp. I wished I'd written more things down. I wish I'd written everything, everything he said, everything I noticed about him. I halfway hoped Opal would pretend to be possessed. I wanted her to roll her eyes back, to write in all the empty margins of the book, to fill it with words, or even just scribbles, just nonsense. I would find a way to interpret.

I didn't really expect Haze to arrive, but I liked getting ready to see him. I kept returning to the shop's one mirror to adjust my necktie's knot, trying for the right combination of dashing and devil-may-care. I was so intent on it, I felt my heart nearly stop when Opal rapped at the glass of the front door.

She stepped into the shop and out of her coat, looking up and up. "How do you know if you want a book at the very top of the shelves? They're all stuffed in everywhere, all the way to the ceiling."

I shook the basket at the front door, rattling my collection of opera glasses and binoculars. She turned to face me, and I saw she'd brought a book of her own, one held tight to her chest. I hoped it wasn't some collection of spells and witchcraft we'd have to consult.

"I'm sure you're wondering why it has taken me so long to get here," she said very gently.

"You said it might be overwhelming."

"Objects act like anchors," she said. "They hold on to the souls that left them behind. A wedding ring. A wristwatch. A china poodle, even. But books especially. Every book you fall in love with keeps a little piece of you. This shop is noisy with voices."

"Is it?" I said. I hoped she could hear the skepticism. I was suddenly ready for the night to be over. *Just disappoint me and go,* I wanted to say.

"I do all this by candlelight," she said as she walked toward the front window.

"So I've heard," I said. I lit a candle, and it caught a draft, its flicker and rasp like the papery rattle of a desert snake. I still had a puddle of wax in my desk drawer, from the candle we spent, Haze and me, on the night we were naked on the bookshop floor. He had promised me he'd stay until the candle burnt down and the flame flickered out, and he did.

"Tommy," Opal said.

"What?"

"The man you're pretending to be. His name was Tommy." She tapped her finger on the glass, where *Library Steward of the Titanic* was etched in.

"Thomas Kelland," I said.

"Did you know him?" By the way she said it, she seemed to hope I had.

"I did not," I said. I only knew his name because it had replaced mine on the lists of the dead. "Did *you* know him?"

"I spent some time in the library," she said.

"Reading?" I said.

She shrugged and shook her head. She sat on the windowsill and leaned back against the glass. "They played cards in there. And games. Gambled. On these ships, the library stewards often manage some of the betting pools, so . . ." She shrugged again. "If you're a family of cheats, you get friendly with someone like that."

"What was he like?"

"Younger than you," she said. "Probably even younger than I am now." She put her fingers to the window again, to trace the *T* of *Titanic*. "Zinnia told me your leg was broken to pieces."

"Oh?" I said.

"A shipwreck onstage," she said. "You got caught up in some rigging and pulled onto a track."

I nodded. I'd never told Zinnia the particulars of the accident. She could only have known if Haze had told her. This didn't feel like disloyalty; it felt like love. They did think of me after all, when they were alone.

"I imagine that must have had a devastation of its own," she said. "Such terrible pain. Something like that would distort your sense of the world."

"Yes."

She held out her book to me.

"What is it?" I asked, but then I recognized it before I even lifted the cover to see the rubber stamp of the White Star Line, with a space for the name of the steward. And there was my signature.

"When I went to the library," she said, "Tommy asked me what my interests were, and I told him I summon ghosts. I think he thought it was cute that such a sweet thing would say something so dreadful. He loaned me that very book, which has two stories in it, and one of them has ghosts." *The Two Magics* by Henry James, with *The Turn of the Screw*—the cloth of the cover was a lovely shade of midnight blue, and there was an indentation of lanky irises, their stems and leaves a series of curves and squiggles.

I'd added it to my library of forbidden books on the basis of a small-town schoolteacher who'd sought to have it blacklisted. It dabbled in the occult, she said.

I was holding in my hands the only book likely to have been carried to shore from the wreck. I'd heard of no Bibles, no prayer books, no pocket-sized volumes of poetry brought onto the life-boats by survivors. Had there even been a diary? A sentimental collection of love sonnets, bound in red velvet?

"When he loaned me the book," Opal said, "he said to be sure to return it, because any books that aren't returned, the library steward has to pay for himself. Is that true?"

"It is," I said, though the books I'd snuck on board were my own contraband. No one, not even me, had a complete list of all the books I'd carried on.

"I guess that's why I still have it," she said. "It was one of the things I took with me into the lifeboat. Isn't that strange? I some-how thought I shouldn't lose it; I worried he'd have to pay."

I held it out to her, but she told me to keep it.

"It belongs to you," she said.

"But it's worth far more as yours than it was when it was mine. It has a story all its own now. There's an underground market for these things, you know." Even the ship's lifeboats were torn apart in the New York Harbor by thieves in the night, to be sold in pieces, plank by plank.

"I kept it so I could give it back to Tommy," she said. "Giving it to you . . . that's the closest I can get to that."

I smiled at her. I thanked her. I opened the cover and looked again at my own handwriting, that of someone familiar, but gone. A man I'd lost at sea.

53

On Opal's last evening in Paris, an enemy zeppelin was spotted above the clouds. The streetlights of the city were doused, and everyone was told, by the sirens that sounded, to hide in their houses under the cover of darkness. We would steal the city right out from under them.

We sat in Zinnia's garden—Zinnia, Opal, Alice, and me—drinking teacups of something Opal fixed, a hot flannel, heated-up gin and beer with sugar and nutmeg, yet another adaptation of the dog's nose cocktail.

We looked at the sky, at the searchlights seeking dirigibles, the flash and flare darting through the clouds like a shudder of lightning.

As we drank more of the hot flannel, the light fell from the sky and I could see stars here and there. I didn't know any astronomy, but since seeing *Castor et Pollux* at the opera, I'd been reading up on the twins and I now knew they were the bright stars of Gemini, the sign of the zodiac that Haze and I were born under in June. The sailors navigated by them, calling their bright lights Saint Elmo's fire.

Everything, even the sky, was always leading me back to Haze and his absence.

"I feel like if we don't act quickly enough, we'll lose him," Zinnia said quietly.

"You have to lose him," Opal said, her voice hushed, too. "There's not another option. I'm here to help you let him go, not to keep him here."

This seemed to surprise Zinnia, despite all the hours the two of them had been spending together. "But what if we tried?" she said.

"You can't, Z. That would be cruel. To leave him in a place without senses. Imagine what that would be like. To kiss someone and not feel it. To reach out to someone and not feel the touch of their skin. You do know what it's like to have longing that won't stop, to be mesmerized by it. Imagine that, but imagine it more painful, physically painful, tearing you apart. If you ever loved Haze, you have to let him go. You have to take comfort in the fact that he came here, to be with you, to get your help."

Not only did Opal not do goodbyes, she said she never kept in touch either. "But I'll think of you fondly," she insisted. Despite my skepticism, I wanted her to stay. I'd fallen into a pattern of doubt that I found that I needed.

In the morning, I went looking for news of the zeppelin—we'd only heard about it from Alice, who had heard about it in the street on her way to Zinnia's. But what I found at the newsstand was what I'd expected: where a dirigible might be was only blank space, the censors having pulled the type and the pictures from the print run. To get a sense of the progress of the war, you had to go to the city streets, the kiosks, to deduce things by the posters, the decrees, the transcripts. There were announcements about vehicles, fundraisers, the requisition of pigeons, the restrictions on the sale of absinthe. We always went looking for all the postings to be gone, hoping for it, really, to see the columns stripped bare of all warnings and edicts. Only then might we go on with our lives.

54

I heard tales of a counterfeit Paris to be built in the countryside, as a decoy, an effort to trick the Germans should they bomb from above. Instead of setting the city ablaze, they'd only destroy a stage set. I imagined a canvas backdrop painted with picturesque scenes, and a stagehand turning a crank, unrolling the seasons: skaters on the frozen ponds of the Bois de Boulogne, the peonies of the Luxembourg Gardens, me with Zinnia and Haze collapsed in the heat of summer in the wicker chairs of the café, consoling ourselves with chips of ice in our gin.

The chatty censor who sat across from me had an actual map of this mirage, which was to have avenues strung with streetlights, and train stations, and wooden boxcars.

After I left the office, I headed home in a roundabout way and, my eyes worn out, Paris flattened before me, its walls turning to plywood propped up on stilts. The birds in the trees were folded from paper, all trilling out tinny tunes from the wound-up music boxes in their beaks of gold foil. Even the people I passed had the glassy eyes of mannequins.

And as I wandered farther away, I found myself closer to Zinnia's house than I was to the shop.

The house was empty when I walked in, but she'd left some confections on the table, atop a lazy susan of black lacquer. It had been a week since Opal had left, and though I saw Zinnia every day, she spent most of her hours in her kitchen. I knew she was intent on going against Opal's advice, hoping to draw Haze closer and closer, to trap his essence in a sugar cage.

The desserts were dainty, pristine, looking made of porcelain and jade, of crystal, topaz, satin. I thought perhaps she'd been expecting me. The first one I tried was a crystal-clear jelly, like a raindrop the size of a saucer, with what looked to be an actual honeybee in the center of it. The wiggle of the confection trembled the bee's wings.

It tasted of weak tea, if it had any taste at all.

I took a bite of the next one, which resembled a lotus flower and tasted like walking through a cobweb. The desserts got prettier and prettier as the lazy susan revolved, even as they came to taste more and more ethereal, of salt water, dust, humidity.

"Those weren't for you," Zinnia gently scolded when she got home. The lazy susan had brought back around the raindrop jelly, which I was picking at with my fork. I'd thought perhaps the bee at its center was the thing to be eaten.

She carried a paper bag in her arms. She'd been out for more ingredients, I suspected. I apologized, but there was no more discussion of who, exactly, the confections were for. Because I knew. This had been an offering to the dead.

Zinnia insisted I stay—she'd fix me something that *was* for me, she promised. "And you can spend the night, like you used to," she said.

I hated telling her no, but I'd come to need my own bed in the shop. More specifically: I was addicted to the deep sleep Opal had provided me, from a copper-colored bottle.

It's quite addicting, she had said, slipping the bottle into my hand on the night she left. She'd meant it as a warning, but the suggestion of addiction just made me crave it before I'd ever tried a drop. She called it a hypnotic. *You need absolute quiet,* she whispered. *The senses drift off to sleep one by one... your hearing is the last to go.*

Having eaten those unsweet sweets Zinnia left for Haze, I dreamt my dream again, the one where the bookshop floods, but this one tipped even more into nightmare, the entire building unmoored, rocking with the water that poured down the walls. And it wasn't just the shop that was flooding; the street was too, water rising up the windows, drowning my twin mermaids. Suddenly all the *Titanic* survivors of our book club were in the shop with me, struggling to pull open the door, pounding their fists at the glass, every woman's elegant gown ballooning up around her as the water pulled her in. Their voices rose up in an opera that thundered more than the rush of the sea through the shop, the aria from *Castor et Pollux*, the renouncing of the light, *ta lumière*.

I dove to the black tiles of the shop's floor, to the bejeweled *Rubaiyat* lost in the *Titanic*, and I lifted its cover, releasing the peacocks from within. They fluttered up into the ocean, their wings embroidered in golden thread.

Leopold swam up to me to hold a mask to my face, and I breathed in the vapor that gave me dreams. It was then that I woke, gasping for air. I sat up in my bed in the shop and lit my lamp so I could study the walls. I touched the bindings of the books. They felt a little damp, but the longer I held my fingertips to them, I realized the cloth was only cool from the cold of the room.

I did what I always did when I tucked my bed back up into the wall: I stood a minute looking at Haze's photographs of La Librairie Sirène, seeing him everywhere in the empty shop. I could see Haze in other photographs he wasn't in, too, like those snapshots he took of Zinnia and me that late-autumn day in Robinson, in the restaurant in the tree. He himself wouldn't pose, not even with Zinnia. *I'm unsightly,* he said, with that mellow smile, his eyes drowsy from wine.

The moments I missed the most were those I had known would never last. Even unaware of all the tragedy to come, I would have chosen, if I could, for us to live forever in that afternoon, the three of us pretending to be shipwrecked, the rest of the world blissfully on the other side of the ocean.

I poured the sleeping tonic down the sink so I wouldn't have a chance to forgive it as the day wore on. Every morning that I'd woken from a nightmare I swore I'd never take the tonic again, but by nightfall I was craving it.

As soon as I knew the office would be open, I called to say I was another victim of the aniline pencils. "Can't see out my right eye," I lied.

At last I returned to the business of selling books, alongside Alice.

I sent Zinnia a blue note by pneumatic tube, and she was at my shop that afternoon with a box of woven bamboo. She lifted the lid. Inside was a graveyard of sugar skulls that were the size of my thumb.

"Alas Poor Yoricks!" I said. On that night we first kissed, passing those candy whistles tongue to tongue, Zinnia had conjured up an idea for sugar skulls in my honor.

"I got the recipe from a Mexican cookbook I found right here in the shop," she said, sauntering in, looking up and around, just like she did on the very first day she visited me. *"Candy for the Feast of the Dead."*

I worried about my teeth, so I bit down with caution, but the sugar broke easily. I popped another one in my mouth. "Cinnamon and chili powder," she said, glancing at me as she sat on the divan. She leaned forward, watching my expression. "Some coconut. Maybe you'll sell them here? At the front desk?"

"I love that idea," I said. I ate another.

I brought out Haze's cognac and poured us each some in the tea party *Titanic* cups the toymaker had brought for our first book club discussion. I put on my record of Beethoven's *Kreutzer Sonata,* and I sat next to her. I'd listened to the music often since

Haze's death, and I could always hear the skip in it, from when we knocked up against it as he kissed me.

"An overripe raspberry," I said of the taste of the cognac, smacking my tongue.

Zinnia took a sip of her own. "Mashed rhubarb," she said.

"Bacon fat in peach syrup," I said.

"So what was the straw?" she said. *Straw.* I squinted, tasting for it. But then she said, "That broke the camel's back. What made you finally quit that office job, something I told you to do a long time ago?"

"You know, I guess maybe it was a map I saw? They're building a sham Paris for Germany to bomb. And I couldn't help but see the real me in the real Paris, and a ghost me in the ghost one, doing double the work. And then I imagined two bookshops, neither one of them with me in it. I didn't like the looks of it. Does that make sense?"

She took another sip, and though she squinted in thought, I knew she was no longer considering the flavors of the cognac. "I kind of like the idea of a cardboard Paris," she said. "Maybe we can move there. In *Genji,* the characters were always saying they felt like they were in a work of art. In a romance, or a painting, or a lyric."

"You can have a candy shop made of sugar. We'll call it 'Ma Confiseuse.'"

After evoking the nickname Haze had for her, I could see her imagining that little shop, the one Haze had told her she should open someday. Right there and then, she snapped it together brick by brick, picturing her confections spoiling prettily in the window.

The *Kreutzer Sonata* record played on, and I could see the notes become ink on the page—we'd come to the part when the staccato of the piano became ellipses to me, the melody of the violin an ampersand. Zinnia leaned her head over to rest against the back of the sofa. "In your next life you won't know any pain," she said. "No unhappiness. We won't have any disappointments at all."

"Let's have a million lives like that," I said.

She drank the rest of her drink. We listened to the music. After a long moment, she spoke. "Can I tell you something?"

"Tell me anything."

"I miss your letters. From before the war, when you were pretending to be Haze. I wish you would write me again. And send me books." When I looked down into my cup, thinking of what to say next, she said, "Not as Haze, of course. Oh, no. As *you*."

It was a simple enough request; I recommended books all the time. But there seemed some danger of such letters striking an old chord. Even so, I wanted nothing more than to stroll through my shop and find all the books that sat waiting for her. I knew already I wanted her to read the works of the new writers taking risks, *Sons and Lovers, The Voyage Out*, the anthologies of Imagist poetry, all destined to feel the spark of a match.

"You have to meet with me after you've read whatever I send you," I said. "We'll talk about the books over a glass of gin."

I could see us sitting in Haze's light and shadow, the pictures he'd take of us in our own little splinter of the city. Within days, Zinnia embarked on her plan for selling her confections, and she bought the building a few doors down, where I'd lived for a time in a room upstairs. She paid much too much, but she considered it a victory to evict my mean concierge. She also paid too much for carpenters, so that she could have the shop open before summer. I gave her the little chairs and tables from the attic, from when my shop's previous owner had considered adding a tearoom.

She didn't call the shop "Ma Confiseuse." She called it "Monoimi," using the Japanese word she'd plucked from the footnote in *Genji Monogatari*. It was meant to evoke Haze's ghost too; *monoimi* was the word for the fasting you do after something supernatural happens.

I did worry about her opening a pastry shop named for a hunger strike.

But Monoimi would become known among the war widows

of Paris, and the mothers and fathers of lost soldiers, and all the people of the city who grieved. She did immaculate work for them, choosing some ingredients less for the flavor than for how they looked: pickled rosebuds, the deep purple ink from the rotten bloom of a dying iris, yellow dust from the pistil of a lily. To assure they were beautiful inside and out, she brought in all her experience from Paper Crane, and she incorporated the tastes of the Parisians, some of them just a touch illegal, thanks to Alice's insights into the black market. Zinnia's sweets took on the flavor of burnt almonds, coffee beans, singed pears, curdled cream, yellow plum, candied angelica and ginger, cognac, kirsch.

With her shop, Zinnia ceased catering to the desires of the dead and returned to the world of the living.

I decided to do the same, by way of Delphine Blanchet. She'd become part of an effort to correspond with soldiers, wounded and not; she signed copies of pocket-sized editions of Shakespeare's plays and sent them to the war front. This led to the Titanic Survivors Book Club gathering every Saturday in my shop, to read and respond to letters, each of us selecting books from my shelves to wrap up and send to the hospitals and to the trenches, not only to soldiers and their generals, but to nurses, ambulance drivers, nuns, cooks, letter carriers. We situated tables and chairs throughout the bookshop, here and there, the best we could, so everyone had a surface to write on. I was able to approve all their letters under my official eyeball as a licensed censor, a title I kept despite never returning to my desk. The letters we sent out from La Librairie Sirène would reach the war front without a word out of place.

My *Titanic* survivors had specific books they liked to send, so I committed myself to keeping the shop properly stocked, thanks to Zinnia's donation of funds. The gambler, of course, saw instructional books on improving your betting skills to be a tool of survival at the front lines, particularly fond of *How to Win at Draw Poker Scientificaly* by "A Retired Card Sharp." Penny Dreadful sent along her own mysteries, and though all her books were full of death, it was death of a harmless sort, every bullet and twist of the knife only an amusing diversion. The orphan surprised us by insisting that the men at war deserved sex and scandal—or so she'd heard from Henry Dew, the fallen evangelist still upright at the front lines—so she liked to send along novels about the illicit love affairs of courtesans and cocottes.

It did seem the war might rage on and on, and once the fake Paris fell, would they keep building it, over and over, until it replaced the real Paris entirely?

In this Paris of our own, Zinnia will have another chance at love—on one of our Saturday nights of sending off books, in a twist of coincidence worthy of a romance, she will come to reply to a letter from the very same sailor who wrote down Haze's thoughts for him on White Star stationery. He was the man who soothed the horses, and he will send her a picture of himself that Haze had taken, every bit as handsome as Haze had said, with a dashing mustache like those worn by bare-knuckled boxers. The sailor will like when she sends him epistolary novels, because a story told in an exchange of letters seems to him closer to fact than fiction. He will like all the drama, the confessions, the expressions of love, but he doesn't want dialogue. *Too much like theater,* he will write to her. *I don't like my novels acted out.*

And I, too, will meet someone. When the French Foreign Legion finally realizes I've slipped free from my shackles at the censorship office, and that I'm not coming back, it will task me with going to the houses of the bereaved, carrying to them the personal effects of the men they've lost. My walking stick makes me well suited for it; the sight of me, someone wounded himself, might soften the blow.

I speak to mothers, wives, fiancées. They often invite me in, for tea, coffee, a shot of brandy, a piece of pie, a slice of cake. They tell me the stories behind the things I return to them. All of it is commonplace—wedding rings, diaries, a cigarette case, a watch chain—but as the survivors lift them from the boxes I bring, these pieces of a life are transformed into the relics of a shrine. Sometimes they will invite me to come back, just to talk.

I will return many times to the kitchen table of a gentleman who's been at the front lines himself. An explosion has left him with not-insignificant tremors and all his hearing robbed from his left ear. I first meet him when I bring him a box of the effects of a fellow soldier newly dead, a man named Étienne. "I'm his only survivor," my new friend will tell me. "And he would have been *my* only one too."

In the box: a pipe, a leather tobacco pouch, and a broken bisque Kewpie doll minus one arm. But best of all, some synchronicity: a very small volume of three Shakespeare plays, including *Hamlet* (abridged, but with the graveyard scene and Yorick's skull intact). This wouldn't be *extraordinarily* coincidental, considering that librarians sent in truckloads of Shakespeare to flood the trenches, but it's nonetheless something to point out, to connect. I will read to him the lines that mention my name.

I know this pocket-sized series, and so does he, but it's not one signed by Delphine Blanchet, from her theater troupe. "*I* gave that book to him," he says. "I put it in his vest pocket myself the last I saw of him."

The cover is made of a calf leather so soft it's bent, perhaps warped by the shape of Étienne's rib cage, his heart beating near.

The edition is very small, but not the smallest Shakespeare I've seen, which was a collection of sonnets set in "fly's eye" type, a type so tiny it could blind the typesetter, "because you're not only setting it, you're setting it upside down, and backward, for the printing press," and I'll apologize for boring him with minutiae about minutiae.

But minutiae is what he's needing; he would prefer to dwell for hours on matters of small consequence. "I like the sound of your voice," he says. "Tell me about the book." But *To be or not to be* is not the question in this particular instance. He doesn't want story, he wants words. All sound, no fury. "I want to know everything I can possibly know about all the parts of that book. I want to know every stitch of it."

I won't tell him that one tug on one stitch will undo it completely, that it's slapdash, published specifically for soldiers at war, a book born with a short life, its spine built to break, its pages poised to fall to pieces after only one read. This was not one of those books that'd stop a bullet.

So I describe instead a more handsome edition. I make it up as I go along, opening the book, closing it, pointing here and there, telling the story of its threads of Irish flax, its perfumed paste made of parchment shavings and vinegar. The name *Shakespeare*, stamped on the leather, is gilded with a recipe of gold leaf and honey. The fadeless ink inside, I say, is of sulfate of indigo and nitrate of silver. I even pretend to know something about the type foundry that designed the shape of the letters, all the craftsmanship of an apprentice named Orlando, in a studio in Venice.

I unswirl the marbling of the end pages, unfeathering it, its ox gall and copper salt, its glair of egg, its berries, turpentine, Brazil dust boiled in rainwater.

"Touch the paper," I say, and he does, and though it's only wood pulp, even flimsier than newsprint, I convince him he's feeling silk and velvet, a paper of linen and hemp.

He'll follow along, nodding, not falling for any of it. But he loves my tender lies all the same.

ACKNOWLEDGMENTS AND

AUTHOR'S NOTE

Many thanks to those who contributed significantly to the development and publication of this novel, most notably the people of Doubleday. Cara Reilly has been profoundly devoted to every page, providing vital support and insights, and Margo Shickmanter was integral to the very concept of the book. Thanks also to Bill Thomas, Elena Hershey, Milena Brown, and Todd Doughty, and to Michael J. Windsor for the jacket design (and those sublime peacocks).

My eternal gratitude to Jennifer Weltz and JVNLA, most especially my dream agent and dear friend, Alice Tasman, whose unflagging spirit has been a great gift these twenty-plus years.

I'm grateful to the University of Nebraska–Lincoln, and to the bountiful UNL libraries. Marco Abel and Mark Button have created avenues of support in a variety of ways, as has the Adele Hall professorship.

Thank you to D'Angelo Simms for his illustrations.

Janet Lura has provided any number of insights into Japanese culture in the twenty-six years I've known her, and the character of Zinnia wouldn't exist without her. Thanks also to her mother, Akemi, for her perspectives.

As always, my husband, Rodney Rahl, provided the exact right advice on plot and character whenever I needed it the most. And I'm forever indebted to my parents, Larry and Donita Schaffert, for their love, guidance, and support.

For research, I relied on the archives of *The New York Times*,

Newspapers.com, *Vogue,* and *Femina,* a French women's magazine. Google Books allowed access to a number of articles on candy making and candy consumption, in periodicals such as the *Confectioners Journal,* some of which included profiles of the Morinaga Confectionery Co., Ltd., of Tokyo. I found additional information on the company in *Moral Foods: The Construction of Nutrition and Health in Modern Asia,* edited by Angela Ki Che Leung and Melissa L. Caldwell (2019).

To learn more about turn-of-the-century and early-twentieth-century bookselling, bookbinding, and publishing, I consulted the archives of *Publishers Weekly, The Book Monthly,* and *Bookseller and Stationer,* and such books as *The Book-Hunter in Paris* by Octave Uzanne (1893). Exploring the individual histories of the books discussed by the Titanic Survivors Book Club led to a number of insights into publishing in general: *The Awakening* led me to *A History of Stone & Kimball and Herbert S. Stone & Company* by Sidney Kramer (1940); *Monsieur Vénus* led me to *Rachilde and French Women's Authorship* by Melanie C. Hawthorne (2001), a publication of the University of Nebraska Press. And I could spend hours reading the catalogs of the dealers of rare books.

There are a number of useful and vivid guides to Paris and its byways, such as *Where and How to Dine in Paris* by Rowland Strong (1900) and *Paris* by Mortimer and Dorothy Menpes (1907). I relied upon *Paris and Its Environs* to get me around the city's main thoroughfares in 1913; but, as Miss Lavish advises in *A Room with a View,* I had to be emancipated of my Baedeker to see beyond the surface. I found a great deal of useful information in *Queer Lives: Men's Autobiographies from Nineteenth-Century France,* translated and edited by William A. Peniston and Nancy Erber (another University of Nebraska Press publication), and in Finn Turner's 2018 master's thesis, "'I Do Not Speak French': Cruising, Magic, and Proust's Queer Sociability."

The role of a library steward in the early twentieth century is documented in a number of travel-related articles and books, including "The Libraries of the Trans-Atlantic Liners" by Calvin Winter in *The Bookman* (1911) and *The Scientific American Handbook of Travel* (1910). (A library steward appears in the first paragraphs of Edith Wharton's 1918 novella *The Marne*.) The good work of Thomas Kelland, the *Titanic*'s second-class library steward (there was no first-class library steward; the lending library for first-class passengers was part of the lounge), is referenced directly in *The Loss of the S.S. Titanic* by survivor Lawrence Beesley (1912), and in *Titanic Survivor: The Memoirs of Violet Jessop* (1997). Though he goes unnamed in both instances, his character definitely emerges. Jessop acknowledges his thoughtfulness in dropping off at her cabin some English magazines such as *Tatler* and *Sketch*. Beesley, meanwhile, describes him as "thin, stooping, sad-faced, and generally with nothing to do but serve out books."

A NOTE ABOUT THE AUTHOR

Timothy Schaffert is the author of six previous novels: *The Perfume Thief, The Swan Gondola, The Coffins of Little Hope, Devils in the Sugar Shop, The Singing and Dancing Daughters of God,* and *The Phantom Limbs of the Rollow Sisters.* He is the Adele Hall Chair of English at the University of Nebraska–Lincoln and coeditor of Zero Street, a literary fiction series of the University of Nebraska Press.

A NOTE ON THE TYPE

The text in this book was set in Miller, a transitional-style type-face designed by Matthew Carter (b. 1937) with assistance from Tobias Frere-Jones and Cyrus Highsmith of the Font Bureau. Modeled on the roman family of fonts popularized by Scottish type foundries in the nineteenth century, Miller is named for William Miller, founder of the Miller & Richard foundry of Edinburgh.

The Miller family of fonts has a large number of variants for use as text and display, as well as Greek characters based on the renowned handwriting of British classicist Richard Porson.